Taken by Storm

Taken by Storm
ROCHELLE ALERS

ARABESQUE®

TAKEN BY STORM

ISBN-13: 978-0-373-83110-4
ISBN-10:   0-373-83110-2

www.kimanipress.com

Printed in U.S.A.

The Whitfield Brides series

You've met Ryan, Jeremy and Sheldon—the Blackstones of Virginia—and now it's time to meet the Whitfields of New York. In this Arabesque trilogy, you will meet the Signature Bridals' wedding divas: Tessa, Faith and Simone Whitfield. These three women are so focused on their demanding careers that they've sacrificed their personal happiness. Within a year, though, each will encounter a very special man who will not only change them but change their lives forever.

In *Long Time Coming,* wedding planner Tessa Whitfield never imagined that opening the doors of Signature Bridals to Micah Sanborn would lead to their spending the next twelve hours together after a power outage hits her Brooklyn, New York, neighborhood. Her vow never to mix business with pleasure is shattered when the Brooklyn assistant district attorney offers Tessa an extraordinary friendship with a few special surprises that make her reevaluate everything she's come to believe about love.

Wedding-cake designer Faith Whitfield, who owns the fashionable Greenwich Village patisserie Let Them Eat Cake, has all but given up on finding her prince, and refuses to kiss another frog. But, when she least expects it, she discovers love in the passionate embrace of pilot to the rich and famous—and modern-day knight-in-shining-armor—Ethan McMillan in *The Sweetest Temptation.*

After a disappointing marriage and an ill-fated reconciliation with her high-school sweetheart, floral designer Simone Whitfield wants nothing to do with men. She's content to run her business, Wildflowers and Other Treasures, in the greenhouses on her White Plains, New York, property. In *Taken by Storm,* Simone witnesses an attack on a federal judge, and suddenly finds her cloistered suburban life turned upside down when U.S. Marshal Raphael Madison from the witness protection unit is assigned to protect her 24/7. Although they are complete opposites, Simone and Raphael come to share a heated desire and a love that promises forever.

Yours in romance,
Rochelle Alers

To Brie Edmonds-Ashton...

Thank you for the exquisite packaging and incredible
marketing of the Whitfields of New York

They that sow in tears, shall reap in joy.
—Psalm 126:5

ACKNOWLEDGMENTS

I would like to thank the authors, editors and photographers of the following books, which proved invaluable in writing the Whitfields of New York's Signature Bridals:

Victoria Romantic Weddings, Hearts Books, 1998;

Bouquets: A Year of Flowers for the Bride
by Marsha Heckman, Stewart, Tabori & Chang, 2000;

The Knot Book of Wedding Gowns
by Carley Roney, Chronicle Books, 2001;

For Your Wedding Cakes
by Bette Matthews, Barnes & Noble, 2003;

Wedding Flowers Made Simple
by Stephen Roberts, Watson-Guptill Publications, 2003;

Martha Stewart Weddings, winter 2004;

InStyle Weddings
by Hilary Sterne, Time, Inc. Home Entertainment, 2005;

Bride's Receptions Special Issue, spring 2006;

Grace Ormonde Wedding Style, spring/summer 2007.

Chapter 1

Simone Whitfield got up at the same time every day regardless of the season. This morning, rather than prepare to work in the greenhouses on her property, she readied herself to go to a nearby park. She'd waited months for spring and the return of warmer weather to resume jogging.

Staring at her reflection in the mirror over the bath-room vanity, she pulled a large-tooth comb through her hair, securing it off her face in an elastic band. It'd been years since she'd worn her hair off her shoulders, but had been reluctant to cut it because her ex-husband said he liked long hair. Their on-again, off-again relationship from high school sweethearts, to marriage, divorce and a failed reconciliation spanned sixteen years, and Anthony Kendrick no longer had a place in her life.

Now at thirty-three, she'd moved on and had no

intention of ever looking back. She'd given Tony more
chances than he deserved to get his act together and his
last plea of *just one more time* had fallen on deaf ears.
Besides, she had other things on which to concentrate.
She was involved in running her own floral business,
Wildflowers and Other Treasures, while planning her
sister's wedding that was only seven weeks away.

Simone couldn't believe her very staid younger sister
was planning to marry. Tessa Whitfield, the preeminent
wedding planner for Signature Bridals and Event Plan-
ners, Inc., and who'd coordinated countless weddings,
was now going to be a Signature bride.

A week before Simone had been maid of honor for
her cousin Faith Whitfield-McMillan, who'd just returned from honeymooning with her husband, Ethan.
Beautiful, elegant Faith had eloped over the Valentine's
Day weekend after a two-month whirlwind courtship;
then two and a half months later, she and Ethan repeated
their vows for friends and family members in a church
ceremony.

Faith had invited her, Tessa and Micah Sanborn,
Tessa's fiancé, to her Englewood Cliffs, New Jersey
home for dinner Saturday evening, and she looked forward to sharing the small, intimate gathering with family members.

Flicking off the bathroom light, she walked into the
adjoining bedroom and scooped up a set of keys and a
cell phone off the dresser. Simone left her bedroom and
took the staircase downstairs to an area of the large
farmhouse where she'd set up a laundry room and work-
shop/mudroom. Sitting on a wooden bench, she slipped
her sock-covered feet into a pair of running shoes. At

the last minute, she decided to take a small canister of pepper spray. Coyote sightings in several Westchester County communities had prompted her to purchase the spray, which she prayed she'd never have to use. Putting on a hooded sweatshirt, she pushed the spray, cell phone and keys into the deep pockets. Depressing a button on the keypad on a wall, she activated the property's security system and stepped out into the warm, spring morning.

The panoramic view from the two-story house with a wraparound porch that overlooked the Hudson River was why Simone had decided to purchase the fore-closed, three-acre dilapidated property for a fraction of its worth. It'd taken more than seven years and an in-calculable amount of money for her to restore the century-old house and surrounding landscape to its original beauty.

She set off down the hill at a brisk walk toward a wooded area that led into a park with a track, tennis and basketball courts and a baseball diamond. A layer of moisture had dotted her body under the sweatpants and hoodie as she increased her pace along the narrow, paved path.

The sound of footsteps behind her prompted Simone to glance over her shoulder. She recognized the tall, slender man with salt-and-pepper hair. "Good morning, Judge Fischer."

"Good morning, Simone," he said, breathing heavily as he joined her, their rubber-soled feet keeping pace.

The greeting was barely out of his mouth when a large form sprang from a copse of trees. Within seconds, Mitchell Fischer's throat was caught in a savage grip.

Early morning sunlight glinted off a shiny object as it came down once, then again.

Simone couldn't move or scream; she stood stunned as she watched the horrific scene. Fear held her in a stranglehold until the limp body of her neighbor crumpled to the ground and his assailant turned toward her. Reacting on instinct, she reached into her pocket and took out the pepper spray. Her gaze locked on a pair of glittering gold eyes before she noticed the large tattoo on the back of his right hand. The blade of the knife he'd used to stab Judge Fischer was covered with blood. Pressing the red button on the canister of pepper spray, she aimed it directly at the man's face. There came a high-pitched scream followed by a gurgling sound. The knife fell to the ground as he stumbled around blindly before falling into the underbrush.

Everything that followed appeared to happen in slow motion for Simone. She remembered taking off her sweatshirt and pressing it to her neighbor's chest at the same time she fumbled in her pocket for her cell.

Don't panic! Get it together, she told herself over and over. "Judge Fischer." The wounded man's eyelids fluttered, then closed. She applied more pressure, dropping her phone and using both hands while attempting to stem the spreading red stain across the jacket of his white tracksuit.

"What happened?"

She glanced up to see two joggers standing over her. "Someone stabbed Judge Mitchell Fischer. Please call 911 and let them know whoever attacked him ran off into the woods."

One of the joggers took out his own cell phone and

gave the 911 operator their location while the other took over for Simone, administering first aid. Within minutes, the wail of sirens, the distinctive whir of the blades of a helicopter and the cacophony of voices disturbed the quiet of the morning as curious spectators crowded around the crime scene, shocked and appalled that someone had attempted to murder one of their most respected residents.

U.S. Deputy Marshal Raphael Madison maneuvered the government-registered SUV into the driveway of the address he'd programmed into the vehicle's GPS. He'd left his Poughkeepsie condo within minutes of receiving an "urgent" call from his supervisor. Racing against time, he took a taxi to the Dutchess County Airport. Passengers on the small commuter plane glared at him, after the announcement that the carrier was being delayed pending his arrival. It seemed as if the plane had just taken off before it touched down at the Westchester County, where he'd been briefed on Judge Fischer's attack and eyewitness Simone Whitfield and picked up the vehicle.

Opening the hatch, Rafe got out and retrieved two carry-ons and a garment bag. Shifting slightly, his gaze swept over the surrounding landscape. Simone Whitfield's house was built on a hill with breathtaking views of the Hudson River, Westchester County and northern New Jersey.

His last three assignments had been in hotels with adjoining suites where he'd ordered room service and spent countless hours watching television with witnesses he was assigned to protect. Closing the SUV hatch, he

climbed the porch steps and rang the doorbell. A stake
on the front lawn and decals on several windows verified
that the property was monitored by a security company.

The door opened and he came face-to-face with
someone from his past. "Well, I'll be damned."

U.S. Deputy Marshal Keven Robbins flashed a wide
grin. "Rafe Madison! How the hell are you?" He and
Raphael Madison had joined the Marshals Service at
the same time.

Dropping his luggage, Rafe shook the other man's
hand, while slapping his back. "I thought you were with
Prisoner Services." Marshals assigned to Prisoner Services assumed custody of those who were arrested by
all federal agencies and were responsible for the
housing and transportation of prisoners from the time
they were brought into custody until they were either ac-
quitted or imprisoned.

"I was, but transferred over to OCS three months
ago. Court security is very different from babysitting
prisoners."

"But not much different from babysitting witnesses.
Speaking of witnesses, where's Miss Whitfield?"

"Come on in. She's upstairs."

"Please let her know that I'm here."

Rafe retrieved his bags while Keven climbed the
stairs to the second floor. Walking into the spacious
entryway, Rafe set his luggage down under a table with
a vase filled with a profusion of white and pink flowers
that resembled roses. The table was crowded with white
candles of different sizes. The seat of a delicate-looking
straight-back chair in a corner was covered with a
cushion in red and white striped ticking. He preferred

more contemporary furnishings, but had to admit that the space was charming *and* inviting.

Seeing movement out of the corner of his eye, Rafe turned, all of his senses on full alert, and stared at the woman whom he'd been assigned to protect until the conclusion of the trial of Ian Benton. Judge Mitchell Fischer's attacker had been captured a short distance from the crime scene by a SWAT team after search dogs found him hiding in a copse of trees. Temporarily blinded by pepper spray, he'd been unable to make it back to where he'd parked his car, which had been reported stolen two days before.

During Rafe's briefing, he'd learned that Simone Ina Whitfield was in her early thirties, but the petite woman with a dusky gold-brown complexion, large, haunting, hazel eyes and a mop of damp, loose, reddish curls appeared closer to twenty-three than thirty-three.

He forced himself not to stare at her full, lush mouth. There was something about her mouth that reminded him of sultry vixen. A pair of loose-fitting sweatpants and an oversized T-shirt made her appear small and fragile.

Rafe strolled across the room and extended his hand. "I'm Deputy Marshal Rafe Madison."

Simone stared at the large, well-groomed hand as if it were a venomous reptile. "May I please see some ID?"

"I can assure you that he is who he..." Keven Robbins's voice trailed off when Simone shot him a warning look.

"I was told by the U.S. attorney at the courthouse that I wasn't to trust anyone or assume they're who they say they are," she said quietly, glaring at the seemingly embarrassed federal officer. Her gaze swung back to the man who'd been assigned to live in her home while monitoring her whereabouts 24/7. Forcing a smile, she held out her hand. "Now, may I see your identification, Marshal Madison?"

Dark eyebrows lifted slightly in Rafe's lightly tanned face as he reached into the back pocket of his jeans for a small leather case. He handed it to Simone, who stared at his picture ID and badge for several seconds, then returned it to him. A hint of a smile tilted the corners of his mouth. "Are you convinced now?"

There was something smug about Raphael Madison's attitude that irked Simone. Her eyes narrowed slightly. "I'll show you where you can put your things."

Keven cleared his throat. He wanted to tell Rafe that he would have his work cut out for him with Simone Whitfield. Although he'd found her very pretty, he detected a toughness in her that wasn't apparent at first glance. And she didn't scare easily. After all, she'd repelled Mitchell Fischer's attacker with pepper spray.

He winked at Rafe. "I'm going back to the courthouse." He nodded to Simone. "Miss Whitfield." Keven slapped Rafe's shoulder as he made his way to the front door. "Good luck, my friend," he said in a quiet voice. "She's a live one," he added sotto voce.

Rafe walked with Keven, closed and locked the door, then picked up his luggage. When he returned to the living room, he realized Simone hadn't moved. When his gaze met hers, he saw uncertainty in the brown-green orbs. Was she in shock? Had the enormity that she could've been murdered or seriously wounded finally set in?

But she hadn't been killed or injured because common sense and quick thinking had saved not only her life, but also that of a federal judge.

Simone blinked once, as if coming out of a trance. "Follow me, Mr. Madison."

Rafe stared at her back as she headed for the staircase. "We have to settle something straightaway, Simone." She stopped her retreat and turned to face him. "Since I'm going to be living with you for a while, I believe we can dispense with the formality of Mr. Madison and Miss Whitfield."

Her naturally arching eyebrows flickered. "How do we address each other?"

"Rafe and Simone will do. It'd be better for everyone involved if you don't advertise why I'm here."

If Simone hadn't been so traumatized by the day's events, she would've reacted to the tall man with a mane of dirty-blond hair and intense dark-blue eyes. He'd been blessed with the most exquisite bone structure she'd ever seen in a man. His perfectly symmetrical features made him almost a little too pretty. He was what her pastry chef cousin, Faith, would refer to as *delicious* or *yummy*. A lightweight black jacket was stretched over his broad shoulders and a pair of well-washed jeans hugged his lower toned body like a second skin. It didn't matter if he was easy on the eyes; she'd never been attracted to blond men.

"How do I explain *you*, Rafe?" There was a hint of facetiousness in her query.

"You can say I'm an old friend from college."

"How do you know that I attended college?"

Rafe's impassive expression didn't change. "I know

everything—well, almost everything—about you," he said, correcting himself.

The Bureau had forwarded her biographical information, along with other data needed for the security, health and safety of their government witness. He knew when and where she'd been born, the schools she'd attended, her marital status and how much income she'd reported to the IRS.

"You do know that I don't want you here."

A slight frown appeared between his eyes. "What you want is unimportant to me. I've been assigned to protect you whether you like it or not. Now, please show me where I can put my bags, then we'll sit down and clear the air about a few things."

Simone decided she didn't like United States Deputy Marshal Raphael Madison. She didn't like his macho attitude *and* superciliousness.

She narrowed her gaze at him while crossing her arms under her breasts. "Why wait until later? Let's clear the air right now. I don't like you and I don't want you living with me," she said. "I only agreed to go along with this witness protection thing because of what that monster did to my neighbor *and* would've done to me if I hadn't pepper sprayed his ass. I am cooperating with the government because I believe he should be locked away where he can't hurt anyone ever again. But that doesn't mean I'm going to become a prisoner with you as my jailer. I have a business to run and that's not going to change just because you're here."

Rafe struggled not to lose his temper. "Either you deal with me, or you'll find yourself in federal detention charged with obstruction. I can assure you that I won't interfere with your personal life or your business, but I want you to remember one thing. Where you go, I go. Those are my orders."

Simone inhaled deeply in an attempt to relieve the constriction in her chest. She felt helpless, vulnerable, but she wasn't going to let her bodyguard know that. "Okay. But try and stay out of my way." Turning on her heels, she headed for the staircase. "Now that you understand where I'm coming from, I'll show you to your room," she said over her shoulder.

Pressing his lips together, Rafe swallowed his sarcastic reply. If Simone Whitfield thought she was going to set the ground rules for what he hoped would be a short-term involvement, then she was quite mistaken. There was one thing of which he was certain, and that was he was very good at what he'd been trained to do.

From the time the Witness Security Program was authorized by the Organized Crime Control Act of 1970 and amended by the Comprehensive Crime Control Act of 1984, no program participant who followed security guidelines had ever been harmed while under the protection of the Marshals Service, and he wasn't about to let Simone Whitfield become the first victim. Not on his watch.

His gaze was fixed on the profusion of corkscrew curls floating down her back. Simone's face and hair reminded him of his sister's favorite doll, which she'd refused to play with because she claimed she hadn't wanted to ruin it. The doll sat in a chair year after year until Rachel Madison packed her away the year she'd turned sixteen. It was the same year that all hell broke loose in the Madison household when Rafe relocated his mother and sister from Kansas and California.

Following Simone up the stairs and down a wide hallway, he pulled his thoughts back to the present. "Do you have an attic or basement?"

"No. There's just the first and second floor."

Rafe smiled. It was the first time she'd spoken to him civilly. "I need to check all of the windows and doors to make certain the locks are in working order."

"The house is wired and monitored by a security company."

"I'm still going to check everything," he insisted.

Simone slowed her pace, stopping at a bedroom at the end of the hall. Shifting slightly, she stared up at Rafe. "I always sleep with my bedroom window open regardless of the weather."

He shook his head. "You can't continue to do that. What you don't want is to make it easy for someone to get to you."

There came a pause as a flicker of fear swept through her. "What makes you think someone is going to get to me? Isn't Ian Benton locked up?"

There was another beat of silence before Rafe said, "Yes, he is. And I doubt whether he'll be granted bail. But there's also the possibility that he may have had an accomplice."

Her eyes grew wide as she mulled over the marshal's words. What if Ian Benton hadn't acted alone? What if someone had paid him to kill the judge? "Are you saying someone paid Ian Benton to murder Judge Fischer?" she asked, voicing her concerns aloud.

"I don't know," Rafe lied smoothly. What Simone

didn't know was that Ian Benton had been added to a domestic terrorist watch list after he'd stabbed a federal prosecutor to death in a Dallas courthouse parking lot. It'd been one of three attacks on federal officials marking the first anniversary of the Oklahoma City bombing of the Alfred P. Murrah Federal Building. Undercover agents had reported the subsequent attacks, like the bombing, was to avenge the Waco siege and Ruby Ridge killings.

The agents had also gathered evidence that Benton was a professional hit man for supremacist groups targeting lawyers and judges involved in the prosecution of hate crimes. However, after his 1996 release following the mysterious disappearance of a government witness, Benton dropped out of sight, only to resurface more than a decade later, this time in the Northeast. If convicted, he would be sentenced to life in prison without the possibility of parole.

Simone exhaled a soft sigh. She didn't want to think or talk about Ian Benton. She wanted to believe she'd imagined everything that had happened to her, that she'd had a bad dream, that when she woke she would be living alone and she wouldn't have to share her house and life with the marshal who'd become her bodyguard.

Opening the door to the room she'd chosen for Rafe, she gave him a level stare. "This will be your bedroom."

"Where's yours?" Rafe asked.

"It's the one on the right at the top of the stairs."

"I can't sleep here."

"And why not?" she countered.

"It's too far from your bedroom." He didn't want to lose time getting to her in an emergency. "I'll take the bedroom across from yours."

"Whatever," Simone mumbled under her breath. She'd chosen the room as much for its spaciousness as for its southeast exposure. If Rafe wanted to sleep in a bedroom with embroidered sheets, lace panels at the windows and frilly pillows, then she didn't want to hear any complaints from him.

They went upstairs, Rafe dropping his bags with a thud when he peered into a smaller bedroom. Lace- and fringe-trimmed pillows were piled high on two twin, four-poster beds draped in more embroidered lace. It was pretty, but Rafe wasn't into butterflies. White-painted furniture and cream-colored coverlets added to the feminine softness of space fashioned expressly for a girly-girl.

He smiled, attractive lines crinkling around his luminous eyes. "Who last slept here? Cinderella or Snow White?"

Simone flashed a Kool-Aid grin. "Very funny, Rafe." She sobered quickly. "I did offer you the bigger bedroom *and* a larger bed."

Rafe eyed the beds again. He was six-three, two hundred and ten pounds, and there was no way he'd be able to sleep comfortably in a twin bed. "I'll take the other room."

A smile of triumph softened Simone's mouth as she averted her face so he couldn't see her expression. It was enough that he was sleeping under her roof, and she didn't want him *that* close to her bedroom.

"I'll leave you to settle in. By the way, *your* bathroom is directly across the hall. You'll find a set of towels on a tray on the bench under the window. There're more in a cupboard, along with grooming supplies. I'll be downstairs in the kitchen if you need me for anything."

"Where's your bathroom?" Rafe asked.

The seconds ticked off as Simone met his questioning gaze. "It's in my bedroom. Why?"

"I'm going to take a shower before I go through the house to familiarize myself with the layout of your property. Activate the alarm, and please don't open the door for anyone."

"What if someone comes while you're still in the shower?"

With wide eyes, he glared at her. "Then come and get me."

Bully! she mused, glaring at him. Rafe reminded her of a bad-tempered dog who'd growl and bare his teeth, but only after he let you pat him. Solitary by nature, she didn't want Raphael Madison around, not only because he reminded her of what had happened earlier that morning, but also because she didn't want to share her space with a man. Once she'd made the decision to give her ex-husband his walking papers, she'd sworn that the next man to sleep under her roof would be the last man in her life.

Rafe would sleep under her roof, but thankfully his stay would be temporary. As soon as Ian Benton was tried, convicted and sentenced, she'd be able to move on with her life unfettered and unencumbered by a man. If her ex's intent was to turn her off on all men, then he'd been successful. Simone realized she didn't want or need a man— not even for sex. She turned and walked away, feeling the heat of the marshal's gaze on her retreating back.

Picking up his bags, Rafe retraced his steps, stopping to peer out the hallway window before walking into

what would become his bedroom. As in the smaller
room, this one also had white walls, pale floors, furniture, baseboard heating, ceiling vents for central air-
conditioning and a wood-burning fireplace. However,
this one came with an added bonus: an incredible view
of the river.

There was built-in storage with shelves and drawers
to minimize clutter. A wicker rocker with a patchwork
cushion was positioned under the vaulted ceiling, while
a matching bedside table cradled a Depression blue vase
filled with fresh sunflowers. A shelf in an alcove held a
television, a state-of-the art stereo system and an assortment of hardcover novels.

The information he'd been given about Simone Whitfield confirmed that she operated her flower business out
of her home. She'd erected greenhouses on her property,
and her reported income and the large, colorful sunflowers were obvious indicators of her skill as a floral designer.

Slipping out of his jacket, he hung it on a wooden
hook affixed to the back of the door. He reached under
his T-shirt and slipped a pair of handcuffs, a holstered
semiautomatic handgun and an extra clip of ammuni-
tion off his waistband. He would unpack later. His first
priority was to shower, change his clothes and then
make it very clear to Simone what he needed from her
to ensure her safety.

Chapter 2

Simone sat in the dining area of the kitchen, her feet tucked under her body. It was the first time since she'd returned home to take a shower that she'd been alone.

She'd been driven to a White Plains station house in a police cruiser where she stood behind a one-way glass and identified Ian Benton as the man who'd tried to murder Mitchell Fischer. Even if she hadn't recognized his face, it was the infinity tattoo on the back of his right hand that sealed his fate. A cadre of marshals transported Ian Benton to a detention center, while she'd lost track of time when questioned by a team of attorneys at the federal courthouse. The lead prosecutor told her that she would be provided with witness security, and until the conclusion of the trial, she wasn't to discuss any aspects of the case on the phone and only her immediate family would know of her protected status.

Simone had just finished her second cup of green tea when she felt the hairs stand up on the back of her neck. Glancing over her shoulder she saw Rafe standing under the entrance, staring at her.

Lowering her feet, she stood up. "I see you managed to find the shower."

Water had darkened his rakishly long hair to burnished gold. He'd changed into a pair of black jeans with a matching V-neck polo and black boots. She noticed the slight bulge at his waist near his left arm. She detested firearms, handguns in particular, yet she was forced to cohabitate with a man who wore one as if it were an appendage.

Rafe angled his head. "You probably think you're very clever. Why didn't you tell me it was hidden in a closet?"

"I just assumed you'd find it. And apparently you did."

"Were you testing me?" he asked, walking into the kitchen.

Simone dropped her gaze before his steady stare. She noticed for the first time that his eyes weren't blue, but an odd shade of violet with dark blue irises. The color reminded her of the delicate purplish-blue flower of the same name, while his hoary lashes and eyebrows were several shades darker than his hair. She wanted to tell him that he was sorely in need of a haircut.

"No. But if I were, then you passed. Have you settled in?"

"Not yet." Rafe glanced around the space that reminded him of the kitchen in the farmhouse where he'd grown up in Kansas. Hanging copper pots and exposed ceiling beams imbued the space with warmth, while open shelves put dishes and decorative serving pieces on display. A country-style table with seating for eight was duplicated with a smaller round one in the cozy nook surrounded by a trio of windows with seating for six. Clay pots filled with flowering plants and herbs lined window ledges, countertops and tables.

"I'd like for you to show me your place now," he said in a quiet tone.

"Where would you like to begin?"

"Upstairs."

"Follow me." Her sock-covered feet were silent as she led the way out of the kitchen. Simone showed Rafe the master bedroom with a king-size antique iron bed and a massive mirrored armoire painted a sunny-yellow. Pale honeycomb shades at tall, narrow windows were raised to let in the bright afternoon sunlight. Framed Audubon prints of birds and flowers and a white vase filled with ferns and lilacs stood out in stark relief to the soft, light colors in an adjoining sitting room.

Crossing the room, she opened a door. "This is my bathroom."

Rafe peered in, feeling as if he'd stepped back in time. A claw-foot tub, a deep upholstered chair in rose-pink toile, floral wallpaper and period scones infused the bathroom with an undeniable sense of femininity. He skirted a white, shaggy rug, lowered and locked the window before raising it again. Pale green sheers billowed in the warm breeze coming in through the screen. The ivy spilling over the sides of clay pots lining the fireplace mantel matched the delicate design on the wallpaper.

His bedroom, the bathroom where he'd showered and Simone's bedroom and bath had fireplaces. "Do all of the rooms have fireplaces?" he asked.

Simone smiled. "Yes."

"How old is this house?"

Simone felt a spark of excitement for the first time that day. She didn't have any children, so she'd focused a lot of attention on refurbishing and decorating her home. "It'll be one hundred next year."

"Did you move here before or after you were married?"

She stared at Rafe as if he'd spoken a foreign language. "What did you say?" Her reaction seemed to amuse him. He was grinning at her as if she'd told a joke, not asked a question.

"What did you say?" he mimicked. Without warning, he sobered. "I'll indulge you this one time, but I don't like repeating myself, Simone. I asked you if you'd moved into this house before or after you married Anthony Kendrick."

His earlier statement came rushing back. *I know everything—well, almost everything—about you.* Simone wanted to scream at the man standing inches from her. It'd been less than six hours since she'd become the only eyewitness to a horrific crime and already the government had a file on her. And Rafe hadn't been bluffing when he raised the possibility of her being charged with obstruction of justice. When interrogated by one of the federal prosecutors, she'd been warned that her failure to assist in bringing Ian Benton to justice would result in her being charged with obstruction, punishable by up to five years in a federal prison.

"After," she admitted reluctantly.

"How long were you married?"

A shadow of annoyance crossed her face. "You tell me, Rafe. You claim you know everything about me."

"I could easily find out."

"Then you do that. Now, if you're finished interrogating me, we'll continue with the tour."

Clasping his hands behind his back, Rafe trailed behind Simone as she made her way to the first floor. Her hands were curled into tight fists, her shoulders pulled up in a defensive gesture. He'd deliberately goaded her to see whether she was quick or slow to anger. He was mildly surprised because she hadn't shouted or lost her temper. What she'd exhibited was controlled rage that compressed her lips, flared her delicate nostrils and caused her breasts to rise and fall heavily under the oversized T-shirt.

Keven had warned him that she was a live one, and she was. Standing only five-three in her bare feet, she'd faced a killer with a can of pepper spray and won. He remembered his grandfather telling him that it wasn't the size of the dog, but the size of the fight in the dog when he'd come home with a black eye after fighting with a boy twice his size who'd attempted to take his lunch money. He'd held on to his money after giving the wannabe thug a bloody nose, split lip and two black eyes. It was the first and last time Raphael Madison used his fists to protect himself and his property.

Simone led him into the room she'd set up as an office/library. A bleached pine antique secretary was littered with invoices. An open planner displayed entries for two weeks. A laptop, printer and PDA occupied another corner of the desk. Floor-to-ceiling built-in bookcases provided a place for books, framed prints and decorative objects ranging from marble busts to painted ceramic vases.

A leather steamer trunk doubled as a coffee table and was the perfect place for a plant with large red flowers in a shiny copper pot. Striped and solid pillows in coffee-brown and eggshell were nestled attractively on loveseats covered in Haitian cotton, which faced each other. Canvas shades at a quartet of windows let in streams of bright sunlight.

Rafe approached the fireplace. The grate behind a decorative screen was filled with fresh bundled herbs rather than wood; he stared at an array of framed sepia, black-and-white and colored family photographs on the mantelpiece. He focused on one of Simone in a gown and hood and another of her with a group of young women wearing royal-blue T-shirts with white Greek letters across the front.

"Are you finished here?" Simone asked softly behind him.

He pulled his gaze away from the photographs. "You pledged a sorority." His question was more of a statement.

She smiled. "Yes, I did."

"Are you still in contact with your sisters?"

"A few of us get together around Christmastime." A neutral expression replaced her smile. Simone was trying to be polite without revealing more than he'd read in her file. As it was, he knew more about her personal life than most. The exception was her family.

Continuing with the tour, Simone opened mahogany pocket doors separating the living and dining rooms that brought together an array of red and white patterns against a neutral backdrop. Rafe found her home lovely, as lovely as the woman who owned it.

"I like your home."

"So, do I," she confirmed without a hint of modesty. "It's taken me a long time to restore it, and I'm still not finished."

Rafe moved closer until their shoulders were within inches of touching, the top of Simone's head coming to his shoulder. "What more do you want to do to it?"

Tilting her head, Simone met his gaze. Rafe stood close enough for her to feel the heat from his body, close enough for her to detect the subtle, tantalizing scent of a very masculine cologne, and much too close for her to feel comfortable knowing it would be just the two of them living in proximity for who knew how many weeks, or even months. Although she'd told herself that Raphael Madison wasn't her type, she had to acknowledge that he was drop-dead gorgeous.

"I'd like to replace some of the furniture with antiques."

Rafe flashed a sheepish grin. "Anything made before 1950 is antique to me."

Simone couldn't help but roll her eyes at him. "I don't think so, mister," she drawled. "If it's from the sixteenth, seventeenth, eighteenth and late nineteenth centuries, then definitely yes. Certain twentieth-century pieces would take their place in antique and collectible history before the end of this century."

Rafe decided the topic of antiques was preferable to arguing with Simone. Whenever she talked about something she liked, the sound of her voice changed. The register deepened to where it resembled a sensual textured husky timbre.

His eyes widened appreciably as he took in everything about her in one, sweeping glance. She was a cat—a sensual, purring feline with her reddish-brown

hair and glowing eyes. He'd grown up with an assortment of farm animals, but it was the cats, he discovered,
that were the most elusive and unpredictable. They'd
climb up on his lap wanting to be stroked, then without
warning either flee or sink their claws into his flesh,
leaving him wondering what he'd done to deserve their
sudden aggression.

"Where do you shop for your antiques?"

"I usually go to Cold Spring. It's close enough so I
don't have to leave the state," Simone added when he
shot her a curious look.

A slight frown creased Rafe's smooth forehead. He'd
caught her innuendo. "You're not on parole or house
arrest."

She wrinkled her nose. "I was just checking, Warden."

He wanted to tell Simone that what she'd witnessed
was hardly a joking matter. Ian Benton and the people
he worked for wouldn't hesitate to eliminate her as
easily as swatting an annoying insect. He realized she
had to make light of her situation or she wouldn't be
able to function normally from day to day. Working out
of her home complicated logistics, because if she hadn't
been self-employed she would've been put up in a hotel
or safe house where her every move would be closely
monitored. But on the other hand, her house had an
added advantage: it was built on a rise that permitted an
unobstructed three-hundred-and-sixty-degree view of
everyone coming or leaving.

"I'm not your warden, and if you cooperate with me
then there's no reason why you should feel like a prisoner."

Her eyebrows shot up. "Oh! How would you like to
change places, Rafe?"

There came a lengthy pause. Simone was physically everything he wasn't: female, petite, dark-haired with dusky brown skin. She was the most beautiful woman he'd ever seen, and if he'd met her under other circumstances he would've made that known to her. She was as beautiful and delicate as the flowers she cultivated.

"Maybe we can—after I complete this assignment."

For the first time in a very long time, Simone was at a loss for words. It was she, not her brother or sister, who was constantly grounded because she didn't know when to stop challenging her parents, her mother in particular. Lucinda Whitfield put up with a lot of things, but wouldn't tolerate sass from any of her children.

Rarely a week passed when she hadn't been banished to her room to *think about what you've just said*. Most times she didn't see what the fuss was all about because she was merely exercising her First Amendment right of free expression.

Lowering her gaze, a wealth of lashes touching the top of her cheekbones, Simone shook her head. "I don't think so." She'd enunciated each word.

"Whatevah," Rafe drawled.

A smile lit up her face. "Oh, no, you didn't go there."

His smile matched hers as he exhibited a set of perfect white teeth. "Yes, I did." Rafe winked at Simone. "You don't know what you're missing."

Her delicate jaw dropped. She couldn't believe his arrogance. "What did you eat this morning? A bowl of ego?"

"No. Froot Loops. Speaking of cereal, do you have any?"

Simone angled her head, not wanting to believe he'd just mentioned Froot Loops. "How old are you?"

"Thirty-five."

"Don't you think you're a little too old to be eating a kiddie cereal?"

He affected an expression of innocence. "No. I just happen to like Froot Loops."

"Well, I'm sorry to disappoint you, because I don't have any in my pantry. However, I do have oatmeal and Grape-Nuts." Rafe made a face as if he'd caught a whiff of something. "Well, if you want Froot Loops, then you're going to have to go to the supermarket."

Reaching for her hand, Rafe cradled it gently. "Let's finish up with the other rooms on this floor before I check outside. Then we'll go to the store."

Rafe was amazed at Simone's transformation. She'd changed out of her baggy clothes and into a pair of jeans, a yellow tee and a pair of navy blue leather mules that added several inches to her diminutive height. The profusion of hair that had framed her face was pulled into a single braid, the curling ends secured in an elastic band.

"Is that you, Simone Whitfield?"

Rafe moved quickly, stepping in front of Simone and sandwiching her between his body and the shopping cart. "Don't move." A rush of adrenaline had all of his senses on high alert.

"I can't," she whispered. Bracing her hands against his broad back, Simone tried moving him, but to no avail. She tried peering around his shoulder. "Will you please let me see who's calling me?"

A hand resting on his holstered weapon concealed under his shirt, Rafe took a step; his gaze lingered on a tall, slender, middle-aged woman with feathery coiffed silver hair that flattered her porcelain complexion. She appeared harmless enough, but when it came to witness security he couldn't afford to trust anyone.

Simone smiled when she recognized the woman who'd called her name. "Good afternoon, Miss Jennings." The retired high school teacher had put her Mount Vernon home up for sale and moved to Tarrytown to live with a widowed sister.

Corrine Jennings offered Simone a warm smile. "I thought that was you. How're your folks doing?"

"Very well, thank you."

"What are they up to?"

"Mama and Daddy are in Bermuda, celebrating their thirty-eighth wedding anniversary."

"When will they return?" Corrine asked. "I'd like to call and drop in on your mother to chat."

"They're due back next week. How's retirement?"

She didn't want to tell her former literature teacher that her father and uncle planned to close Whitfield Caterers at the end of the summer. The identical twin brothers were currently negotiating with the city's planning board to open an upscale bowling alley in an area of downtown Mount Vernon slated for gentrification.

The older woman's dark eyes sparkled like polished onyx. "To say I'm enjoying it is an understatement." Her gaze darted between Simone and the tall man standing beside her. "Aren't you forgetting your manners, Miss Whitfield?"

Simone paused before glancing up at Rafe, who lifted his eyebrows questioningly. Leaning into him, she put an arm around his waist. "This is my friend, Raphael Madison."

Corrine studied Rafe thoughtfully. "I don't remember you as one of my students."

"That's because I didn't go to school in New York," he said.

"We met years ago in Virginia Beach during spring break," Simone added quickly, knowing it was a lie she would repeat before her association with Rafe concluded.

Corrine Jennings smiled at the attractive couple. "It's nice meeting you, Mr. Madison. Well, you two have fun."

"We will," Simone and Rafe chorused.

"Now, that was easy," he crooned when Miss Jennings made her way down the wide aisle. "All we have to do is tell the same story and no one will suspect we aren't friends."

Dropping her arm, Simone backed away from Rafe. She wanted to remind him that they weren't friends and would never be friends. Raphael Madison was a stranger and interloper who'd insinuated himself into her life.

"I don't like lying."

"You really didn't lie," he countered.

"Why would you say that?"

"I did spend one spring break at Virginia Beach."

She knew she didn't have to tell him that she'd spent several spring breaks at Virginia Beach. Even when it wasn't spring break, she could be found at the beach studying or relaxing. It was one of the reasons she'd decided to attend Hampton University.

"Where did you go to college?" There was a long silence, which Rafe didn't seem inclined to break. "Now you know how I feel when you ask me my business," she chided in a tone pregnant with contempt.

Rafe glared at her in disbelief. Like quicksilver, Simone had come at him like a hissing cat because he refused to answer her question. He much preferred her soft and purring. Leaning closer, he pressed his mouth to her ear. "When we get back to the house we'll talk about *us*."

Simone resisted the urge to push him away. She wanted to tell him that he was wrong because there was no *us*. "Are you finished shopping?" she asked instead.

Her protector's idea of grocery shopping was going to a supermarket warehouse. She'd given him the directions to a Sam's Club in nearby Elmsford, where he'd filled a shopping cart with fresh fruit and vegetables, peanut butter, meat, fish, poultry and dairy products. When they'd gone down the cereal aisle he'd selected the largest box of Froot Loops available.

"I need to pick up some milk, then we can leave."

Two young women, both with toddlers seated in the front of their shopping carts, slowed, turned and stared openly at Rafe. His hair had dried and flowed down around his strong neck like sun-streaked wheat. Lifting their eyebrows in approval, they shared knowing glances. Without warning, their smiles faded when they noticed Simone standing a short distance away.

"Do you think he's here with *that?*" one whispered.

"Yes, he is," Simone spat out recklessly. Both women blushed noticeably with her comeback. Under another set of circumstances, she wouldn't have said anything, but it was the first time someone referred to her as if she were an inanimate object.

Rafe turned when he heard Simone's voice. "Is something wrong?"

"No, darling. I'm good." Her smile was as sweet as the words dripping facetiously off her tongue. The women raced down the aisle as if in a timed supermarket shopping competition.

Rafe placed a gallon of milk into his cart. "What was that all about?" he asked Simone.

Tucking a wayward curl behind her left ear, she affected an expression of unadulterated innocence. "What are you talking about?" She'd answered his question with one of her own.

Rafe studied the large hazel eyes staring up at him, enthralled by what he saw. "Do you make it a habit of talking to strangers?"

"No."

"Do you know those women?"

"No," she repeated. "And they don't want to know me. I hope you're ready to leave because I have to take care of some paperwork."

Eyes narrowing suspiciously, Rafe knew something had gone down between Simone and at least one of the women, but it was apparent she'd defused whatever it was before it got out of control. What he didn't want was for her to draw attention to herself before she was to appear in court. Once the trial began, the proceedings were certain to draw a lot of media attention.

Simone sharing her home with him was nothing compared to how her life would change, not only drastically, but also dramatically, the moment he escorted her into the courthouse. The government's lead attorney had begun building a case against Ian Benton, while taking the necessary steps not to leak the name of their witness until the trial.

* * *

Half an hour later, Rafe maneuvered into the drive-way of Simone's home. When she'd shown him around the outside of the house, he hadn't known what to expect. It certainly wasn't the enclosed back porch that was perfect for a gathering at any time of the year. The space was filled with wicker furnishings and a natural-fiber rug that set the tone for a gardenlike romantic setting. There were an assortment of floral and red-and-white striped throw pillows, vases of fresh flowers, potted plants and dwarf lemon trees.

She'd added an expansive deck that led from the back porch out to a distance half the length of a football field on which sat a Victorian-style gazebo with a cozy settee, white wicker chairs, a small round table and flowering plants positioned on a periwinkle-blue and white rug. A gas grill, picnic table and chairs were protected from the weather by custom-made, heavy-gauge waterproof fabric. He hadn't been able to conceal his surprise when seeing the hot tub with a maintenance-free redwood cabinet.

Two large, barnlike greenhouses, the life's blood of Wildflowers and Other Treasures, were erected on the southeast end of the three-acre property. The structures were clearly visible from his bedroom window, not that he planned to let Simone work there alone. He intended to stick as close to her as a permanent tattoo.

Shutting off the engine, Rafe reached over and caught Simone's wrist. "You're not to get out of the car or go into the house until I give you an all-clear signal. And please don't ever leave the house without me."

"Rather than checking in with you, I'll give you a printout of my schedule for the next two weeks," she volunteered. Simone knew she had to go along with whatever Rafe proposed or he was certain to make her day-to-day existence a living hell.

Smiling, he nodded. "That'll do."

She resisted the urge to salute him. "I'm glad you approve."

Rafe stared out the windshield. "It's not about you getting my approval, Simone. It's about making my job and your life less stressful."

"That's not going to happen until Ian Benton's locked up for the rest of his life."

"Let's hope that's sooner than later. And another thing…" His words trailed off.

"What is it, Rafe?"

His head swung around and his indigo-hued eyes bore into her. "Don't call me darling unless you mean it."

"And don't you flatter yourself, Raphael Madison," she countered as he opened the door and stepped out of the truck. Smiling broadly, he winked at her over his shoulder seconds before he closed and locked the SUV with a remote device.

Arrogant pig! Simone fumed silently. She hadn't meant to call him darling, but once the endearment slipped from her lips she hadn't been able to retract it. Slumping against the leather seat, she grunted softly. There was no way Rafe would ever become close to what she considered her darling.

Chapter 3

"I'll put the groceries away," Rafe told Simone in a no-nonsense tone while at the same time giving her a don't-challenge-me look. He'd unloaded the government-issued Yukon Denali.

What Rafe did not know was that Simone didn't want to challenge him or anyone. During the ride back from Elmsford, all of her spirited spunk had dissipated. Although the images were still as vivid as they'd been hours before, she hadn't wanted to believe what she'd become involved in. She knew she was in denial, because like so many who lived in suburban neighborhoods, she believed *crimes like this don't happen here.* Not only had she witnessed a heinous assault, but she was also drawn into circumstances not of her choosing.

In a moment of weakness she wanted to tell Rafe to drive her to Mount Vernon, but then remembered that her parents were in Bermuda, celebrating their wedding anniversary. She needed their reassurance that she would cope with this crisis as she had when the man with whom she'd fallen in love and married turned out not to be who she'd wanted him to be. The only difference was it wouldn't take sixteen years to resolve the case of *U.S. v. Ian Benton.*

"I'm going to print out my schedule for the next two weeks before I go upstairs and lie down," she told Rafe.

"Are you all right?"

Simone gave him an incredulous look. Of course she wasn't all right. Would he be all right if he'd seen someone nearly get murdered? "Yes," she said instead, walking in the direction of her office.

What she didn't want or need was his sympathy or pity, because she'd lost count of the *poor Simones* or *isn't it too bad she wasted her life with a man who was so wrong for her* when her marriage fell apart. A few times she had to tell off a few folks when they spoke as if her life were over and that she would never find another man. She would celebrate her thirty-fourth birthday in September and she certainly wasn't too old to remarry *or* have children.

Fifteen minutes later, Simone had entered her schedule from the planner to the PDA, downloaded it into her computer and printed a hard copy for Rafe.

"Do you need help?" she asked, strolling into the kitchen.

Rafe glanced over his shoulder at Simone as he dried his hands on a paper towel. "No, thanks. I think I have everything under control."

Closing the distance between them, Simone placed her schedule on the countertop. "That's my schedule for the next two weeks."

He quickly scanned the top sheet. "What's happening in the Bronx tonight?"

"I'm in a bowling league."

"Who do you bowl with?"

"Cops." She smiled when he gave her a stunned look. "My sister and her fiancé, who's a former NYPD lieutenant, are in a bowling league with a group of officers from a Bronx precinct."

"Do you bowl every Wednesday?"

"Yes."

"What about Englewood Cliffs Saturday night?"

"I'm having dinner with my cousin and her husband."

"Can you cancel it?"

"No!"

Rafe reached for the cordless wall phone, handing it to Simone. "I suggest you call your cousin to let her know that you're bringing company. It'd be in poor taste for me to show up unannounced."

A flicker of apprehension swept her as she processed what she'd been instructed to do. She wouldn't be able to go anywhere, see or talk to anyone without Rafe being present. Her life as she knew it was no longer hers.

She closed her eyes, struggling with the gamut of emotions shaking her confidence. Whenever her sister and cousin wanted to do something daring, it was always Simone Whitfield who accepted the dare and came out a winner.

She was the Whitfield girl, not Faith or Tessa, who preferred hanging out with the boys, climbing trees, hopping fences and playing baseball. It was she who had mixed it up with the boys in their Mount Vernon neighborhood, and it was she who had never run from a fight, even if her opponent was older or bigger.

When she'd announced to her family that she was getting married, no one believed her until the day she exchanged vows. The running family joke was they'd expected Tessa or Faith, the Whitfield princesses, to marry before designated family tomboy Simone.

Depressing a button on the speed dial, she rang Faith's cell phone, which she used exclusively for her business. The call was answered after the second ring. "Let Them Eat Cake. Faith speaking."

"Faith, Simone. I'm calling to ask if it's all right if I bring a date Saturday night."

"Why, Simi Whitfield, do you insist on working my nerves? Of course you can bring a guest." A soft chuckle came through the earpiece. "Who is he?"

Simone smiled. Faith was the only person who shortened her name. "You'll see," she said cryptically.

"Simone Whitfield!"

"Goodbye, Mrs. McMillan." Ending the call, she gave Rafe the phone. "She'll be expecting you."

He placed the receiver in its cradle. "You listed a party for Thursday evening. Where is it?"

Crossing her arms under her breasts, Simone leaned against the counter. "Manhattan. I'm doing the floral arrangements for a dinner party."

Rafe gave each item a mental check. "You also listed a consultation for tomorrow at eleven in Central Valley."

"I'm meeting with a prospective bride to discuss her wedding flowers."

"What's Monday in BK?"

"Every other Monday I get together with my sister and cousin. This coming Monday, we're meeting in Brooklyn at Tessa's house. The next meeting will be here, then after that we'll meet in Greenwich Village at Faith's apartment. The only time we don't meet is when one of us is out of town."

"Doesn't Faith live in New Jersey?"

Simone realized that not only did Rafe have a quick mind, but there were probably very few things that would get past him. "She and her husband stay in Manhattan during the week, and spend the weekends in New Jersey."

Rafe fixed his dark blue stare on Simone's delicate features, taken aback by her fragility. He didn't know why, but there was something about her that appealed to his protective instincts that had nothing to do with the assignment.

"How often do you go out of town?"

"Not too often. The last time I left the state for business was when I was commissioned to provide the floral decorations for a charity affair in D.C. Most times it's within the tri-state area."

Scanning the second sheet, he noted she'd listed a number of visits to Mount Vernon. "If you don't mind, I'd like for you to curtail your personal social engagements."

What was he talking about? Simone fumed inwardly. If she didn't bowl on Wednesdays with her sister and future brother-in-law or commit to their bimonthly get-togethers she wouldn't have anything remotely resembling a social life. What if she'd had a boyfriend? Would she have to stop seeing him, too?

"I'll see what I can do to accommodate you. I'm

going upstairs to relax." She walked out of the kitchen, leaving Rafe staring at the space where she'd been.

Simone pressed her face into the softness of a mound of pillows on her bed. How could her life have changed with a single incident? Why now, when she was attempting to get her life *and* head together?

She'd spent years wishing, praying and hoping the man she'd come to love more than she'd loved herself would change. She'd tried over and over to make her marriage work. Even after divorcing Tony she'd attempted reconciling, yet in the end she knew she had to let him go.

Her emotions, vacillating from frustration to fear, made her a prisoner in her own home. If and when she ventured out of doors, she would never be alone, free to walk down to the greenhouses and linger long enough to lose track of time. Even if she were to end her day sitting on the porch, it would be under the sharp gaze of a man whose job it was to see that no harm came to her until the conclusion of the trial of a man charged with attempted murder. Questions assaulted her like missiles, questions to which she had no answers, questions she wanted to ask, but feared the answers to.

What she actually wanted was to go to sleep, then wake up and find it was all a dream. Rolling over on her back, she stared up at the ceiling. Simone knew wishing, hoping or praying wouldn't change the fact that what she was experiencing wasn't a dream, but a reality as real as the man moving around her kitchen as if he belonged there. She closed her eyes, willing her mind blank, and within minutes she succumbed to the comforting embrace of Morpheus.

It felt as if she'd just closed her eyes when she came awake suddenly to find Rafe sitting on the padded bench at the foot of the bed. She popped up like a jack-in-the box. He stood up and came to sit on the side of the mattress; it dipped with his added weight. Lengthening afternoon shadows made it difficult for her to see his face.

"What's wrong?"

"Nothing's wrong, Simone." Rafe's voice was soft and comforting. He'd come to her bedroom and, not wanting to startle her, sat on the bench, waiting for her to wake up.

She blinked once. "What are you doing here?"

"I came to ask you if you wanted something to eat."

He leaned closer, his warmth and scent sweeping over her; suddenly Simone felt smothered, trapped. Unconsciously she moved back against the mound of pillows propped against the headboard. She wanted to escape from Rafe, but there was no place to go. Was she just now undergoing delayed post traumatic stress?

She shook her head. "I don't think I'll be able to keep anything down."

"You're going to have to eat."

"I know." She closed her eyes for several seconds.

Rafe didn't think he would ever get used to hearing her husky voice. Not only was it sensual, but also hypnotic. "Are you a vegan?"

With wide eyes, she gave him an incredible stare. "No. Why would you ask me that?"

"There was no meat in your freezer."

Simone's expression softened. "I eat red meat three times a week, and this was my week to call in an order to the butcher."

"Do you pick up the order or have it delivered?"

"They deliver."

"That's going to change. The less company you have, the better."

She moved off the bed, walked over to a window and stared at the verdant landscape. Rarely a day passed when she didn't find herself in one of the greenhouses pruning branches, stripping wilted leaves from flowers or weeding vegetable flats.

"You mention company as if I have a steady stream of people traipsing through here. Aside from the butcher, there's only a courier service I use to deliver plants or flowers to family and clients."

Rafe left the bed and stood behind her. "What I want is to control the number of people you come into contact with."

Crossing her arms under her breasts, Simone turned and stared up at him. Blond or not, he was gorgeous. His features weren't too broad or thin, and his coloring wasn't washed-out, but a tawny gold that afforded him a look of being perpetually tanned. And when her gaze met and fused with his, she felt as if she were drowning in water the color of Ceylon blue sapphires.

"Why do I feel like a prisoner even though you claim I'm not one? You're wearing a gun, follow me around—"

"I'll try and make certain you don't see the gun," he said, cutting her off.

Exhaling, she managed a smile. "Thank you."

"What else is bothering you, Simone?"

"Why do you think something's bothering me?" she asked rather than answer his question.

"You're tense."

"Well, well, well," she drawled. "It looks as if my lawman is also a therapist." Her mood changed quickly. "I'm more than tense, Raphael Madison. What I am is scared. When I woke up this morning I never would've imagined that I'd see someone that I know almost murdered, or that a marshal would take up residence in my home and he would become a constant reminder that my life is not my own, that every phase of my existence is to be shadowed for heaven knows how long."

Rafe curbed the urge to pull Simone into his arms to offer her tangible protection. "I can't tell you not to be afraid, but what I need is for you to trust me. I've been protecting witnesses for ten years and I've never lost one. In fact, no program participant who follows security guidelines has ever been harmed under the active protection of the Marshals Service."

Simone smiled in spite of her predicament. "You sound like a recruitment ad."

"You think?" he teased.

She nodded. "I know."

He extended his hand. "Come with me."

Placing her hand in his, Simone felt the power in the fingers that closed over hers. "Where are you taking me?"

"We're going to the kitchen."

"It's too late for lunch, so I suppose it'll have to be an early dinner."

"What are you cooking?" Rafe asked.

Simone stopped suddenly, causing him to lose his

balance before he managed to regain his footing. "You came to get me because you want me to cook for you?"

"For your information, I don't need you to cook for me."

"You cook?"

He nodded. "Some."

"How much is some?"

"Enough." He started walking, pulling her gently along as they descended the staircase.

"Where did you learn to cook?"

"I decided to learn when I went to college. It was either eat ramen noodles or go hungry."

"What's on tonight's menu?" Simone asked.

"Do you eat seafood?"

"Yes."

"I bought lobster tails, so I thought I'd make lobster over linguine."

Simone's smile was dazzling. "Talk about luck. I get a bodyguard who cooks."

Rafe returned her smile. "You don't cook?"

She wrinkled her nose at him, unaware of the endearing gesture. "I cook, but it's not fancy."

"Define fancy."

"I'll season a chicken with salt and pepper, then put it in the oven to bake, while other people will prepare broiled chicken breasts stuffed with herbs, green peppercorns and prosciutto."

"You may not cook what you consider fancy dishes, but you do grow incredibly beautiful flowers."

"Thank you." His compliment buoyed her sagging spirit. "Speaking of flowers, if you don't want them in your bedroom I'll take them out."

"No, please don't. Sunflowers remind me of home."

Easing her hand from Rafe's loose grip, Simone stopped at the entrance to the kitchen. "You're from Kansas?"

He nodded. "Yes."

"I don't believe it," she whispered.

"What don't you believe?"

"I never would've taken you for a Jayhawker."

Rafe winked at Simone as he stood aside to let her enter the kitchen. "That's because you're biased and into stereotypes."

"No, I'm not!"

"Yes, you are. And I'm going to prove it before this assignment ends." He held up a hand when she opened her mouth to refute him. "Please don't say anything else that may incriminate you. And I promise not to say I told you so when you realize I'm right. I don't know about you, but right about now I'm hungry enough to eat a side of beef."

"You make the lobster and linguine, and I'll put together a salad and set the table."

"I don't like bottled dressing," Rafe said as he opened the side-by-side refrigerator.

Simone's gaze lingered on the breadth of his wide shoulders before moving down to the denim fabric hugging his slim hips. "I have all the ingredients you'll need to make your own."

Taking the packaged lobster tails from the refrigerator, Rafe closed the door using his hip. "Aren't you going to help me cook?"

"I offered to make the salad."

Rafe gave Simone a direct stare. "Perhaps we can

work out a schedule where we can take turns cooking. I usually have cereal, toast and coffee for breakfast, so that lets you off the hook for that meal. I don't mind preparing dinner if you take care of lunch."

"I...I don't believe you," Simone sputtered as a rush of color suffused her face.

"What don't you believe?"

"You take over my kitchen, then proceed to tell me what to do."

Rafe angled his head. "We can easily remedy that situation."

"How?"

"You can pack some clothes and personal items, and we can check into a hotel and order room service."

Her jaw dropped slightly. "You know I can't do that. I have a business to run."

"And I have a job to do," Rafe countered, his voice low and cutting, "but I don't intend to go hungry or tiptoe around you whenever you go into diva mode. We're going to be living together for several months, so I suggest you make the best of what you deem an uncomfortable situation."

Simone recoiled as if Rafe had struck her. She wanted to scream at him, but didn't want to give him the satisfaction of knowing how much he'd upset her. She closed her eyes, suddenly feeling as if a crushing weight had settled on her chest.

Rafe moved quickly when he saw the color in Simone's face change. She was hyperventilating. He held her close to his body. "Breathe, Simone," he crooned softly. "That's it, baby. Take deep breaths. In and out, in and out," he repeated over and over until she finally let out a trembling gasp.

It didn't take a psychiatrist's evaluation to identify Simone Whitfield's behavior not as hostility, but fear. He knew from past experience that if a person didn't break down within minutes of witnessing a violent crime, then it would come later. In Simone's case, it was the latter.

Picking up Simone as if she were a child, Rafe sat down, settling her across his lap. He had to convince her that she was safe, that he would forfeit his life in order to protect her. When he'd been assigned to protect Simone Whitfield it'd become his responsibility to shield her from harm—physically and emotionally—because when he escorted her into the courthouse, the U.S. attorney expected her to give an accurate eyewitness account of Ian Benton's attempt to murder a federal judge.

It was Rafe's turn to hold his breath when Simone snuggled closer to his body, burying her face against his throat. What he was sharing with her was so acute that for a brief moment he felt what she was feeling: fear.

Lowering his chin, he buried his face in her soft, fragrant curls. "You're safe, Simone. I'm not going to let anything or anyone hurt you."

It was a promise he'd made only once in his life, when he rescued his mother and sister from an existence where they'd become prisoners to Gideon Madison's slow descent into a world of madness. Now, ten years later, he'd repeated the vow to Simone Whitfield, a woman with whom he would live for an unspecified time period, then walk away from when he accepted his next witness security assignment.

Simone heard the deep, comforting voice mouthing

the words she wanted and needed to hear to ease her angst. Looping her arms around Rafe's neck, she fed on the strength emanating from him as naturally as breathing.

"I'm sorry," she mumbled.

Rafe smiled. "What are you apologizing for?"

She pulled back, but didn't break contact. "For losing it."

He stared at the shimmer of unshed tears. "You're allowed, Simone."

Sniffing and smiling, she nodded. "Thank you, Rafe."

Attractive lines deepened around his eyes. "You're welcome."

A slight frown formed between Simone's eyes that were now a vibrant green. "You must think I'm silly—"

"Stop it," Rafe chided softly. "What you went through today would take the nerve of the bravest man, so don't you dare apologize for being human."

"What…what would you've done in my situation?" she asked tentatively.

A muscle tightened his lean jaw. "I would've shot the bastard."

Rafe had said it so matter-of-factly that Simone shivered noticeably, as if cold air had swept over the nape of her neck, and in that instant she wondered if he'd ever killed another human being. She felt herself withdrawing although she hadn't moved.

"Would you have killed him, Rafe?"

He nodded. "I would've if he'd come at me with a knife."

"Did you…have you ever killed someone?"

Rafe smiled at Simone as if she were a small child. "Thankfully I haven't had to."

She returned his smile. "That's good to know."

"Why?"

"Because I'd feel uncomfortable living with you knowing you'd taken someone's life."

Within seconds, Rafe's expression became a mask of stone. "I don't ever want you to forget who or what I am. I'm not a school crossing guard protecting children from motorists who disobey the twenty-mile-per-hour school zone speed limit. I know my living with you is a constant reminder of what you saw this morning, but it's not a permanent arrangement. Think of the Supreme Court Justices who live every day of their lives under the protection of the U.S. Marshals Service."

Simone shook her head. "I don't think I could live like that, knowing that some crazy may be planning to take me out because they don't agree with my decision."

"You wouldn't have a choice if you were confirmed and accepted the position. Don't forget that everything we do or say has either conditions or consequences."

She knew Rafe was right. Easing out of his embrace and off his lap, she flashed a shy smile. "Thank you for your shoulder. I'm okay now."

Pushing off the chair, Rafe studied the too-bright smile and false bravado of the woman who for several minutes had slipped under the professional facade he wore like a badge of honor. Always the consummate professional, he'd never let any witness affect him emotionally.

However, when he'd held Simone he hadn't wanted to acknowledge that she'd felt so right in his arms that he hadn't wanted to let her go. He also hadn't meant to call her *baby*. He had to be careful, very careful, not to cross the line and risk compromising his assignment.

What he couldn't tell her was that she reminded him of a woman who'd captured his love and passion a year after he'd joined the Marshals Service. But his world came crashing down when she'd informed him that she was carrying another man's child. Although they'd lived together, she'd also been sleeping with another man. Their two-year liaison had ended without incident when he moved out, checked into a motel and submitted a request to his regional director—he wanted to be reassigned to witness security. Traveling kept him busy, and a single-minded focus on protecting witnesses proved advantageous to his emotional healing and growth.

A wry smile twisted his mouth as he walked over to the sink. Simone Whitfield's hair may have reminded him of Dorene, but that was where the similarities ended. The woman under whose roof he would sleep had an in-your-face attitude that said she was no shrinking violet. She'd proven that when she pepper-sprayed Ian Benton.

There was no doubt that if she were in law enforcement, the taxpayers of New York wouldn't have to foot the expense of the thirty-plus thousand a year it cost to incarcerate an inmate. Rafe knew that if Simone had been armed, she would've shot and probably killed Benton.

He gave her a sidelong glance when she stood next to him. "I'll make the dressing tonight. Tomorrow you're on your own."

Simone rolled her eyes at him. "Bully," she said under her breath.

Rafe lifted his eyebrows. "You think?"

She flashed a smile that looked more like a grimace. "I know."

The seconds ticked off as they stared at one another. Rafe was the first to break contact. "I'm going to need some fresh parsley, a green onion and two shallots."

"The parsley's in the second pot on the left on the window ledge. But I'm going to have to get the onion and shallot from the greenhouse." She'd set up one greenhouse to grow her flowers and half of the second one for herbs and vegetables.

Reaching for the keys to the house Simone had left on the window ledge, Rafe slipped them into the pocket of his jeans. "I'm ready whenever you are."

"You're going to have to change your shoes if you're going to the greenhouse."

He glanced down at his boots. "What's wrong with my shoes?"

"I don't want you to track fertilizer and insecticide into the house. There should be a pair of clogs or garden boots in the mudroom that should fit you."

Rafe wanted to ask Simone why she had men's shoes in her house if she wasn't living with a man, but thought the question much too personal. He followed her to the mudroom and discovered a shelf filled with wooden clogs and rubber boots in varying sizes and heights. He found a dark green pair of clogs in his size and slipped into them at the same time Simone pushed her sock-covered feet into a pair of rubber boots.

He waited for her to activate the alarm before they took off, walking side by side down the hill to the greenhouses. For a brief moment of madness, Rafe wondered how it would've been if he'd met Simone under other circumstances. He dismissed the traitorous thought as soon as it came to mind, knowing that if he allowed himself to see her as someone other than a witness, then he would lose his edge.

Ian Benton and the men who'd hired him weren't small-time hoods robbing gas stations and convenience stores for a few dollars. They were a well-organized group of dissidents whose intent was to eliminate anyone who opposed their beliefs.

Unconsciously, he reached out and took Simone's hand. She stiffened momentarily, then relaxed her fingers as she met his unflinching gaze. *I'm going to make certain nothing happens to you,* said a silent voice. She flashed a shy smile, and he returned it with a confident one of his own.

He'd made her a promise, one that he intended to keep, just like he'd kept the one he made to his mother and sister.

Chapter 4

"Park next to the gray Beemer convertible," Simone instructed Rafe, pointing to the empty parking space in the bowling alley lot. "That's Micah's car," she added when he gave her a questioning look.

"Who's Micah?"

"Micah Sanborn is engaged to my sister Tessa."

"The former NYPD lieutenant and soon-to-be brother-in-law."

Smiling, she nodded. "Yes." Rafe maneuvered the large SUV into the space in one motion and shut off the engine. "I know," Simone drawled when he turned to look at her. "Don't get out until you give me the all-clear signal."

Rafe winked at Simone. "Smart girl. You're a quick learner."

Simone wanted to tell him she wasn't a girl, but didn't want to ruin what had become an undeclared truce between them. She'd recovered from her temporary meltdown to assist Rafe in preparing dinner. His admission that he could cook was grossly underestimated when he concocted an incredibly scrumptious dish—lobster over linguine—with flavors that exploded and tantalized her palate. She'd sat on a stool watching him melt butter in a large skillet to which he added garlic, shallot, mushroom and chicken broth.

When her grandmother had informed her, Tessa and Faith that she was going to teach them to cook the dishes that had been passed down through generations of Whitfield women, it was Simone who always skipped cooking lessons because she had better things to do than stand over a hot stove. Faith and Tessa had become the recipients of an invaluable tradition of secret recipes that were repeated time again when her father and uncle added them to the menu at Whitfield Caterers.

Simone had become the brunt of family jokes when everyone said that if she cooked as well as she designed floral arrangements, then she would be an award-winning chef. She no longer had her grandmother, but what she did have was a live-in replacement: Raphael Madison.

Rafe was a patient teacher when he showed her how to chop green onions and fresh parsley, and dice tomatoes, all which she grew in her greenhouse, with the facility of a professional chef. She was transfixed by the power in his hands when he removed the lobster meat from the tails without using a knife to crack the shells. At that moment, she'd imagined the side of his hand coming down on the back of someone's neck, rendering him unconscious within seconds.

Although they hadn't been together more than twelve hours, Simone found her bodyguard a study in contrasts. He'd warned her never to forget who or what he was—a U.S. Deputy Marshal licensed to carry a firearm and kill, if needed, with deadly force. However, when she'd lost her composure, he'd held her as if she were fragile porcelain, whispering words that calmed her fears, knowing she could trust him with her life. It was only at that moment that she realized that her life was in his charge.

"Why are you so cautious when you've said that only the Feds and a few members of the White Plains Police Department know that I'm the only witness?" she asked Rafe when he helped her out of the Yukon.

Rafe stared at Simone staring up at him. Brilliant gold-red rays from the sun turned her into a statue in shades of umber, honey and henna. Suddenly he found himself transfixed, hypnotized by the petite woman with the mesmerizing eyes and lush mouth who, within a matter of hours, had seeped into a part of him he hadn't known existed. Other than her overt beauty and a sensuality he wasn't certain Simone knew she possessed, he wanted to know what was it about her that made him feel as if he were a deer caught in the headlights of an oncoming vehicle.

"Training," he said after an interminable silence. It was training, and the possibility that someone could inadvertently leak her name. Even a file labeled *TOP SECRET* wasn't that if more than one person was privy to the information.

"Can't you relax just a bit?"

"Why?"

Simone dropped her gaze, staring at the middle of

Rafe's chest. "We're never going to fool anyone into thinking we're friends if you act like a bodyguard."

"For the lack of a better word, that is what I am, Simone." He opened the rear door to get the bag with her bowling ball and shoes, but when he closed it he found that she was heading for the ultramodern two-story building. He caught up with her, reaching for her hand. "How relaxed do you want me to be?"

"You don't have to tell me not to get out of the car before you, because that's something that I do with any man."

Rafe gave her fingers a gentle squeeze. "In other words, you want me to pretend that I'm your boyfriend?"

She gave him a sidelong glance. "The operative word is *pretend*. How am I going to explain you living with me if we don't *pretend* there's at least something happening between us?"

"Have you taken up with other men other than your husband?"

Simone's eyelids fluttered wildly. It was a question her cousin and sister had asked on occasion, and the answer was always the same. *No.*

"What do you mean by 'taken up with'?"

"Date."

She thought about a man who bowled with her that she'd recently gone out with. She probably would've consented to see him again if he hadn't talked incessantly about his ex-wife. "I've dated, but the dates never progressed to a man living with me."

"What about men sleeping with you?"

A shock swept through Simone with the power of a sirocco, her retort wedging in her throat. Who the hell did he think he was to ask her something that personal? "That's none of your business." she said, her voice lowering as she struggled to contain her quick temper.

Rafe flashed a devastatingly sexy smile. "The fact that you won't answer the question says you're celibate."

A soft gasp escaped her parted lips. "Whether I'm celibate or not is none of your damn business."

"Oh, but it is, Simone," he said softly. "If you're sleeping with someone, then you'd better tell him that there will be no knocking boots until after I'm gone."

"Oh, now I'm not permitted to date?"

"You can date."

Her smile was dazzling. "Why, thank you."

Rafe sobered quickly. "The only person you'll be dating is me. If you want a pretend boyfriend, then you have one. Let's practice to see if we can get it right."

He dropped her hand and looped an arm around her waist, pulling her flush against his body. Lowering his head, he fastened his mouth to her parted lips, breathing in her breath and deepening the kiss. Rafe hadn't consciously thought of kissing Simone, but he found her sultry mouth was like the open blooms of flowers beckoning insects to taste the sweet nectar within.

Simone tried pushing Rafe away, but she was no match for his superior strength. The shock of his mouth on hers melted away, replaced by a warming that started at her toes and eddied slowly up her legs. Her thighs warmed and the hidden place at the apex throbbed with long-forgotten sensations that threatened to make her faint. Thankfully it ended as quickly as it'd begun.

With wide eyes, she stared at the sardonic grin on his face. He knew! He knew his kiss had affected her more than she wanted it to when his gaze moved down to her heaving chest. She was struggling vainly not to succumb to the delicious sensations coursing throughout her body.

"How did I do?" he asked, winking at her.

"Okay."

Rafe's dark eyebrows lifted slightly. "Just okay? Perhaps I need more practice." He reached for her again, but she stepped nimbly away from him.

"Don't you dare touch me," she said between clenched teeth.

"Are you all right, Simone?"

She whirled around at the sound of a familiar voice. It belonged to one of the police officers in her bowling league. "I'm okay, Mark."

His bright red eyebrows met in a frown, as clear blue eyes shifted between her and Rafe, who'd switched the bowling bag from his left hand to his right. "Are you sure?"

She nodded. "Very sure." The last thing she wanted was for bullets to start flying if the two lawmen drew down on each other. Moving closer to Rafe, she went on tiptoe and brushed a light kiss over his firm mouth. "We were just having a lover's spat."

Mark nodded. "If that's the case, then I'll see you inside."

Waiting until the other man walked away, Simone rounded on Rafe. "What the hell are you trying to do? Get yourself shot?"

"Do you really think he would've drawn a gun on me without identifying himself as a police officer? No, Simone," he said, answering his own question. "By that time, I would've told him the same. Despite what you might think, there is police protocol. Let's go," he continued. "I don't want to make you late for your game."

Simone shot him an angry glare as she waited for him to open the door. Rafe was several steps behind her when she made her way past an area where bowlers were exchanging their street shoes for bowling shoes.

"This place is really nice," Rafe drawled behind her.

"It is," she concurred.

It was nice, but the one her father and uncle planned to put up in Mount Vernon would surpass this one in square footage and other amenities. She spied Tessa and Micah as they sat together at the far end of the building. Simone knew she had to get her sister alone to tell her why she'd come with a strange man in tow.

She placed a hand on Rafe's shoulder. "Let me talk to my sister alone before I make the introductions."

"Okay. I'll be over there." He pointed to a corner where bowlers had left their bags.

Smiling, Simone approached her sister. Tessa's fiancé, Micah Sanborn, stood up and kissed her cheek. "Hey, Simone. How's it going?"

She returned the kiss, smiling at the tall, dark, handsome and incredibly masculine Kings County assistant district attorney whom she'd come to regard as her brother. He was dressed casually in a pair of jeans and a navy-and-white-striped rugby shirt.

"It's all good," she lied smoothly. "How's your family?"

"They're well, thank you. By the way, my folks wanted me to ask you if you're available Sunday to come for a cookout. Faith and Ethan have already committed."

Tessa Whitfield stood up and hugged her sister. Two

years younger than Simone, she was taller and darker in coloring and the modified flyway Afro hairstyle she'd worn for years was replaced with a short chic cut that flattered her soft, delicate features. Light caught the sparkle of blue-white prisms in the magnificent cushion-cut center diamond on her left hand.

"Please say you're coming, Simone. Micah and I are spending the night at his parents' house after we leave Faith and Ethan. You can come with us, and that way you won't have to drive back to White Plains just to turn around and come back to Jersey the next day."

Simone met Micah's intense dark gaze, and knew he was waiting for her answer. She gave him a warm smile. "Excuse me, Micah, but I need to tell Tessa something before I commit."

Tessa gave her a perplexed look. "What's the matter?"

"Come with me," she said cryptically. Taking Tessa by the hand, she pulled her away from the people who'd begun crowding into the neighboring lanes. In another fifteen minutes, balls would be hurtled with astonishing speed, drowning out conversations.

Rafe took a step when he saw Simone with a woman who looked enough like her to be her sister, but settled back against the wall when he realized they weren't moving out of his line of vision.

He watched Tessa Whitfield's expression change as Simone whispered close to her ear. After a full minute, both women turned and stared at him. He acknowledged Tessa with a barely perceptible nod before she threw her arms around Simone's neck. He mentally concluded that Simone and Tessa must have incredibly attractive parents to have produced not one, but two beautiful daughters. Straightening to his full height he was ready when Simone led Tessa over to him.

She extended her hand. "Hello, Rafe. I'm Tessa Whitfield, your *girlfriend*'s sister. It's a pleasure to meet you."

Rafe shook her hand. "The pleasure is mine, Tessa." He noticed their voices were similar, but Simone claimed a slightly lower register.

"Come, Rafe. I'd like you to meet my fiancé before we start bowling."

He wasn't certain what Simone had told her sister, but if she was going to pass him off as her boyfriend then he would willingly play out the charade until the game ended. What he didn't want to think about was kissing her again. He knew Simone hadn't been expecting the kiss, but once his mouth touched hers he hadn't wanted to stop.

Rafe's gaze swept over Micah Sanborn. He was tall, slender, with close-cropped dark hair sprinkled with flecks of gray. Although he wasn't in uniform there was something about the way he carried himself that silently blared *Cop!* Once a cop, always a cop. He wondered if it would be same with him when he retired.

Tessa looped her arm through Micah's. "I'd like you to meet Simone's boyfriend, Raphael Madison. Rafe, my fiancé, Micah Sanborn."

Smiling, Micah gave him a firm handshake. "Nice meeting you, Rafe. Is it Rafe or Raphael?"

"Rafe will do."

Micah's dark, penetrating eyes took in everything about Raphael Madison in one sweeping glance. "Are you on the job?"

Rafe knew he was asking if he was a cop. "How did you know?"

"After putting in twenty years on the force, I can spot one fifty feet away."

"What are you doing now?" Rafe asked, not admitting or denying he was in law enforcement.

"I'm a Kings County ADA."

"I'd like to talk—"

"Yo, Sandy, you guys are short one man tonight," called out Justin Jamison, a short, but solidly built man with a shaved head. "Harris had a collar, so he's stuck at the station with paperwork."

Micah stared at Rafe. "Do you bowl?"

"Not in a while."

"Do you mind filling in tonight?" Micah asked

Rafe preferred bowling to standing around looking and acting like a bodyguard. "I wouldn't mind at all." Placing a hand on Simone's shoulder as she sat changing her shoes, he leaned over her. "I'll be back."

"Where are you going?"

"I'm going to be your bowling partner tonight."

She wrinkled her nose. "If you spoil our winning streak I'm going to hurt you, Rafe Madison." Not only was her team undefeated, but she and Micah had earned highest league scores among the men and women.

"Whatcha gonna do to me, baby?" he whispered.

"You don't want to know." She gave him a sassy grin when he winked at her.

Knowing no one was going to harm Simone with dozens of police officers around her, Rafe went to select a pair of shoes and a ball. It was apparent she'd adjusted to her present situation because she was smiling more than scowling, joking rather than protesting. He'd enjoyed cooking with her, even if he'd done most of it.

* * *

Simone was on her feet, her gaze fixed intently on Rafe. Whenever it was his turn to bowl, those in nearby lanes stopped whatever they were doing to watch him. She wasn't certain whether it was technique or luck, but the results were awesome. He'd just bowled his seventh consecutive strike.

"I'm impressed," she said, complimenting him when he sat down. "And I'll have you know that I'm not very easily impressed."

A dazzling smile deepened the lines around his eyes. "Neither am I."

"What's that supposed to mean?"

"You've impressed me, too."

Simone gave him a skeptical look. "I'm not the one on track to bowl a perfect game."

"Have you ever bowled a three hundred?"

Shaking her head, Simone watched Tessa's follow-through. She'd knocked down her spare. "I've come close. What about you?"

Rafe lifted a broad shoulder. "I've done it once or twice."

NYPD Sergeant Justin Jamison took a long swallow from a bottle of beer, narrowing his gaze at Rafe. "Look, Sandy, you know the rules. No ringers."

Simone popped up like a jack-in-the-box. "Who are you calling a ringer, Justin?"

He'd asked her out once, and she'd accepted. Although divorced, he couldn't stop talking about his ex-wife. And what Justin refused to understand when he called to ask Simone out again was why she'd turned him down. It was apparent he was unable to accept rejection because after that he'd suddenly turned on her as if she were a bitter enemy.

The homicide detective glared at her. "I wasn't talking to you, *Curly Sue*."

Rafe rose slowly to his feet and took Simone's arm. Even though he didn't need Simone to defend him he wasn't going to stand by and let the obviously inebriated man get in her face.

"Look, man, you need to watch your mouth," he threatened softly.

Micah shot the man a warning look. "And I think you should lay off the beer." A female vice detective forcibly pried the beer bottle from Justin's hand.

The others on Jamison's team groaned in unison while rolling their eyes at him. "What the hell are you looking at?" he asked his teammates.

The vice detective rubbed Jamison's shaved head, then kissed it. "They're spanking us, Sarge, so suck it up."

"Let go of my arm, Rafe," Simone whispered angrily when he steered her a short distance away.

"Only if you promise me you won't go after someone who's had a little too much to drink."

"But he accused us of cheating."

"It's okay."

"But it's not okay, Rafe."

He angled his head and glared her. "Let it go, Simone."

"I—"

"Enough, Simone." His warning was spoken softly. "If I haul you out of here now, then your team is going to have to forfeit the game. Remember, the *ringer* is only filling in for tonight."

The fact that Rafe referred to himself as a ringer made her pause. "You're not a professional bowler, are you?"

"No, I'm not. Please, let's finish this game so we can go home."

"I need to tell you something."

"What is it?"

"We've been invited to Micah's folks' house on Sunday for a cookout and…"

"And what?" Rafe asked when her words trailed off.

"After we leave Faith and Ethan's I'm not going back to White Plains."

"Where are *you* going?"

"Franklin Lakes. I've been invited to spend the night with the Sanborns."

Rafe shook his head. "Not without me, Simone. Remember, where you go, I go."

She gave him a facetious smile. "Why did I know you'd say that?"

"Probably because you know that I'm not going to succumb to your seductive wiles."

Her delicate jaw dropped. "What are you talking about?"

"You've got more than half the men here lusting after you. All you have to do is smile and they melt like butter."

With wide eyes, she shot him an incredulous stare. "I'm not interested in any of these men."

"That's a good thing because I'd hate to act a fool every Wednesday night."

Rafe didn't miss the admiring male stares directed at Simone, or the whispered innuendos about her face and body. He wanted to tell them that the woman he'd been assigned to protect was not only forbidden and unobtainable, but also unavailable. What he found objectionable was that most of the men were married.

"You won't have to act a fool much longer because next Wednesday is our last night."

"Good. Now, what's up with Saturday?"

"I'll let Micah know that you're coming, too."

He wanted to ask Simone if they were expected to share a bedroom because if they were, then it would complicate everything. It was one thing to sleep in the same house and quite another to sleep in the same bed.

The next-to-last game of the season ended with Rafe bowling a perfect three hundred and Simone a two thirty-eight, her highest score to date, allowing her team to remain in first place as the only undefeated team in the league.

Simone moved closer to Rafe, her hand cradled protectively in his as they stood in the parking lot talking to Tessa and Micah.

"Are you ready for some football?" Micah crooned singsong.

"I think I should warn you that whenever the Sanborns get together on Sundays there's always a friendly game of football," Tessa said to Rafe. "Do you think you're up to the task?"

Staring down at Simone's upturned face, Rafe found himself mesmerized by the glowing eyes under the overhead lights in the brightly lit lot. There was the faintest glimmer of a smile on his lips when his gaze met and fused with hers. "Not only am I ready, but I'm looking forward to it."

Micah extended his hand. "Thanks again for filling in."

Rafe shook his hand. "I'm glad I could help out."

"You were awesome," Tessa complimented softly. "Are you certain you're not a professional bowler?"

"Why is everyone asking me that?"

"Who else asked you that?" Micah asked.

"Simone. I just happen to have excellent eye-hand coordination."

Micah chuckled. "How's your throwing arm?"

A swollen hush ensued before Rafe said, "It'll do."

As he bade Micah and Simone's sister good-night, he replayed the former cop's query about his throwing arm. It'd been more than ten years, but he still could throw an eighty-mile-an-hour fastball. His curve and sinker balls weren't too bad, either. There'd been a time in his life when throwing a baseball had become as vital to him as taking his next breath. He'd openly challenged his father when he skipped his chores to spend hours with his high school's pitching coach perfecting sinkers, sidearm curves and fastballs. Major and minor league scouts came to every game to watch him strike out batter after batter with ninety-plus-per-hour fastballs.

The Superman character had come from fictional Smallville, Kansas. But the great state of Kansas had spawned a real superhero in the likes of Raphael Madison. The Ks hanging from the high school outfield bleachers representing the number of strikeouts belonged to their local hero: Captain Kryptonite.

Baseball had saved him, his mother and his sister. The money he'd been paid when he signed a MLB contract saved his father's farm, but all the money in the world couldn't save Gideon Madison from an illness for which there was no cure.

The two couples bid each other good-night with a

promise to see one another on Saturday before making their way to their respective vehicles and heading out in opposite directions. Rafe made it back to White Plains in record time, exceeding the speed limit by more than fifteen miles an hour. He maneuvered into the driveway to the house ablaze with light from first- and second-story windows.

"You can hold on to that set of keys," Simone said when Rafe locked the door behind them. "I have an extra set."

Pocketing the keys, Rafe set the alarm. "I'm going to put up a pot of coffee. Would you like some?"

She gave him a long, penetrating look. Rafe living with her was a persistent reminder that her life was not her own to live as she'd planned. And his presence was also a constant reminder that it'd been years since she'd shared her home with a man.

Simone forced a smile. "No, thank you. Good night." She walked out of the entryway and made her way to the staircase.

The seconds ticked off before Rafe said, "Good night, Simone."

Chapter 5

After his third cup of black coffee, Rafe felt the caffeine racing through his veins like jet fuel, firing his body's sensory receptors. The feeling of agitation was preferable to ruminating about the woman under whose roof he would reside for an indefinite amount of time. She wasn't the first female he'd been assigned to protect, but there was something about Simone that made him blatantly aware of their gender differences.

Time stood still and everything around him ceased to exist when he'd kissed her in the bowling alley parking lot and, for a nanosecond, she'd responded. And what he couldn't forget was her shocked expression. Was it because she hadn't expected him to kiss her or was it because she was aware that he'd enjoyed tasting her mouth?

Rafe closed his eyes, and in his mind he could still see

her incredibly beautiful face. It was ironic that he hadn't known Simone Whitfield twenty-four hours, yet could mentally recall everything about her: the way the light played off the varying colors of her curly hair, full lips with a perpetual pout and a lush, curvy body designed to drive any normal man crazy. He opened his eyes and glanced over at the clock on the microwave. In another twenty minutes, it would be midnight. He had to get at least five hours of sleep or he would be less than alert.

Pushing to his feet, he walked over to the sink, rinsed the coffee mug, leaving it in the sink. It took another ten minutes to check all of the windows and extinguish the lights throughout the first level of the house. His footfalls were heavy when he climbed the staircase to the second story. Slowing, he stopped outside the door to Simone's bedroom. Listening intently, he encountered silence before continuing down the hallway to his bedroom.

Rafe's motions were automatic, almost mechanical as he undressed. He removed his firearm from the holster and placed it under one of the pillows on the bed before he made his way out of the bedroom to the bathroom across the hall. It took less than fifteen minutes for him to brush his teeth and shower. He reentered the bedroom, got into bed, then reached over to switch off the lamp on the bedside table.

This time when he closed his eyes, it was to sleep.

Rafe felt warmth seconds before he detected movement on his left. All of his senses kicked into gear as he opened his eyes, rolled over, reaching for the Glock at the same time.

With wide eyes, he looked at Simone staring back at

him, her shocked gaze fixed below his waist. He looked down, groaning inwardly. His flesh had betrayed him. It wasn't a full erection, but close to it.

Simone didn't know what had shocked her more— seeing the deadly-looking gun pointed at her or the flesh hanging heavily between Rafe's muscular thighs. When she'd walked down the hallway to his bedroom, she realized he hadn't closed his door. He had been in bed, his bare back to the door, so she wasn't certain whether he was awake or still asleep.

Hoping not to disturb him, she'd crept quietly into the room to tell him that she was going jogging.

Then the unthinkable happened. She hadn't been more than three feet from the bed when he sprang up, naked, gun in hand and the evidence of his maleness in full view.

"I'm...I'm sorry," she sputtered, her face burning in embarrassment. Turning on her heels, she raced out of the room with Rafe calling her name.

"Dammit!" Rafe hissed between clenched teeth. Placing the firearm on the bed, he reached for his jeans and slipped into them. Simone had come up on him so quietly that he hadn't had time to react. He'd been assigned to protect—not frighten—her.

He took off after her, his bare feet muffled in the carpeted runner that extended along the length of the hallway. A quick search of her bedroom revealed nothing. She'd made her bed and the calming, seductive scent of lavender lingered throughout the space.

What Rafe didn't want to think of was that Simone had left the house without him. It was too late to turn back to get his gun, so he bounded down the stairs two at a time.

"Simone!" The sound of him calling her name

echoed throughout the house as he searched each room, his heart pounding painfully against his ribs. Then he found her. She was sitting on a love seat in the enclosed back porch, eyes closed and her breasts rising and falling heavily under a long-sleeved tee.

"Simone?" This time his voice was softer, barely above a whisper. Rafe felt his heart turn over when he saw her tears. They trickled slowly down her face as she cried without making a sound.

Simone heard the deep voice, but was loath to open her eyes for fear of seeing the gun in Rafe's hand. She'd managed to push the events of the prior day to the dark recesses of her mind when she pretended it hadn't happened, but all of the horror and fear came rushing back when she saw the deadly weapon pointed at her.

In that instant, it wasn't a gun, but the bloody knife that had been plunged into her neighbor's chest, a knife that could've possibly been plunged into her to hit a vital organ, rendering instantaneous death. Would she, she mused, have been given time to say a silent farewell to her parents, sister, brother and other family members? Would the bright lights of life have gone out as quickly as someone flipping a switch? Every macabre thought had raced through her mind when she ran away from Rafe and all he represented.

Her eyes fluttered open when she felt the power in the hands easing her gently off the love seat. The brave front she'd affected twenty-four hours before dissipated like a thick fog being blown away by a strong wind.

"It's all right," Rafe repeated over and over when Simone buried her face against his bare chest. "I'm not going to let anything or anyone hurt you."

He didn't know what it was, but she felt so right being in his arms. She smelled delicious and the soft curves of her feminine body fit into the contours of his body although he was a foot taller.

Simone snuggled closer, feeding off the warmth and strength in the arms around her. It was the second time that she'd found herself in Rafe's arms and it felt so right, as if she belonged there. She knew if her father had been around, she would've crawled up in his lap as she'd done as a little girl in order to feel safe. But Malcolm Whitfield wasn't here, and Rafe wasn't her father, yet she felt safe, protected.

And in all the years she'd known Anthony Kendrick he'd never protected her or made an attempt to make her feel safe. She'd always been the tough girl, the tomboy who'd been able to take care of herself. Then came a time when she was tired of taking care of Simone and wanted someone else to assume that responsibility. It was one of the reasons she'd married Anthony.

It'd taken sixteen years for her to come to the realization that she'd selected the wrong man for her life partner. Anthony wasn't going to and didn't want to change because he couldn't. He was who he was.

Lowering his chin, Rafe buried his face in the profusion of curls floating around Simone's face. He didn't know why, but he liked seeing her hair falling down around her shoulders and back. Maybe because it made her look like a sultry vixen, reminding him why he'd been born male.

"I'm sorry I frightened you," he said in a soft, soothing tone. "You have to give me a bit more warning the next time you creep up on me."

Bracing her hands on his chest, Simone pushed Rafe back until he dropped his arms. Tilting her chin, she stared up into the brilliant violet-blue eyes that reminded her of tanzanite. "I didn't know if you were asleep. And if you were, then I hadn't wanted to wake you up."

A smile tilted the corners of his mouth. "I'm a very light sleeper."

Her gaze lowered as a flush suffused her cheeks. "I found that out the hard way." Heat singed her body when she realized she'd used the wrong adjective.

Rafe's smile widened. Simone Whitfield was blushing, the deepening color a shade that made her appear innocent and demure. But he had to remind himself that she'd been married, and that married women usually weren't *that* innocent or naive.

He hadn't found Simone brash, but she had an in-your-face attitude that probably intimidated a lot of men. And he'd suspected there was something more between Simone and Justin Jamison than just their bowling in the same league. There was no doubt the man wanted more, and she wasn't biting.

"I'm sorry you had to see me like that, but I always sleep in the nude."

"I wasn't talking about your hard-on." The word was out of her mouth before she could stop it.

It was Rafe's turn to blush. His face turned a deep red as he averted his gaze. "I'm not going to apologize for having, as you say, a hard-on, because I'd rather wake up with one than not."

"I'm not talking about your state of arousal or lack there of."

"Just what are you talking about?"

"You pointing a gun in my face. Yesterday it was a knife, and today it's a gun. You're supposed to protect me, Rafe, not scare the hell out of me!"

He took a step, but Simone put up a hand to stop him from coming closer. "I'm sorry, baby."

"Don't you dare *baby* me, Raphael Madison. I am not your *baby*."

Rafe closed his eyes, berating himself for the endearment. He opened his eyes, silently pleading with her to understand. "I won't call you *baby* again. But I'm sorry about the gun. When you startled me, I reacted the only way I know how. The next time you come into the bedroom, either say something or knock on the door."

Simone saw something in her bodyguard's eyes that hadn't been there before—humility. He was sorry that he'd frightened her, sorry that he'd pulled a gun on her, but he wasn't going to apologize for his physical exhibition that left nothing to her imagination. She hadn't had a lot of experience with the opposite sex, and if she were being truthful, she'd have to admit that her ex-husband was the only man with whom she'd slept. What made that so pathetic was that she couldn't remember a time when she'd actually enjoyed sleeping with him.

She'd lost count of the number of times she'd pleaded a headache, it was her time of the month or she didn't feel well. But her excuses never bothered Anthony. He'd simply turn over and go to sleep without a word of protest. If she'd revealed the intimate details of her marriage to her sister and cousin, they would've said that her ex was even too lazy to make love to his wife.

Crossing his arms over his chest, Rafe stared at

Simone, wondering what was going through her mind. "Why did you come to see me?"

Her eyelids fluttering as if she'd just come out of a trance, Simone trained her gaze on Rafe. He looked incredible with his clothes on and magnificent out of them. Broad shoulders, defined pectorals, a six-pack abdomen, narrow hips and muscular legs were the perfect complement to his drop-dead gorgeous face. Why hadn't the Justice Department assigned her an older, less attractive or even a female bodyguard?

"I wanted to tell you that I'm going jogging."

"You're going jogging," he said. It was more a statement than a question.

"Yes, Rafe, I'm going jogging."

"At five o'clock in the morning." Again his query was a statement.

"Yes."

Rafe shook his head. "Not today, Simone."

"What do you mean 'not today'?"

"First of all, it's too early to go jogging, and secondly I didn't bring jogging gear."

A slight frown appeared between Simone's eyes. "What gear? All you need is a pair of running shoes, shorts or sweats. We're only going to jog around a track, not run a corporate-sponsored marathon."

Rafe rolled his eyes. "I have everything you mentioned, but if you happen to have an extra jockstrap handy, then I'll go jogging with you—*later.*" He'd stressed the last word.

Simone blushed for the second time in a matter of minutes. "No, I don't happen to have an extra jockstrap around. What I do suggest is that you purchase one, because I don't intend to modify my schedule because of your lack of *gear.*"

"You have a meeting in Central Valley at eleven. What time do you have to be in Manhattan tonight?"

"I estimate getting there around four. Why?"

"We'll leave here a little earlier so that I can stop at a sporting goods store to pick up a few things."

Simone nodded. "That shouldn't be a problem. After breakfast, I'm going down to the greenhouse to select the flowers I'm going to need for tonight's dinner party."

Grinning broadly, Rafe ran his fingers through his hair, pushing thick, sun-streaked waves off his forehead. "What's for breakfast?"

"For you—Froot Loops. I'm having waffles with strawberries."

"I want what you're having."

"What's wrong with your Froot Loops?"

"I'll eat them tomorrow."

"When I make omelets tomorrow, I bet you'll want those, too."

"Instead of arguing about who'll make what, let's set up a schedule," Rafe suggested. "You can make breakfast, while I'll be responsible for dinner."

It took Simone only seconds to mull over his suggestion. She was much more proficient with breakfast foods than she was at preparing dinner. "Okay."

Rafe expelled an inaudible sigh at the same time he winked at Simone. "I'm going upstairs to shave and shower. Please don't leave—"

"The house without you," she said, finishing his statement. "I get the message."

He winked at her again. "I was just checking."

"Yeah, right," Simone drawled as a hint of a smile parted her lips.

As Rafe walked out of the kitchen, she stared at the broad back that tapered to a slim waist and hips. It was the first time that she noticed he had a slight swagger to his walk. A knowing smile softened her features. Raphael Madison was the total package from head to toe, and that meant it was virtually impossible to ignore him. She had to make certain to keep busy or else she'd find herself drawn to the hunky lawman with a magnetism that came off him in sensually charged waves.

Having changed from her jogging attire into a pair of well-worn jeans and a faded sweatshirt, Simone carefully poured batter onto the heated plates of the waffle iron before closing the top. Hot steam and the warm, sweet smell of baking waffles mingled with the aroma of brewing coffee made from freshly ground beans.

Without warning, a shiver shook her. She couldn't fathom the eerie feeling because she hadn't opened any of the windows in the kitchen. And if she had, then it would be warm, not cold air coming in through the screens. Simone didn't want to imagine that she was losing her mind because twenty-four hours before her life had irrevocably changed, and she doubted whether she would ever be the same.

"Something smells good."

Peering over her shoulder, she watched Rafe walk into the kitchen. The light blond stubble on his jaw was gone, his damp hair clung to his scalp and he'd changed into a pair of light blue jeans and matching shirt. This morning he wore a pair of running shoes instead of boots.

"It's the coffee."

Rafe came closer and wrinkled his nose. "It's more than the coffee."

Simone returned her attention to the waffle iron. The light indicating doneness had gone out. Reaching for a fork, she opened the top and removed two perfectly crisp waffles and placed them on a platter.

"How many waffles do you want?" she asked Rafe.

"How many did you make?"

"Eight. I usually freeze the leftovers and use them for ice cream sandwiches."

Rafe reached over her shoulder to take the platter. "That's ingenious."

She wrinkled her nose at him. "They're even better when you roll them in chocolate chips or nonpareils."

"How often do you eat them?"

"I can assure you not too often, or I won't be able to fit into my clothes."

Rafe wanted to tell Simone that he doubted that even if she had an ice cream sandwich every day that she'd put on a lot of weight. She had a nervous energy that made her almost hyper. The only time she wasn't busy or moving was probably when she was asleep.

"Go sit down and I'll bring everything to the table," he said instead.

They sat at the table, eating silently while the music from a radio on the countertop filled in the blank spaces where conversation was unnecessary. Fragrant brewed coffee and fresh squeezed orange juice provided a perfect accompaniment to the crisp waffles and fresh, tart strawberries, bursting in their own juices and topped off with lightly whipped cream.

Rafe cleared the table, while Simone rinsed and stacked dishes and flatware in the dishwasher. "I only have two pet peeves, and dishes left in the sink tops the list."

"Are you talking about the cup I left in the sink last night?"

She nodded. "If you're going to rinse it, then please put it in the dishwasher."

"What if I don't rinse it?"

Simone rolled her eyes at him when she saw the smirk playing at the corners of his mouth. "You don't want to find out."

He took a step, bringing them within mere inches. "What are you going to do to me?"

Resting her hands on her hips, she rose on tiptoe. "I'll jack you up, Raphael Madison."

"Never happen, Simone Whitfield. Don't you realize I'm exactly a foot taller and weigh a hundred pounds more than you?"

Her delicate eyebrows lifted. "I'm certain you've heard the expression about the bigger they come the harder they fall."

"Of course, but that's not the case with you and me."

"I—" Simone wasn't given the chance to finish what she was going to say when she found herself hoisted effortlessly above his head as if she were a barbell. Her heart beat a rapid tattoo against her ribs. "Put me down! Please, Rafe. I'm afraid of heights!" He'd unknowingly found her Achilles' heel.

Lowering her slowly, Rafe set her on her feet and pulled her to his chest. "What else are you afraid of?"

Burying her face against his shoulder, she shook her head and waited for her heart rate to slow down. "That's it."

"What about snakes, worms or spiders?"

She shook her head. "No."

Smiling, he dropped a kiss on the fragrant hair covering her head. "You're a girl after my own heart." Rafe didn't know why, but he preferred women who didn't shriek or faint if they saw a bug or reptile. He found those who constantly played the vapid female boring *and* tiring.

A frown found its way over Simone's face. It was the second time Rafe had referred to her as a girl. She knew she wouldn't be so sensitive about the word if she'd come close to looking her age.

"The last time I checked my driver's license, it indicated that I was over the legal age."

Rafe's frown matched hers. "What are you talking about?"

"I'm not a girl, Rafe. If you claim you know that much about me, then you'd realize that I'm a full grown woman."

Gently easing her back, he studied the face that belied her age, but not her body. "You think I don't know that," he said quietly. "You may have issues about looking younger than you actually are, but once you're over forty you'll gladly accept the comments and the compliments."

She scrunched up her nose. "I'll be certain to look you up the day I celebrate my big 4-0, so you can see for yourself if I look my age."

He shook his head. "That'll never happen." There

was a solemnity in his voice that sounded ominous. "Once I leave here, chances are our paths will never cross again."

Simone sobered. "You're so right about that. Let's finish up here, because I have to go to the greenhouse to pick the flowers I need for tonight's dinner party."

Chapter 6

Rafe, sitting on a low stool, long legs stretched out in front of him, watched Simone's fluid motions as she made her way along rows of flats and potted flowers growing in wild abandon in the greenhouse. The structure wasn't as large as those in commercial nurseries, but its contents yielded enough to ensure success for Wildflowers and Other Treasurers. The hinged doors provided easy entry into the temperature- and humidity-controlled environment equipped with a security system and a small boom box.

He'd promised himself that he had to make a concerted effort to think of Simone as his witness because it would serve to keep their association on a less personal level whenever they weren't out together. To the world they would present themselves as a couple, but behind closed doors he had to make certain to keep as physically far away from her as possible. There was something about Simone that made him react to her with a little less professionalism. At first he'd thought it was because of their living arrangements, but if he were truly honest with himself, then he'd have to admit it had nothing to do with residing under the same roof.

The reality was that he'd found himself enthralled with Simone Whitfield. Everything about her had become his ideal as it pertained to a woman: her looks and her spirited personality; but there was something else—a latent sexiness he was certain she was totally unaware she had. And what Rafe couldn't understand was why she downplayed her sexiness when it wasn't as obvious with her sister.

Tessa was stunning, and she knew it. But on the other hand, Simone was sensually ravishing, but appeared totally unaware of her effect on men. Each and every time she'd gotten up to bowl, most of the men within twenty feet of her stopped what they were doing to stare at her—and he was no exception. Rafe still hadn't figured out whether it was her hair, her eyes or her tiny, lush, compact body, but whatever it was it had him fantasizing about things that had nothing to do with his job. In fact, he'd been dreaming about Simone when she'd come into his bedroom earlier that morning. If she'd seen him in a state of arousal, then she'd been responsible for his lack of control.

Rafe pulled his gaze away from her to stare at the butt of the small automatic in the holster strapped to his ankle. Leaning over, he adjusted the hem of his jeans to conceal it. Simone had admitted to her fear of heights, but neglected to include firearms in her declaration. He made a silent promise do everything possible not to let her see the weapons.

"Are these roses?" he asked, running his fingertips over the delicate petal of a white flower growing in a large clay pot.

Simone halted cutting the stems of a delft-blue hydrangea. Her client had requested varying shades of hydrangeas, her favorite flower, for her dinner party. "No. They're camellias, or better known scientifically as *camellia japonica*."

"Do you use them in wedding bouquets?"

She nodded. "Occasionally I do. But I prefer using them in garlands for decorating staircases, in urns or as centerpieces with other blush-colored flowers like rhododendron or cherry blossoms."

Rising slightly, he moved his stool closer to her. "What made you get into the flower business?"

Simone placed each bloom into a large straw basket gently, as if she were collecting eggs. "Every summer Tessa, my cousin Faith and I went to South Carolina to visit my grandmother. Whenever it came time for cooking lessons, I conveniently found something else to do. I preferred climbing trees, playing ball or swimming in the lake. One day my grandfather took me with him on a nature walk. He showed me which berries were edible and the ones that were poisonous. Grandpa knew the name of every tree, bush, weed and flower. He was the first one to show me crossbreeding through propagation.

"I'd forgotten everything he'd taught me until I got to college and took several botany courses. I'd dabbled in the humanities before changing over to a liberal arts concentration. But it was the math, science and social sciences I liked best."

"Did you go into college to be liberal arts major?"

There came a beat before Simone said, "No. I'd decided beforehand to become a psychologist. After two years, I changed my concentration because my personal life was in disarray. I signed up for courses that I believed would be fun. It turned out that botany had become the magic cure. After I broke up with my ex, I started buying plants and flowers because having them around also managed to lift me out my funk. After a few months, the house looked like a nursery and smelled like a funeral parlor. When I ran out of room, I bought this greenhouse. Then when I took a course on floral arranging I knew I'd found my niche."

"How did you get your clients?" Rafe asked.

"My first client was a childhood friend. I'd offered to do her wedding flowers for a fraction of what I should've charged. And as the saying goes, 'the rest is history.'"

"So most of your business comes from referrals?"

"All of it is referrals."

"Pretend that I'm a bride. Don't look at me like that," Rafe said when she gave him a dubious stare. "I did say *pretend*."

Simone shifted her stool over to a large pot filled with pale-hued hydrangeas and expertly clipped off half a dozen flowers. "I'm trying very hard to imagine you in a wedding dress."

"If Dennis Rodman can put on a wedding gown—"

"Don't you dare go there, Rafe," she interrupted, grinning. "It's easier for me to imagine Dennis Rodman on his book jacket butt-naked than seeing him in a wedding gown."

"Whatever floats your boat," Rafe whispered under his breath. "Okay, scrap that image. What if my sister came to you for wedding flowers? What would you suggest?"

"What's her favorite flower?"

"She likes roses."

"What color roses?"

"She prefers white."

"I'd probably suggest a bouquet of all white roses, or a mix with ranunculus, lilac and lily of the valley."

"What is ranunculus?"

Simone pointed to a pot in a far corner. "That's ranunculus. It's called the little frog flower, because *rana* is Latin for frog and because it grows near the water."

Rafe crossed his arms over his chest. "Do you know the Latin names for most of the flowers?"

She nodded. "Their Latin derivation, history and what they represent. Louis IX brought ranunculuses to his mother after the Fifth Crusade, but unfortunately for him they didn't flourish. Several hundred years later, its corns were stolen from a sultan's garden in the Ottoman Empire and traded in the Marseilles flower market."

"What about different colors? Does a white rose have the same meaning as a pink?"

Simone exhaled slowly. She didn't know whether Rafe had kept up a steady stream of conversation because he was actually interested in what she did, or he was bored and he wanted her to entertain him. "Pink roses represent perfect happiness, and the white rosebud signifies worthiness and purity.

"If you want to know more about flowers I'll let you read Charlotte de la Tour's 1918 version of *Le Language de Fleurs*. It was very popular during the

Victorian period, because at that time flowers became
a means of clandestine correspondence between chape-
roned lovers. Secret messages were communicated in
the bouquet based on chosen flowers. The flowers in a
bridal bouquet, known as a *tussie mussie,* told a groom
what his shy bride wanted him to know about her."

"Give me an example," Rafe said, totally engrossed
in the history of flowers.

"Name some flowers," Simone countered.

"White roses, violets, irises and daffodils." They were
only flowers he could think of off the top of his head.

"Irises mean I have a message. The white rose says
she's bringing him her girlhood innocence, the violets
represent fidelity in the marriage and the daffodils
promise devotion and a sweet disposition."

Rafe's gaze moved slowly over Simone's delicate
profile. Suddenly it hit him. Not only was she a pretty
face and sexy body, but she was smart—very, very
smart. Lowering his arms, he pushed to his feet and
picked up the petal of a white rose that had fallen off its
stem. He cupped Simone's elbow, easing her to her feet.
Their gazes locked as he pushed wisps off her cheek and
tucked the bloom behind her left ear.

Simone closed her eyes against his intense stare.
"What are you doing?" Her voice was barely a whisper.

His lids came down, hiding his innermost feelings.
Rafe wanted to tell Simone that she was as beautiful
and as breathtaking as the delicate flowers in her
greenhouse. "I didn't want to see something so pretty
go to waste."

Reaching up, Simone pulled the petal from behind
her ear, dropping it into the basket with the hydrangeas.

"It won't go to waste. When we go back into the house I'll show you what I do with them."

She sat down on the stool again and snipped smaller blooms of blue and green hydrangeas until she had enough flowers to fill two straw baskets. She took off her gloves and left them and a pair specially angled clippers on a built-in shelf. "I'm going to take these inside. Then I have to change before we leave for Central Valley."

Rafe eased the basket from Simone and waited until she set the code to the greenhouse, then escorted her across a manicured field to the main house.

Rafe lay in bed, his head resting on folded arms as he stared up at the shadows on the bedroom ceiling. The glowing numbers on the clock on the bedside table read 2:17 a.m. He was as wide-awake as he would've been at two in the afternoon. Although not prone to bouts of sleeplessness, he now knew what insomniacs experienced.

He'd accompanied Simone to Central Valley to meet with a prospective bride to select the design for her wedding flowers, spending three hours on the porch while the two women deliberated. The mother of the bride-to-be had offered him lunch, but he'd opted for a tall glass of sweet tea.

They left Central Valley, stopping at a sporting goods store in a nearby mall where he purchased socks, sweats, T-shirts, three tracksuits and a pair of running shoes. He wasn't looking forward to jogging with Simone because he preferred running on a treadmill.

He'd driven back to White Plains, and Simone spent

an hour in the mudroom where she'd stored the hydrangeas in a built-in refrigerator. When she emerged it was with six round glass vases filled with hydrangeas. Around the lip of each vase she'd tied contrasting ribbon with a decorative bow. Her client had invited six couples and wanted to welcome them with hydrangea centerpieces they would take home as parting gifts at the conclusion of the dinner party.

It'd been some time since Rafe had been to Manhattan, so he'd suggested eating dinner at a restaurant that featured outdoor dining. There was an instant when he'd sat across the bistro table from Simone that he felt as if they were actually on a date. But when he'd asked himself whether under another set of circumstances he would've liked to date her—and the answer was a resounding yes.

Turning over, he punched the pillow. He had to get at least three hours of sleep in order to keep up with Simone's busy schedule. He tried counting backward from one hundred, taking slow, deep breaths and then willed his mind blank. It was when streaks of light pierced the veil of darkness that sleep claimed his mind and body.

Rafe opened his eyes, blinking at the glowing red numbers on the clock and sprang from the bed. It was after one in the afternoon, and it was raining. Reaching for a pair of boxer briefs, he slipped them on and headed for the bathroom. The fact that he'd overslept wasn't as upsetting as not knowing where Simone was or what she was doing.

He managed to brush his teeth and shower in less than ten minutes. Not bothering to shave, he pulled open dresser drawers for clean underwear, shorts and a T-shirt. Not bothering to put on socks, he tucked the holstered gun into the waistband of his shorts, covering it with his shirt, and raced out of the bedroom and down the stairs. He found Simone sitting on the enclosed back porch, thumbing through a magazine. Rafe hadn't realized how fast his heart was beating until he saw her.

Simone, seeing movement out of the corner of her eye, turned to find Rafe staring at her. A hint of a smile parted her lips. "Good morning. Or should I say good afternoon?"

He gave her a sheepish grin. "Good afternoon. I'm sorry I overslept."

"So did I," she admitted. "I think it was the rain."

Rafe walked into the room and sat opposite Simone. "I can't blame the rain. I couldn't fall asleep."

"That's because you drink much too much coffee." After dinner, he'd drunk two cups of strong, black coffee to her one cup of decaffeinated herbal tea.

"You're probably right." He'd told her a half truth. There were occasions when he'd drunk coffee nonstop, but it usually didn't affect his ability to fall asleep. What had disturbed and continued to disturb him was the woman with a mop of curly hair sitting a few feet away.

Simone closed the magazine and placed on the cushion next to her. "You must have either dressed in a hurry or in the dark because your shirt is on backward."

Rafe pulled at the neckline of his white T-shirt. Reaching for the hem, he pulled it up and slipped his arms from the sleeves. Without taking it off, he turned the shirt around and put it on correctly. "What do you have planned for today?" he asked Simone when she gave him a wide-eyed stare.

"You're really uninhibited, aren't you?" she asked, ignoring his question.

His eyebrows furrowed. "Why would you say that?"

"This is the second time I've seen you half-dressed or completely nude."

An expression of incredulity crossed Rafe's face. "I would never take you for a prude. But if my showing some skin bothers you, then I'll make sure it won't happen again."

"I'm not a prude," Simone said in protest, a rush of heat stinging her cheeks.

"Yesterday morning was unavoidable and I explained that I always sleep—"

"I understand about yesterday, Rafe. I'm talking about today."

Rafe stared at Simone, trying to understand where she was coming from. The seconds ticked by as they regarded each other. "Simone, are you a prude?"

"No!"

"You said that much too quickly."

Her eyes flashed fire. "And what's that supposed to mean?"

"That the lady doth protest too much."

"Hel-lo. I was married."

"There are a lot married prudes."

"And I doubt if you're one of them," she spat out angrily.

"I'm not a prude, nor am I married." He looked at her, gazes locking, then he turned away. "Since I've been assigned to witness security, I get to learn a lot about people when there's just the two of us day in and day out. People can take so much isolation. After a while they talk about any and everything."

Simone rolled her eyes at the same time she sucked her teeth. "Well, if you think I'm going to spill my guts, then you'd better think again, because I'm not going to tell you any more than what's written in the file you have on me."

Rafe ruffled his damp hair with his fingers. He wanted to tell Simone that she was no different from the countless other witnesses he'd protected. At first, most would barely speak to him, but after a week they would come looking for him to say something to break up the monotony of staring at the same four walls. What most had come to understand was that human beings were social creatures and needed contact and interaction with other humans in order to maintain one's mental and emotional equilibrium and sanity.

"You still haven't answered my question."

"And exactly which one is that, Rafe?"

He ignored the thread of hardness that'd crept into her voice. "What are your plans for today?"

"I'm expecting something to be delivered today."

"What is it?"

Simone counted slowly to three to keep from blurting out that it was none of his business. She had to keep reminding herself that her life had changed, that the barefoot man glaring at her would monitor every phase of her life regardless of whether she was awake or asleep. She woke at five, but hadn't gotten out of bed until seven because of the steadily falling rain. Even if it hadn't been raining she'd been reluctant to walk down the hall to knock on Rafe's bedroom door to wake him for fear of finding him naked again. The vivid image of his magnificent male body was imprinted in her mind—forever.

Unconsciously, she'd mentally compared Rafe to Anthony Kendrick, and Tony had come in a distant second. Once she'd been able to emotionally distance herself from her ex-husband, she realized all he'd been was a pretty face. And there was nothing about his physique to indicate that he worked out, because if breathing hadn't been involuntary then he would've expired a long time ago.

What Simone couldn't understand was how Tony was content to get up every day and not leave the house. The few times he'd attempted to hold down employment he'd complain incessantly about commuting into Manhattan. Even when he'd managed to secure a job in White Plains, the complaints continued—complaints about his boss and/or coworkers. After a while, she realized Tony was responsible for putting the Z in lazy.

"Construction plans."

Rafe's eyebrows lifted. "You're having work done on this house?"

"No—I mean, yes. But not until the fall." She gave him a hopeful look. "Do you think the trial will be over before September?"

"There's no way of predicting that. I'm certain the U.S. attorney wants to gather enough evidence before he takes it to trial."

"What more do they need? They have me as an eyewitness."

"The government's going to want more than just your eyewitness account. Forensic evidence must be substantiated, along with footage from close circuit cameras in and around the park at the time of the attack."

"Are you telling me that I'm going to be a prisoner in my own home for at least the next three to four months?"

Rafe shook his head. "No, I'm not, Simone. First, Benton has to be arraigned, then the evidence on him will have to be presented to a federal grand jury, and if there's a backlog on the calendar, then we'll have to wait."

A shiver snaked its way up Simone's back when she recalled the feral look in Ian Benton's eyes as he came toward her. "Do you think he'll be granted bail?"

"I doubt that any judge will agree to bail. What they'll probably do is set the amount so high that only someone like Bill Gates will be able to come up with the money. After all, the man's accused of trying to kill one of their own, so I doubt if he'll find one sympathetic judge in all of Westchester County."

"What if his attorney asks for a change of jurisdiction because he believes his client won't get a fair trial in this county?"

"Whether he's tried in the Southern or Eastern District, it doesn't matter. It's up to a jury to find him guilty or innocent."

"What if he cops a plea?"

"I hope he does, because he'd save the taxpayers the cost of a trial. Regardless of whether he accepts a plea or is found guilty of attempted murder, he's still going to spend the rest of his life behind bars without the possibility of parole."

There was a pregnant silence as Simone closed her eyes. She opened them to find Rafe watching her intently. "What if something goes wrong and he's found innocent?"

"Nothing's going to go wrong, Simone." Rafe wanted to tell Simone that Ian Benton had dropped off the government's radar screen before, and there was no way they were going to let him slip away again.

"What about jury tampering?"

"You've been watching too many gangster movies," Rafe chided softly.

"Don't try and pretend it doesn't happen, because it does."

"I know it does. But if it happens, then he'll be retried and I'll get to play your boyfriend a little while longer."

Simone didn't know whether Rafe was teasing her in an attempt to belie her anxiety. "Why do I get the impression that you like pretending to be my boyfriend?"

Rafe's eyes smoldered with a fire he'd successfully concealed from Simone within seconds of coming face-to-face with her. He'd called her a prude when he should've referred to her as naive, or perhaps even innocent. But what he couldn't wrap his head around was the fact that she *had* been married for four years, yet was still uncomfortable with the male body.

"Do you want me to lie or do you want the truth?"

She blinked once. "I would like the truth."

"I like pretending to be your boyfriend." His lips were parted in a smile that did not reach the blue eyes darkening with a foreign emotion Simone couldn't identify.

Simone felt a languorously sensuous shiver pass between them and she shuddered noticeably when she recognized the sexual magnetism coming off Raphael Madison in a vortex sweeping her up in its force field, refusing to let her go. How, she wondered, could she find herself drawn to a man who physically looked nothing like the men to whom she'd been attracted, or to a man who'd spent only two nights under her roof.

"Why?" she asked when she found her voice.

Rafe shook his head in a motion that was barely perceptible. "I don't know, Simone. Perhaps before I leave you, I will have figured it out." A clock on a side table chimed the hour, breaking the soporific spell from which neither wanted to escape. He forced a smile. "It's a little late, but right about now I'm fittin' to go get a big bowl of Froot Loops."

A smile crinkled her eyes. "Fittin'?"

"You've never heard of the word?"

"Yes, I have. But I never figured you would use it."

Pushing to his feet, he approached her and pulled gently on her hair. "That's because you don't know me." Turning on his heels, he walked out of the sunporch, leaving her staring at his back.

"You're right, Rafe," Simone whispered, "I don't know you."

She didn't know him and she didn't know herself. One thing she did know was that she definitely wasn't a prude, but frustrated—seeing Rafe's nude body was a reminder of what she hadn't experienced in eight years: sex.

She'd met Tony the year she'd celebrated her sixteenth birthday, began dating him at nineteen, married him at twenty-one and by the time she was twenty-five she'd filed for divorce.

The sound of the doorbell echoed throughout the house. By the time she'd made her way to the front door, Rafe had the mailing tube with the schematic for connecting outbuildings that would conform to the design of the farmhouse and replace the greenhouses. He handed her the tube, his gaze lingering on her mouth. "I signed your name."

"Forgery is a crime, Mr. Madison."

Rafe, pressing his palms together, extended his hands. "Then, cuff me, Ms. Whitfield."

"That sounds kind of kinky."

His grin was dazzling. "Don't knock it unless you've tried it."

Returning his smile, Simone winked at him. "Go eat your Froot Loops."

Rafe reached for her free hand. "Come keep me company."

"Why?"

"I don't like eating alone."

Simone wanted to tell him that she, too, didn't like eating alone, but after eight years she'd come to accept it. She didn't know how long Rafe would live with her, but within seconds resigned herself to enjoy his company *and* his protection.

Chapter 7

Simone went completely still, her brow furrowing when she heard the deep, pumping sound. She couldn't believe she could hear music coming from down the hall and into her bathroom's dressing area. There was no doubt Raphael Madison had lost his mind playing music that loud. And the music was a genre that wasn't one of her favorites!

Slipping her bare feet into a pair of fluffy pink slippers, she went to close the door connecting the bathroom with her bedroom. It muffled the sound, but hadn't eliminated it completely.

She'd managed to spend Friday indoors with Rafe without incident. If it hadn't rained all day, she would've asked him to drive her to Cold Spring to browse through the many antique shops, but resigned to catch up on her reading. Her hands halted smoothing a perfumed crème on her smoothly shaven legs as a frown found its way between Simone's eyes when she registered the misogynistic lyrics of a popular hip-hop performer singing that all women were good for was sex.

"Oh, hell, no!" she whispered angrily.

If Rafe Madison thought he was going to play that garbage in her house, then he was sorely mistaken. Reaching for a short, red silk wrap, she slipped her arms into it, belting it tightly around her waist. She flung open doors and made her way down the hallway. Her rage escalated the closer she came to Rafe's bedroom. He'd closed the door, but it did little to reduce the pounding, driving bass line. She'd purchased the component system because the brand had come highly recommended, but hadn't turned the volume up to its highest setting, which was what Rafe had probably done.

She alternated knocking on the door with calling his name. "Open this damn door! Now!" She was poised to hit the door again, this time with a closed fist, when it opened suddenly. "What do you think you're doing?" Simone screamed at Rafe.

Rafe didn't register the frown distorting Simone's delicate features because he was mesmerized with the high color in her cheeks and the cloud of damp, curly hair floating sensuously around her face to her shoulders. She looked and smelled good, good enough to eat.

"What's the matter?"

Simone was too enraged to take in the stark white shirt, tailored navy blue slacks and a perfectly knotted dark blue and off-white checkered silk tie. When she'd reminded Rafe that they were going to a dinner party at her cousin's house, it was obvious he'd opted not to wear jeans.

"Turn the music down!" That said, she turned on her heels in her fluffy slippers and retraced her steps.

"Keep the robe, but lose the slippers!" Rafe called out to her stiff back.

"Turn it down," Simone repeated without turning around. The volume decreased by the time she walked into her bedroom and closed the door. She hadn't thought it was necessary, but it was apparent she had to reiterate *and* establish a new house rule: no dishes in the sink, greenhouse shoes are not to be worn inside the house and no loud music. She didn't want to censor Rafe's music choices, but there was no way she intended to put up with him playing his music so loud that the prints on the walls vibrated.

The nerve of him talking about her slippers. At least she hadn't come to his bedroom wearing nothing more than her birthday suit. An impish gleam sparkled in her eyes. How would he have reacted, she mused, if she'd knocked on his bedroom door completely naked. Simone was willing to bet his reaction time would've slowed considerably, to the point where he wouldn't be so quick to draw a gun on her. Glancing at the clock on the fireplace mantel, she realized she had less than fifteen minutes to finish dressing. She'd told Rafe to be ready to leave at six-thirty.

Simone walked out of her bedroom at the same time Rafe stepped out into the hallway. They stood motionless, staring at each other.

Simone's vermilion-colored lips parted in a smile when she realized it was the first time she'd seen Rafe's hair combed into a semblance of a style. He'd brushed the thick tawny strands off his forehead and ears, the curling ends brushing the collar of his shirt. It was a little too long to suit her tastes, but then she had to remind herself that he wasn't her type, so how he wore his hair was his business.

Rafe walked the length of the hallway, carrying a leather overnight bag, his gaze widening as he approached Simone. He forced himself not to stare at her bare legs in a pair of chocolate-brown, fabric-covered high-heel pumps. He hadn't realized he'd been holding his breath until he felt tightness in his chest.

Simone Whitfield was breathtakingly beautiful in a silky stretch-knit lime-green tank dress with alternating narrow bands of brown and green at the hem ending at her knees. The clinging fabric accentuated every curve of her petite body, while the scooped neckline displayed her full breasts to their best advantage. She hadn't pinned up her hair, and a cloud of gold-red curls floated over her bare shoulders and down her back.

Rafe stared at Simone under lowered lids. "You look beautiful."

She angled her head, giving him a bright smile. "Thank you. You look nice, too."

Simone hadn't lied to Rafe. The suit jacket fit his broad shoulders as if it'd been tailored expressly for his body. Even his leather slip-ons were made of the finest leather. "I'll drive tonight," she said softly.

Rafe shook his head. "No. I'll drive."

"I know how to get there."

"I have GPS," he countered.

Simone rested her hand over his sleeve. "My car has been parked in the garage for days. I—"

"Okay, Simone. You can drive your car." Rafe didn't want to argue with her—not tonight. Now when all he wanted to do was enjoy their time together without being reminded that he was her bodyguard.

She gave him a dazzling smile. "Thank you." Tightening her hold on a small brown crocheted purse, she started toward the staircase.

Rafe followed Simone down the stairs. The first time they'd left the house together, he'd turned off the lights, but Simone insisted the house remain lighted because she didn't like coming into darkness. An hour before sunset, lamps in the many rooms would come on, activated by programmable timers. Bending down, he picked up the bag Simone had left by the front door, along with a large bouquet of pale pink roses, lilies and wild pink and purple heather wrapped in clear cellophane and tied with streamers of curled pink and purple ribbons.

Instead of making one trip to the car, he'd have to make two because of the decorative shopping bag filled with bottles of red, white and a blush wine for the McMillans. He also had to transfer a case of champagne he'd purchased from the Sanborns from his vehicle to Simone's. They would spend the night at Franklin Lakes, then return to White Plains Sunday evening.

Simone left Rafe to lock up the house while she tapped in the code on the keypad affixed to the molding of the two-car garage. The door opened smoothly. She got into the sport utility vehicle and backed the Toyota Sequoia out of the garage. Pulling a lever, she unlocked the hatch so Rafe could load their luggage, flowers and wine.

"Don't forget to buckle up," she teased Rafe as he got in beside her after he'd hung his jacket behind the front seats. The garage door lowered when she touched a button on the remote device attached to her visor. Out of the corner of her eye, she saw him reach for the dashboard. "And don't you dare touch my radio."

Shifting slightly on the leather seat, Rafe stared at Simone's profile as she maneuvered out of the driveway, the hem of her dress inching up smooth, firm thighs. Suddenly he regretted giving in to her request to drive because instead of focusing on the road his gaze would be drawn again and again to her exposed skin.

"Don't you drive with music?" he asked.

"Yes. But not what you were blasting back at the house." Soft jazz flowed from speakers when she pressed a button on the steering wheel.

"What's wrong with hip-hop?"

"There's nothing wrong with it if I'm not bombarded with lyrics that put down women."

He ran his fingers through his hair and stared out the side window. "Hip-hop has a bad rep. Not all of it is misogynistic."

"That may be true, but somehow I had you figured for a country music fan."

He turned around to glare at Simone. "Because I'm from Kansas?"

"Yup."

Rafe gave her a pointed look when she took her gaze off the road for several seconds. "I'm sorry to disappoint you. Gospel music was the only music I was allowed to listen to when growing up. My father was a fire-and-brimstone, Bible-thumping zealot who told me I was going to hell so many times that I'd decided why go to church or pray if I was already condemned to eternal damnation."

"What did your mother say?"

"Her father was a preacher, so she was used to the incessant preaching. She goes to church three or four times a week, doesn't wear makeup, swear, listen to secular music or imbibe the devil's nectar."

Simone smiled when he'd mentioned the *devil's nectar*. The last person she'd heard refer to wine or liquor as the devil's nectar had been a devoutly religious great-aunt. "Why did your father say you were going to hell?"

"I suppose it was because I used to challenge him. He said I was insolent and disobedient."

A slight smile parted Simone's lips. "Were you insolent, Rafe?"

"Were you, Simone?"

Her mouth made a little popping sound when she pursed her lips. "Ah—I don't think I was."

Leaning to his left, Rafe pressed his shoulder to hers. "Admit it."

"Admit what?"

"Admit that you were a bad girl."

Simone wrinkled her nose, unaware of much Rafe had come to look for the gesture. "Never."

He dropped a kiss on her bare shoulder. "You don't have to admit it because I know you were."

"Were you a bad boy?"

Rafe pulled back and exhaled. "My father and I never agreed on anything, and the downside was that he punished me by doubling my chores. Instead of getting up at five to gather eggs and muck out the barn, he'd get me up at four to help him milk the cows."

"Did you grow up on a farm?"

He nodded. "I grew up on land that's been in my family for more than a hundred and fifty years. My great-great-grandfather started out growing wheat, and over the years whoever managed the farm added barley and hops when beer companies sprang up throughout in the Midwest. Now it's corn and soybeans."

Simone signaled and then accelerated as she sped past a slower-moving car. "Does your dad still run the farm?"

Rafe recalled the last time he'd gone to visit Gideon Madison. All he'd talked about was the farm. Who was living on his land? Had he sold it to strangers? Had someone plowed over the corn and soybeans? "No," Rafe said after a marked pause. "The farm was sold to a distant cousin because we wanted to keep it in the family."

"Where do your folks live now?"

"My folks are no longer together. My mom lives in San Diego with my sister and her family, while my dad still lives in Kansas." Esther Madison had left her husband, yet refused to divorce him. She claimed divorce went against her beliefs.

Simone noticed it was the first time Rafe referred to his father as "dad," and she wondered if a rift still existed between father and son. She also wondered why his parents were now living in different states. She wanted to know more about the man living with her, but decided not to pry.

She'd been on the receiving end of countless questions, had become an object of scrutiny the day she'd become Mrs. Anthony Kendrick, and the result was that she'd become a very private person. And she knew the spotlight would be on her again when she introduced Raphael Madison as her boyfriend.

"Slow down, Simone, before we're pulled over," Rafe warned when he noticed the speedometer inching above eighty.

"I ain't afraid of no po-po," she teased. "Not when my boyfriend is po-po." Her foot eased off the gas pedal. "By the way, do have your shield with you?"

"Yes. But—"

"Then don't sweat it, darling. Even if we're stopped, they're not going to give me a ticket."

He frowned. "I thought I warned you about calling me darling."

Simone sucked her teeth. "Lighten up, Rafe, or you'll never convince anyone that we're involved with each other. After all, we are living together."

"Living, yes, but not sleeping together, *darling*," he drawled.

"Don't push it, farm boy," Simone warned. "That's where I draw the line. There'll be no sex."

Rafe angled his head as if deep in thought. "Hmm— no sex," he murmured softly. "It's not going to be easy with my girlfriend looking like she does, but I guess I'm going have to go along with her decision not to give me any and continue with the cold showers."

"Are you really taking cold showers?"

Winking, Rafe gave Simone a Kool-Aid grin. "You saw what I looked like when you surprised me in bed the other morning."

"I can't believe you're bringing that up again. You're downright disgusting!"

He sobered quickly. "You're wrong, Simone. What

I am is a normal man who thankfully can still get it up without the aid of pills or other mechanical devices. You're thirty-three years old, you were married, and you have the face and body that most men fantasize about, so cut out the innocent-little-girl act. Not only is it tired, but it's not becoming."

Simone's temper flared as fury choked off the words poised on the tip of her tongue. "Who the hell do you think you are to talk to me like that?"

"I'm someone who's not afraid to tell you the truth," Rafe countered, his own temper rising. "You've probably heard poor little Simone so often that you're content to wallow in an ocean of self-pity. So what if your marriage failed. Join the millions who couldn't make a go of what they thought was going to last forever."

"Why are you talking about my marriage?"

"Because you're the one who admitted that your personal life was in disarray when you were in college and you got into floral design to pull yourself out of the doldrums. Unless you're prone to depression, which I suspect you're not, then whatever crap you've gone through would have to be because of your ex."

The sounds of measured breathing, the slip-slap of tires on the roadway and the hauntingly beautiful sound of Chris Botti's muted horn filled the SUV as Simone stared through the windshield. She wanted to tell Rafe that he was wrong, that she'd accepted that she'd made a mistake to marry Tony. The ensuing silence between them was deafening as she took the exit leading to the Palisades Interstate Parkway.

"I don't blame Tony because my marriage didn't

work out," Simone admitted when she crossed the state line from New York into New Jersey.

"Who do you blame, Simone?"

Her eyelids fluttered wildly. "I…I blame myself for hoping and praying for a miracle that never manifested itself." Tears filled her eyes, and she blinked them back before they fell.

Rafe, hearing the catch in her voice, said, "Pull over, Simone!"

"What?"

He placed his left hand on the wheel. "I said pull over. I'll drive."

She maneuvered over to the shoulder and they exchanged seats, he adjusting the driver's seat to accommodate his longer legs. After securing his seat belt and repositioning the rearview mirror, he pulled out into traffic as Simone rested her head against the seat rest and closed her eyes.

"I'm sorry, Simone."

She didn't open her eyes. "What are you sorry about?"

"I had no right to bring up your past."

"It's all right. I need to talk about it with someone other than my family."

"You don't have to tell me."

"But I want to tell you," she insisted. "Perhaps talking about what happened with you is like going to a therapist. You'd be impartial."

Rafe wondered how impartial he could be when he realized he was beginning to have feelings for Simone Whitfield. He could say his feelings were purely physical in nature, but that wasn't entirely true; what he was beginning to feel for Simone went beyond his wanting to sleep with her. The truth was he liked her—a lot. She was beautiful, bright, sexy and above all spirited. And it was her spunk and fire that he admired most.

He'd grown up challenging his father because his mother wouldn't or couldn't. Rafe didn't doubt that Gideon loved his wife, but his need to have everyone submit to his will was a source of ongoing contention between father and son.

"Even if I wasn't impartial, I still have no right to cast judgment on you."

Simone opened her eyes and stared at Rafe's distinctive profile. "Have you ever wanted something so badly that you refuse to accept the truth? Well, that was the basis of my marriage to Anthony Kendrick," she continued without waiting for his reply. "I met Tony when I was sixteen and he was in his first year of college. He'd asked to take me out, but Father said he was too old for me and that I had to wait until I graduated high school. However, Daddy did let him take me to my senior prom."

"Had you dated other boys while you were in high school?"

She nodded. "I went out with a couple, but it was nothing serious. I was saving myself for Tony. The day I moved into my dorm room at Hampton, he called and left a message that he was driving from D.C. to see me the following weekend. We spent most of our free time together and when he asked me to marry him, I said yes. He was the first and only man I've ever slept with," Simone admitted when Rafe gave her a sidelong glance.

Rafe groaned inaudibly. He'd accused Simone of being a prude when in reality she wasn't *that* sexually experienced if she'd been with only one man. "How long were you engaged?"

"Not long. I wanted to wait until after I'd graduated college, but Tony said he'd waited long enough for me, so we returned to New York and married. I didn't want to transfer from Hampton to Howard, where Tony was a business major, so we continued to commute on the weekends to be together. The first indication that my marriage was in trouble was when Tony called to say he couldn't see me every weekend because his GPA was slipping, and proposed we get together the first weekend of the month. We alternated calling each other every night, but when I couldn't get in touch with Tony for a week I borrowed my roommate's car and drove to D.C."

"Did you find him?"

"Not really."

Rafe gave Simone an incredulous look. How naive had she been? It was apparent her husband was doing more than trying to pull up his GPA. "What do you mean 'not really'?"

"His roommate told me that Tony had hooked up with several other students who were in a study group, and he hadn't seen him in days. When I told him to give Tony a message that his wife had come looking for him, I thought he was going have a stroke. It was apparent that my loving husband had neglected to tell anyone at Howard that he was married."

"What excuse did he give when he finally surfaced?"

"That he was studying and that he'd lost track of not only the time, but the days."

"Excuse me for saying it, but that's a lot of bullshit, Simone."

"I know that now. I'd heard that he'd been seeing a girl, but he swore on his father's grave that he hadn't been sleeping with her."

"So you forgave him."

Biting down on her lower lip, Simone nodded. "Like a fool, I did. I returned to Mount Vernon for the summer, but Tony stayed at school to take some graduate courses. When I returned to Hampton, I changed my major and continued with what'd become a slowly eroding marriage. I graduated the same year Tony got his MBA. We came back home, rented an apartment and he applied for a position with an auditing firm to prepare for the CPA exam. He put in the hours, took the test, passing it on his first attempt.

"Meanwhile I went to work for Whitfield Caterers, while dabbling in designing wedding flowers. I also began saving to buy a house. Those plans were dashed when Tony came home one night and announced that he'd quit his job, and that we didn't have to worry because his mother was going to subsidize him until he found another position."

Rafe curbed the urge to laugh out loud. Simone had given Anthony Kendrick more chances than he deserved. "Did he ever go back to work?"

"Would you if your mother gave you a weekly allowance?"

"That's a rhetorical question because I'd never take money from my mother."

"That's where you differ from my bum-bitch ex." Simone smiled when Rafe chuckled. "He thought he was doing something when he signed up to do taxes during one tax season, but on April 15 at the stroke of midnight, he put away his pencils and slept in late until the next tax season. He'd go through the motions of looking for work, but if he got something it never lasted more than a week or two, because there was always something wrong with his supervisors or coworkers. The pièce de résistance came when I overheard gossip from tenants in our building that he was having an affair with my next-door neighbor. He was too lazy to work, but not too lazy to cheat on me.

"I'd had enough. I moved out, called a lawyer and served him with divorce papers. Even after we were divorced, I second-guessed myself because I never was able to prove that Tony had actually cheated on me."

"You didn't need proof, Simone," Rafe countered angrily. "The fact that he refused to support you should've been enough to give his trifling ass the boot."

Simone laughed, the low throaty sound filling the vehicle. "Now you sound like my cousin. She says she would've paid someone to beat the hell out of him, but I told her then I'd be left with the responsibility of taking care of baby boy."

It was Rafe's turn to laugh. "You could've always sent him back to his mother."

"That's where he is now."

"Do you still see him?"

Simone shook her head. "It's been more than six months since we've talked."

Rafe concentrated on the signs indicating the number of miles to Englewood Cliffs. "Did he call to tell you that he had a job?"

"When did you become a comedian?" she asked Rafe.

"Well, did he?"

"No. He wanted to know if I'd changed my mind about reconciling."

"Had you?"

"No. I'd given Anthony Kendrick sixteen years of my life with nothing to show for it but disappointment and dashed dreams. I kept telling myself that I loved him, that I'd taken a vow to support him through sickness and health, for richer or poorer. It's taken me a long time to accept that I don't need a man to feel complete."

You are complete, Rafe mused. Simone was the total package, because she'd been blessed with looks and brains. It'd taken her a long time to accept that her marriage was over before it had begun, but thankfully she'd found the strength to end it.

"Do I make a right or left turn at the exit?" he asked as the signs for Englewood Cliffs came into view.

"Make a left. Go straight for two miles, then I'll tell you where to turn off to get to their development."

Ten minutes later, Rafe drove up to the gatehouse leading to the exclusive community where Simone's cousin lived with her husband. Lowering the driver's-side window, he nodded to the attendant.

"We're here to see the McMillans."

The man punched a button on the keyboard and McMillan came up on a computer screen. "Name, please."

"Simone Whitfield."

"You'll find visitor parking on your left." He pushed another button; retractable stanchions lowered automatically and Rafe drove through.

Rafe counted the number of houses in the private enclave. Eight two-story town houses were set one hundred feet back from professionally manicured lawns.

Top-of-the-line luxury cars parked in circular driveways attested to the affluence of the enclave where the McMillans had chosen to live.

He maneuvered into an empty space set aside for visitors, turned off the engine, and came around to assist Simone. Reaching for his jacket, he slipped his arms into the sleeves. "Go and let your cousin know we're here. I'll be there as soon as I get the wine and flowers."

Simone pointed to her left. "Their house is the one with the black Mercedes-Benz coup in the driveway."

Lowering his head, Rafe dropped a kiss on her hair. "Go on in. I'll see you in a few minutes."

Chapter 8

Rafe watched Simone walk, his gaze on her bare legs in the heels. When he'd first seen her in the dress, he was afraid he was going to embarrass himself because he never could've imagined the perfection of her petite, compact body. The fitted dress revealed what had been concealed by her jeans, slacks and sweats. Even when he'd cradled her body to his, he still hadn't been able to discern the lushness that lay under layers of fabric.

He'd kissed Simone—once—and was living with her, and now he about to step into the role to play her love interest. The difference between his prior relationship with Dorene and Simone's was that the latter would be pretense.

Walking around to the rear of the SUV, he took out the bag filled with the bottles of wine and the bouquet of flowers, closing the hatch and activating the remote. He hadn't taken more than two steps when a dark gray BMW convertible maneuvered into the space next to Simone's car.

Smiling, he nodded to Tessa. Her dewy skin radiated good health. "How are you?" Shifting the flowers to the crook of his arm, he leaned over and opened the passenger-side door. Rafe extended his hand, easing her gently to her feet.

"I'm good, thank you. How are you?"

"Wonderful." The single word was pregnant with warmth.

Tessa returned Rafe's smile, her admiring gaze taking in everything about him in one sweeping motion. He looked different in tailored attire. Her sister had confided the reason for her association with Raphael Madison, but that didn't stop Tessa from reading more into their arranged relationship.

She'd watched the interaction between Rafe and Simone when they were bowling together and felt something intangible that communicated that their closeness went beyond witness and bodyguard. She suspected her sister and the marshal were totally unaware of it.

Tessa loved her older sister passionately, but felt that she'd wasted so many years of her life trying to make the impossible possible. Tony Kendrick was a spoiled, trifling man who always looked to a woman to take care of him. She knew of Simone's aversion to blond men, but there was something about the gorgeous lawman that would have *any* woman giving him a second look.

Micah stepped out of the two-seater, slipped his arms into his suit jacket, then came around to greet Rafe, giving him a one-arm embrace. "What's up?"

Rafe lifted a broad shoulder under his suit jacket. "I don't know. This is my first Whitfield get-together."

"Let's hope it won't be your last," Micah said, clapping a large hand on his shoulder. "Aren't you and Simone staying over at my folks' place tonight?"

"Yes, we are."

He and Simone had packed overnight bags, but his concern was whether they would be forced to share the same bed. Rafe thought of himself as an honorable man, but he wasn't certain how honorable he would remain sleeping with Simone Whitfield after seeing her in the body-hugging dress. He wondered if she'd chosen the garment to tease him, or if she'd have worn it even if he hadn't accompanied her.

Tessa looped her arm through Micah's. "Let's go, darling. I'm certain Faith and Ethan are waiting for us."

Rafe exchanged an amused look with Micah. It was obvious that the Whitfield sisters liked the word *darling*. However, it was different with Tessa and Micah because they were each other's darlings and were about to become husband and wife the following month.

The door opened as Simone reached for the doorknocker. Faith McMillan stood in the entryway, her dark eyes shimmering like onyx. Although she was as beautiful as ever, there was something about the model-turned-chef that was different. Her black curly hair was longer than it'd been in some time, but every few years Faith let her close-cropped hair grow out. She wore a white, loose-fitting sheer peasant blouse over a lace-trimmed camisole, a pair of black cropped slacks, and had pushed her bare feet into low-heel black leather mules.

"Oh, my goodness, you look amazing!" Leaning forward, she kissed her cousin's cheek. Faith looked as if she'd gained some weight.

"So do you," Faith countered, returning the kiss. Straightening, she stared over Simone's shoulder at Tessa, Micah and the tall man walking in their direction holding a bouquet of flowers at an awkward angle. "Now, that's what I call yummy," she whispered next to her ear. "Where did you find *him?*"

Simone knew Faith was talking about Rafe. "He found me," she said, lowering her voice to a whisper.

"Talk about nice on the eyes," Faith continued sotto voce.

"Have you no shame, Faith Whitfield-McMillan?"

"No. Not when it comes to a good-looking man." Faith kissed Tessa and Micah, and then smiled politely at the tall man who was her cousin's mysterious date. "Welcome. I'm Faith."

Rafe studied the tall, slender woman who looked as if she'd just stepped off the pages of a glossy fashion magazine. Her flawless dark skin, large eyes that tilted at the corners and delicate features were mesmerizing. He returned her smile.

"Thank you. Rafe Madison." He handed Faith the flowers. "These are for you, compliments of your cousin."

Faith cradled the bouquet in the crook of her arm. "It's nice meeting you, Rafe." She glanced at the profusion of delicate flowers wrapped in cellophane. "I don't know how Simi does it, but she can make weeds look like rare orchids."

"Who's dealing weed?" asked a deep voice behind them.

Faith and Simone gave Ethan McMillan an incredulous look as he strolled into the entryway.

"Shame on you, Ethan," Faith whispered. "Talking about drugs will give Simone's friend the wrong impression. I can assure you that neither of us is into illegal substances," she said to Rafe.

Deep dimples caressed Ethan McMillan's tanned, tawny face as he looped an arm around his wife's waist after he'd kissed Tessa and exchanged handshakes with Micah. Tall and slender, he was his wife's physical counterpart. Close-cropped mixed-gray hair, a deep, resonant voice, luminous gold-brown eyes afforded the former Air Force–trained pilot a second look whenever he entered a room.

He smiled at his wife's cousin. "The flowers are beautiful, as usual. Thank you."

Simone affected a mock curtsy. "You're welcome." She smiled up at her bodyguard. "Rafe, this is Ethan McMillan. Ethan, Rafe Madison." The two men exchanged handshakes and polite greetings as Rafe handed off the bottles of wine to Ethan.

"Everyone's welcome to hang out in the family room before we sit down to dinner."

"I'm going to see if Faith needs any help in the kitchen," Tessa volunteered.

"Me, too," Simone added.

Ethan lifted his eyebrows at Micah and Rafe. "Well, it looks like we'll get to do some male bonding."

"Don't bond so much that you'll be too pie-eyed to

see how to get to the dining room table," Faith warned in a quiet voice that indicated what kind of male bonding her husband was talking about.

"Ah, baby. Both of them have designated drivers, so it's all good."

"It'd better be all good," Tessa mumbled under her breath.

"Ditto," drawled Simone.

She didn't mind driving from Englewood Cliffs to Franklin Lakes, but what kind of bodyguard would Rafe be if he was too drunk to protect her? Then she remembered what he'd told her about growing up in a home where alcohol was forbidden. She wasn't certain whether he even drank alcoholic beverages, because when they'd eaten in the Manhattan restaurant he'd opted for coffee rather the complimentary glass of wine that came with dinner.

The three women exchanged skeptical glances with their men before they turned and walked in the direction of the kitchen.

Ethan, waiting until Micah and Rafe were comfortably seated in a room with a leather seating grouping and wall-mounted television, slowly shook his head. "Don't tell me the two of you were coerced into wearing nooses tonight." As if on cue, Rafe and Micah released the top button on their shirts and removed their ties *and* jackets.

Rafe rolled his head from side to side. "Oh, yeah, that feels better."

Rubbing his hands together, Ethan smiled at his guests. "Now, what can I get you to drink while we watch the game?"

Micah folded his arms over his chest. "Who's playing?"

"Boston and the Yankees," Ethan whispered as if revealing a classified secret.

Reaching for the remote on a nearby table, Micah clicked on the television and flipped to a sports channel. It was a pregame segment where the sportscasters were debating the pros and cons of the lineup of the teams with a rivalry dating back nearly three-quarters of a century.

Resting his elbows on his knees, Rafe leaned forward, his gaze fused to the large television screen with incredibly sharp images. A jolt of excitement pulsed through his body when he saw the steady stream of spectators filling the seats at Yankee Stadium. It'd been years since he'd turned his back on what had been a promising Major League Baseball career, but at twenty-two he hadn't been mature or emotionally stable enough to cope with pro baseball, and Gideon Madison's slow descent into madness that had put his mother and sister at risk.

"What are you drinking, Rafe?" Ethan asked.

"I'll have Jack and Coke."

Ethan nodded. "What are you drinking, Micah?"

"I'll have the same," Micah mumbled. He hadn't taken his eyes off the screen.

Making his way over to a bar, Ethan opened a door to a built-in refrigerator, filling old-fashioned glasses with ice, cola and whiskey. He handed Micah his drink and a cocktail napkin, then did the same for Rafe. "Do I hear a little Kansas City in your speech pattern?"

Two pairs of eyes met him. "It depends on which Kansas City you mean." Rafe decided he wasn't going to make it easy for Ethan McMillan. Simone had mentioned that her cousin's husband had had a career as a commercial airline pilot.

"Missouri."

"Kansas," he confirmed. "You've got a good ear, Ethan."

Micah lifted his glass in a mock salute. "Here's to a good ear and a steady hand. The drink's perfect."

Ethan took a sip of his own cocktail. "I can't take all of the credit. Faith's an excellent teacher."

"She samples every drink you mix?" Micah asked Ethan.

"She did until she became pregnant." Ethan knew he'd made a faux pas as soon as he said the *P* word. A scowl twisted his handsome features. "Damn, I wasn't supposed to say anything until later on."

Scooting to the edge of his chair, Micah peered closely at his host. "Is that why you and Faith invited us over? To tell us you guys are going to have a baby?"

"Man, keep it down," Ethan warned Micah, placing a forefinger to his mouth. "I promised Faith I wouldn't say anything until dinner."

Micah angled his head. "But you decided to let the cat out of the bag—"

"Please lower your voice, Micah."

Rafe gave Tessa's fiancé a knowing glance, then burst into laughter. He'd just met Ethan and it was his second encounter with Micah, but he felt a camaraderie with the two men he hadn't experienced in years. He took another sip of the Jack and Coke, enjoying the smooth taste of premium whiskey on his palate.

"Look, my brothers, I need ya'll to help me out here," Ethan pleaded.

Looping one leg over the opposite knee, Micah affected a bored expression. "It's funny, but I don't remember any of my brothers looking like you, Brother McMillan. What about you, Rafe?"

"Don't have a brother," he crooned in his best Kansas drawl. "Sorry, Ethan, but I can't seem to help you out."

The sweep hand on the mantel clock made a full revolution before laughter filled the room, this time Ethan's joining Rafe and Micah. The three men touched glasses, silently acknowledging their secret would go no farther than the four walls.

Faith lifted the lid off a large pot and gently turned over its contents with a slotted spoon. "Simi, do you think your man will eat Southern-style greens and black-eyed peas?"

Simone halted arranging flowers in a magnificent crystal Waterford vase Tessa had given the McMillans as a wedding gift. "He's not my man."

"If he's not your man, then what is he to you?"

She wanted to tell Faith that Rafe was her bodyguard, but wanted to wait until an appropriate time to tell her about how witnessing a crime in progress had irrevocably changed her life. "He's a good friend."

"I'm not asking if you're sleeping with him, Simi."

Tessa made a cutting motion across her neck when she met Faith's gaze. "It doesn't matter whether she is or isn't, but what's important is that he's not a scrub."

Faith's eyebrows lifted with Tessa's disclosure that Rafe Madison had a job. "What does he do, Simi?"

Simone had the federal prosecutor's approval to inform her immediate family of her security witness status.

Although Faith was her first cousin, they were more like sisters. She'd told Tessa and would tell Faith, but not now. Not before they sat down to eat, and not before what she'd suspected about her cousin could be confirmed.

"I'll tell you later." She held up a hand when Faith opened her mouth. "I can assure you that he does have a job."

"Yes, he does," Tessa confirmed, deadpan.

Faith's gaze wavered between Simone and Tessa. "What are you two hiding from me?"

A hint of a smile softened Simone's lips. "No more than you're hiding from us."

A soft gasp escaped Faith's parted lips. "You know?"

"Know what?" Tessa queried. "What am I missing?" she asked, continuing with her questioning as Faith and Simone were engaged in what appeared to be a stare-down.

"Tell her, cousin."

Faith took a deep breath, held it and then let it out slowly. "I'm pregnant."

Tessa and Simone threw their arms around each other, jumping up and down as they'd done when little girls. "Yes! Yes! Yes!"

"Simone! Tessa! Please tone it down," Faith pleaded. The sisters stopped their impromptu happy dance. Excitement shimmered in their jewel-like eyes. "Ethan and I promised each other that we wouldn't tell anyone until we all sat down together tonight."

Simone sobered quickly. "So, it's supposed to be a surprise?"

Faith nodded. "We have a wager that the first one to break the promise will forfeit the right to name the baby."

"No!" the sisters chorused.

"Yes," Faith countered. "I'd suspected I was pregnant a couple of weeks before we had the church ceremony, but I didn't want to say anything."

Simone walked over to Faith and wrapped her arms around her waist. "So when I mentioned that your gown did wonders for your cleavage, you knew then that you were having a baby."

Faith giggled like a little girl. "And remember me telling you that I had enough, because I was spilling out of my bras." She motioned for Tessa to come closer. "Pinky swears that you won't say anything about the baby before Ethan and I make the announcement." The three linked pinkies.

A slight frown furrowed Tessa's smooth forehead. "Have you told your parents?"

"Not yet. We're meeting them for early mass tomorrow, so we'll tell them then."

"But I thought you were coming with us to Franklin Lakes," Simone said.

"We are coming," Faith confirmed. "Ethan said he wants to get there in time for the football game. Of course, yours truly will most happily sit on the sidelines."

Tessa rolled her eyes. "I don't have an excuse for not playing."

"Yes, you do," Simone insisted. "Just don't play."

"Not with one Whitfield sitting out. After all, we Whitfields have to represent."

"Hel-lo," Faith crooned.

Simone went back to the counter to put the finishing touches on her flower arrangement. "Faith, do you mind if I set the table?"

"Of, course not. Come with me and I'll show you where we keep the china and silver."

"Wow! Everything looks incredible!" Ethan announced as he entered the dining room, Micah and Tessa following.

Faith, standing behind a chair at one end of the table, smiled at her husband. "Simone can take the credit for setting the table."

Rafe's amused gaze locked with Simone's for several seconds before he gave her a wink. Their host was right. Fragile bone china, silver and crystal stemware on a white lace cloth over a matching liner shimmered under the glow of an overhead chandelier. Lighted tapers in crystal holders and the exquisite bouquet of flowers in a leaded crystal vase set the stage for exquisite dining. The McMillans had a beautiful home designed for comfortable living and ultimate relaxation.

As if choreographed in advance, the men pulled back chairs for their women, seated them, then took their seats, Ethan sitting at the opposite end of the table from Faith. They shared a look before she nodded.

"I'd like to say a few words before we begin eating." All gazes were directed at Ethan. "Faith and I invited you to our home tonight because we wanted you to be the first to hear what we believe is wonderful news. We are expecting our first child."

Reaching for his water goblet, Micah pushed back his chair and came to his feet, the others following his lead. "Congratulations."

· Faith, blinking back tears, whispered, "Thank you."

Simone extended her glass to Faith, then Ethan.

"Many blessings as you await your special gift. I'm here to let you know that Auntie Simi is available whenever you need a babysitter."

Tessa nodded. "I second that."

All eyes were trained on Rafe. They expected him to say something. "When Simone isn't available I'll be more than happy to stand in as her backup."

"I hope you know what you just committed to," Simone said, laughing.

"Here, here!" Micah and Ethan chanted.

"Sit down and stop teasing Rafe," Faith ordered in a tone filled with laughter. "Don't let these folks rope you into anything you don't want to do."

Rafe retook his seat next to Simone. "I've never made a promise I didn't keep." The seriousness of his tone sobered everyone.

Tessa stared across the table at her sister's dining partner. "It's a pleasure to know someone who can make and keep a promise." Her fiancé didn't believe in making promises.

Micah recoiled as if Tessa had stuck him with a sharp object. "I did promise to marry you."

"That's because you're smart enough to recognize quality when you see it," she said, giving him a saucy look.

"I'm not going to lie about that," Micah stated without a hint of guile.

Ethan raised his goblet again. "I raise my glass in a toast to Faith, Tessa and Simone—the sexiest and the most beautiful Whitfield women on the planet."

Leaning over, Rafe touched his glass to Ethan's, then Micah's. "I'll second that."

Simone placed a hand on his thigh under the table,

feeling the warmth of his flesh through the fabric of his trousers. "Careful, darling, or you'll have a problem differentiating between reality and make-believe."

Turning, Rafe gave her a long, penetrating stare. "Wrong, Simone." His voice was barely above a whisper. "I've never had a problem with reality. The only decision I've had to make was whether to deal with it or walk away."

"And there's going to come a time when you're going to have to walk away from me. So, let's make it easy on both of us. Keep it light."

Rafe kept his expression deceptively closed for fear of letting Simone see what he'd denied from the very beginning. He liked her—a little too much to remain professional *and* indifferent to her beauty and feminine lushness. She was like a gaily wrapped package under a Christmas tree that he had to wait to unwrap. He wanted to strip away the layers of her affected tough-girl exterior to find her soft core. Every once in a while he glimpsed her vulnerability before she replaced the shield to keep men at a distance. And once the shield was in place, it was virtually impenetrable.

He pressed his shoulder to hers. "What are you afraid of, *darlin'*?" Much to his surprise, a sudden light came into her eyes.

"Definitely not you, love."

"Are you challenging me to a throw-down?" he whispered.

Simone detected alcohol on Rafe's breath, so she attributed his teasing to his drinking and decided to play along. "Yes, I am."

She jumped slightly when the fingers of his right

hand feathered down the length of her spine before splaying over her hips. His hand had lingered only seconds, leaving her body warm and tingling. "If you play, then you have to pay, Simone."

Had she, Simone mused, gotten in over her head? She'd admitted to Rafe that her experience with men was limited, and she wondered if he would use her inexperience against her if she didn't use him first.

Why not Rafe? a silent voice taunted her. There was no doubt that he'd be the perfect candidate on which to practice the art of seduction. He was single, transient and once he was reassigned, she never had to see him again.

Her left hand came up, she resting it against the small of his back. He stiffened slightly before relaxing against her palm. They exchanged sidelong glances, smiling.

"Are you asking to date me?"

He nodded.

"Then, let the games begin," she mouthed.

Rafe nodded again as an expression of supreme male satisfaction crossed his face, a look that wasn't lost on the others sitting at the table.

Serving bowls filled with Southern-style greens, hopping John and a platter of garlicky crisp roast pork, were passed around the table, along with a garden salad tossed with herb-infused vinaigrette. The question whether Rafe would eat greens and black-eyed peas was answered when he had two helpings.

Simone wanted to tell Faith that Kansas wasn't the South, but it was close enough to Missouri for Southern influences to overlap state boundaries: *Brown v. Topeka*

Board of Education, Bleeding Kansas and Quantrill's Raiders. He'd managed to fit in without trying, Micah and Ethan interacting with him as if they'd known one another for years rather than a few hours. It was apparent the male bonding session had gone well.

Chapter 9

Rafe didn't take his gaze off the taillights of Micah's car as they turned off a side road and onto a private path leading up a steep hill. There were no lights along the path, and the towering copse of trees lining both sides of the unpaved surface concealed what little illumination there was from the windows of an occasional house off in the distance. It would've been completely dark if not for a near-full moon. Slowing, he came to a complete stop behind the roadster; iron gates, rising more than twenty feet, protected the Sanborn property from intruders.

The gates opened smoothly. The gray BMW picked up speed, Rafe accelerating to keep pace with the low-slung sports car. They continued along a paved surface, maneuvering into a parking area behind the rear of a three-story manor-style house with a four-car garage.

Rafe realized there wasn't another house in sight. "I suppose the Sanborns don't have to worry about nosy neighbors."

"You're right," Simone concurred. It was the first time she and Rafe had made an attempt at conversation since leaving Englewood Cliffs.

She had said all she had to say when she'd agreed to date him for the duration of their forced cohabitation. She knew she'd shocked Rafe, but she'd also shocked herself with the realization that she hadn't slept with a man in eight years. Eight long years where she'd denied her femininity because she'd chosen to hold on to a fantasy, a fairy tale where she and Tony would live happily ever after.

Even to this day, she still hadn't discerned what it was about Anthony Kendrick that'd made her turn a blind eye to his shortcomings. At first she'd thought it was his good looks, but once she was able to move beyond the superficiality, she'd concluded it was because he was the first man with whom she'd slept. Most people didn't know that beneath her tomboy exterior beat the heart of an incurable romantic.

Simone had grown up believing in only one true love in one's lifetime. Tony had been that love until he disappointed her over and over. After a while, even she grew tired of his excuses and his promises to do better, but she hadn't wanted to admit to her parents, her mother in particular, that she'd made a grievous mistake to marry the first man who'd shared her bed.

So many times she prayed she could be more like her sister and cousin. Faith's mantra of "if they're not acting right, then kick them to the curb" never penetrated her consciousness. It was only when her parents, Tessa and Faith stopped nagging her about her on-again, off-again relationship with her ex that she was able to take a step back and see what she'd refused to see: she'd wasted more than half her life with a ne'er-do-well.

Spoiled, pampered, indulged baby boy Anthony Kendrick would never become the man she wanted him to be, never be the supportive husband he should've been, and never be the man whom she could count on to take care of the children she'd hoped they would have together.

She sat, staring out the windshield, while Rafe got out and came around to assist her. Her hands went to his shoulder when his fingers circled her waist, lifting her effortlessly off her feet.

"Don't look at me like that," he said softly.

"Just how am I looking at you?"

"You make me feel like the wily alligator who's contemplating eating the gingerbread man."

Simone tightened her grip around his neck. "Do you really think I'm afraid of you?"

"I don't know."

"Well, I'm not," she shot back.

"Good," he said, lowering her slowly until her shoes touched terra firma.

There was enough light from strategically placed flood lamps for Simone to make out Rafe's face when they shared a smile. The expression made her heart beat a little too quickly.

"Are you guys ready to go inside?" Micah's deep voice shattered the moment and the silence of the warm spring night.

Rafe's head came up. "I just have to get our bags."

* * *

"Simone, are you awake?"

Simone opened her eyes and smiled at Tessa as she got into the bed beside her. "Yes. Where were you?"

"I was with Micah. We were talking about including jumping the broom in the ceremony."

Rosalind Sanborn had left a note for Micah outlining assigned bedrooms, because Bridget and her husband, Seth Cohen, had arrived earlier and were sleeping in Bridget's old bedroom. Rafe was given a bedroom on the third floor, and Tessa and Simone were given the bedroom across the hall from Edgar and Rosalind Sanborn.

"Are you sure that's all you were doing?"

"There's no need for that now. Micah's moved in with me last weekend."

"How is it living with a man?"

"I like it," Tessa confirmed. "We decided to live together to make for a smoother transition once we're married." Reaching over, she turned off the lamp on her side of the bed. "How are you getting along with your sexy lawman?"

Simone smiled in the darkness. "We're doing okay."

"From what I saw tonight I'd say you're doing more than okay."

"What's that suppose to mean?"

"There's no need to get defensive, Simone."

"I'm not, Tessa. I just don't want you to read more into something that's not happening."

"Do you want something to happen?"

Simone pondered her sister's question. "I don't know."

"Why can't you make up your mind?"

"He's a federal police officer assigned to protect a government witness, and I'm certain fraternizing is a no-no."

Tessa sucked her teeth. "It's hard not to fraternize. After all, you're living together. And how would they know? Do you plan to dime him out?"

Turning on her side, Simone tried making out her sister's expression in the moonlight coming through the window sheers. "Why are you throwing Rafe at me?"

"Because I can see what you can't or won't. Rafe can't keep his eyes off you and vice versa. If it's that bad when you're around other people, then it must be sizzling whenever you're home together."

"It's just the opposite. We're only together during meals, when I have to go to the greenhouse, or if I have something business-related outside the house."

"Do you like him?" Tessa asked after a comfortable pause.

"What's not to like?" Simone countered.

"I don't know. You tell me."

Simone closed her eyes while she composed her thoughts. "Even if Rafe wasn't carrying a gun, I'd still feel safe with him," she said quietly. "He's the only man other than Daddy who's ever made me feel that way. He also has what Mama considers good home training."

"Rafe sounds like a keeper."

"That's debatable," Simone said. "Remember, we're only going to be together for the duration of his assignment."

Shifting into a more comfortable position, Tessa rested her head on her arm. "Why can't you just enjoy your time together?"

If you play, then you have to pay. Simone replayed Rafe's riposte. If she was going to play, then she knew she had to protect her heart. She would enjoy her time with Raphael Madison, and when it ended she would move on with her life, and he with his.

"I'm going to try, but it's not going to be easy."

"Why not, Simone? He's only a man."

"Yeah, right. He's only a man who's so potent that I feel as if I'm always holding my breath around him." A beat passed. "What I don't understand is that Rafe hasn't even touched me intimately yet…" Her words trailed off as a surge of heat washed over her body when she thought about what she wanted him to do to her.

Reaching for her sister's hand, Tessa squeezed her fingers. "The problem is you've been alone for far too long."

Simone smiled. "I think you're right, Tessa."

The two women talked quietly well into the night about the mistakes they'd made and hoped not to repeat. They talked about Faith, her pregnancy and Tessa's upcoming wedding. After a while, the responses were slower in coming, then stopped altogether when both drifted off to sleep.

Rafe sat up and swung his legs over the side of the bed. Walking on bare feet, he made his way over to the window. The rumpled blanket and twisted sheets evidenced his restlessness. He was tired, yet hadn't been able to fall asleep. Every time he closed his eyes, his mind conjured up images of Simone Whitfield with her hair floating around her face, a single braid falling down her straight spine and her wide-eyed stare that seemed to look through him to see the real Raphael Madison and not the one he presented to the world.

To the U.S. Marshals Service, he was Deputy Marshal Madison. He was son and rescuer for Esther Madison and Uncle Rafe to his sister Rachel's twin boys. As for Gideon Madison, he was Judas, heathen and the devil's spawn. It'd been years since he'd saved Gideon from himself, yet each time he went to see his father he'd been unresponsive because he'd been heavily sedated.

Rafe knew he would've been better able to accept Gideon's illness if his father's body had been afflicted with a disease, because either he would recover or succumb to the malady, but science had yet to come up with a cure for paranoid schizophrenia.

Bracing his hands at the sides of the window frame, he stared down at the flowers dotting Rosalind Sanborn's garden. The flowers reminded him of the lush, colorful blooms growing in the controlled environment of Simone's greenhouses. He knew he'd never look at flowers the same way since meeting her. And of all the blooms she cultivated, she was the most exotic of them all.

He'd come to look for the red-and-gold highlights in her curly hair, the pinpoints of green in her brown eyes and the velvety sheen of her alizarin-brown skin. It was the second time in his life a woman had tugged at his heart, but his relationship with Simone would differ greatly from the one he'd had with Dorene because it would be short-lived.

A soft buzzing garnered Rafe's attention. Turning away from the window he made his way to the nightstand and picked up the vibrating cell phone. The name and number on the display reminded him that he was "on the job."

Pressing a button, he spoke quietly into the mouthpiece. "Madison."

His expression didn't change as he listened intently to the voice on the other end of the line. Ian Benton was scheduled to be arraigned at the White Plains federal courthouse Tuesday morning at ten.

"Thanks for the update." Depressing a button, he ended the call.

It was about to begin. Benton would be arraigned and no doubt denied bail. The next phase would be a grand jury hearing. Rafe didn't want to think of a grand jury not coming back with an indictment in the attempted murder of a federal judge. If not, then Simone Whitfield's life wasn't worth the cost of recycled kitty litter.

He got into bed, pulled a sheet up over his naked body and closed his eyes. What he didn't want to think about was Benton coming after Simone, because if the man even came close enough to breathe on her, he'd put him on his back.

Simone woke up two hours later than she normally would have, and attributed that to the two glasses of wine she'd drunk at the McMillans'. She managed to slip out of bed without waking Tessa. She completed her morning ablution in the adjoining bathroom and then slipped into a pair of well-worn jeans, an oversized T-shirt and a pair of running shoes.

Her footsteps were silent as she walked the length of the hallway to the staircase leading to the third floor. She wanted to take an early morning walk, but knew she had to apprise Rafe of her whereabouts.

There were two bedrooms on the upper level, one unoccupied and the other with a closed door. Stopping at the door, she knocked lightly, waited for movement, then knocked again.

"Who is it?" asked a muffled voice on the other side.

"Simone."

"What a minute, Simone."

"Whatcha doing, Rafe?" she drawled teasingly.

The door opened, and she wasn't given time to react when she found herself in Rafe's arms, his mouth slanting over hers in a kiss that robbed her of her breath. He smelled of soap and aftershave, and tasted like toothpaste. The kiss ended as it'd begun—quickly.

Simone clung to Rafe's neck as if he were her life-line, her gaze moving lazily over his face. "What was that all about?"

He smiled, deep slashes appearing in his lean cheeks. "That was good morning."

She lowered her lashes in a demure gesture. "Well, good morning to you, too."

"I assume you want to go jogging."

"I'd rather walk this morning." Rafe's hands slid down her arms as he pulled her gently into the bedroom, closing the door. "How did you know I wanted to go out?"

Rafe tugged playfully on her braided hair. "You're not *that* mysterious, Miss Whitfield. In fact, you're pretty parochial."

Simone sat on a padded bench at the foot of the queen-size bed, watching Rafe as he sat in an armchair putting on a pair of socks. Jeans and a T-shirt failed to conceal the power in his lean, muscled physique.

She noticed details about him that weren't apparent

before or that she'd chosen to ignore. He had beautiful hands and feet for a man. They were long, slender and delicately formed. Peering over her shoulder, she saw the twisted sheets. It was obvious he hadn't had a restful night's sleep.

Rafe saw the direction of Simone's gaze, and longed to tell her that if she'd shared the bed he doubted whether he would've tossed and turned throughout the night. Slipping into his running shoes, he leaned over to tie the laces.

"I'm ready," he said, rising to his feet. He'd left his firearm in his overnight bag. The fence and closed-circuit cameras served as deterrents for trespassers seeking access to the multimillion-dollar estate.

Hand in hand, they left the bedroom. "I really enjoyed myself last night," Rafe told Simone as they made their way down the winding staircase to the first floor. "You have a wonderful family."

She smiled up at him. "Thank you."

"What's on today's agenda?"

"You'll see."

"I take that to mean you're not going to tell me."

"Bingo."

"Be like that, Simone."

"I will," she said, teasingly, flashing a saucy grin.

"How did your sister meet Micah?"

"She was his sister's wedding planner. Bridget was married here this past New Year's Eve. Tessa had less than three months to coordinate a formal wedding, but she managed to pull it off with rousing success."

Rafe stared up at the massive chandelier, trying to imagine the brilliant lights reflecting off the marble floor, the mansion decorated with exotic flowers and filled with guests in their holiday finery who'd come to witness a wedding *and* to welcome in the beginning of a new year.

"This house is magnificent."

"It is," Simone agreed. "I can't imagine growing up in a house with six bedrooms, six full baths, two half baths, two kitchens, formal living and dining rooms, ballroom, full theater, pool and a pool house, all set on six and a half acres. It would take six of my parents' three-thousand-square-foot house to fit into this place."

Rafe shook his head in amazement. "Sleepovers here must have been a blast." There was a hint of regret in his voice.

He'd grown up in a large farmhouse-style home, but neither he nor his sister ever had sleepovers, nor were they permitted to sleep over at their friends' homes. There'd been so many limitations and restrictions that he'd become a virtual prisoner. The exception was school. Having been blessed with above average intelligence and physical prowess, he took advantage of both, earning academic and athletic scholarships to several prominent colleges throughout the country. Sitting down with his parents, he narrowed the choices to two, and decided to accept a full scholarship to Florida Memorial College in Miami, Florida.

"I'm sure they were," Simone said in agreement.

She recalled her sleepovers in Mount Vernon. The ones held at her home were in the attic that'd been designed to replicate a discotheque, including a glittering ball, and the sleepovers in the finished basement at Faith's made them feel as if they'd retreated to the tropics, with large pots of palm and banana plants, rattan furniture covered with tropical-patterned cushions and a two-hundred-gallon aquarium filled with colorful tropical fish.

They left the house through a rear door, stepping out into warm, bright sunshine. Droplets of dew shimmered on the manicured lawn and meadow like diamond dust. Simone inhaled a lungful of air, holding it for several seconds before exhaling.

Rafe gave her a sidelong glance. "What are you doing?"

"Smelling the air. I love the smell of moist earth and grass early in the morning."

He inhaled and then exhaled. "I don't smell anything."

"That's because my olfactory sensory glands are more sensitive than yours. I can close my eyes and identify the smell of a rose from a tulip or lily," she admitted. "I've been experimenting with extracting the essence of oils from flowers for crèmes and lotions. That's why I've decided to add the outbuildings. I want to use the larger one as a greenhouse and the other as a laboratory to cook and blend my concoctions."

His respect and admiration for Simone just went up another notch. She'd become quite an entrepreneur. "How do you plan to market your perfumed crèmes?"

"It will be strictly mail-order. I don't want to get caught up in distributors or retailers."

Releasing Simone's hand, Rafe looped an arm around her waist, pulling her close to his side when she put an arm around his waist as they made their way along a brick-paved path that led to the southwest end of the sprawling property.

"What are you going to do if demand exceeds supply?"

"I'll hire an assistant or assistants."

"Do you like working from home?" he asked.

Simone's eyes sparkled with excitement. "I love it. I set my own hours and, more importantly, I don't have to concern myself with an overbearing boss or catty coworkers."

"Can you see yourself as a boss?"

Shaking her head, she smiled. "Not yet. If or when I become one, I pray I'm not as hard on my employees as I am on myself. I've been accused of being a perfectionist, or too anal, but when a client spends thousands of dollars for something as fragile as fresh flowers my focus is complete satisfaction."

"Have you ever had a client complain about your work?"

"I've had a few. But there's one in particular who I'll never forget. I knew she was going to be a problem during our initial consultation because she tried to nickel and dime me on everything. She wanted orchids that had to be flown in from Tahiti, but she didn't want to pay the added cost for shipping them overnight. In the end I ordered the orchids from Puerto Rico. They still were expensive, so I gave her a break. Her younger daughter had planned a wedding for the following year."

"How were the flowers?"

"They were spectacular. I'd put together streamers of pink and white orchids and suspended them around the inside of an enormous tent so that it resembled a seraglio. Everyone complimented the bride on the flowers, but her mother continued to bitch and moan about the cost."

"Did you give her a refund?"

"No. I did one better. I refused to do the wedding

flowers for her other daughter. She pleaded and begged, but I was done with her. I've never come that close to cussin' out a client, but she'd really worked my last nerve."

"Ah, the pitfalls of dealing with the finicky public," Rafe drawled. "How do you get your clients?"

"Most of them are referrals. I own a twenty percent share of Signature Bridals, so if a bride signs with Tessa, then I'm commissioned to do the flowers and Faith the cake. But I also have several private clients. Every Monday morning, I deliver flowers to a law firm for their reception area and conference rooms. I also provide the flowers for Whitfield Caterers and send weekly arrangements to Tessa, my mother and my aunt Lucinda."

Rafe didn't have to ask Simone whether Wildflowers and Other Treasurers was doing well because the profits on her tax returns bore witness that she ran a very successful enterprise.

"How was it growing up in Kansas?" she asked after a comfortable silence.

"It's odd living in a state where human beings are the minority. There are two and a half cows for each person in the state," he said when Simone gave him a puzzled look. "Most people believe that Kansas is flat, but it isn't. In the northeast portion of the state, there's the Smoky Hills where the Kansas and Missouri rivers meet. Unfortunately, Kansas is also known as the cyclone state because weather conditions are conducive to tornadoes or cyclones. But the fact is Oklahoma has more devastating wind storms than Kansas."

"Have you ever seen a twister?"

Rafe nodded. "Too many to count. The sound of the wind is similar to that of a speeding freight train. The rule in our house was the moment you see a funnel cloud, head for the storm cellar. Unfortunately, whenever it touches down there's always devastation: human life, livestock and property. I spent my eighth grade in trailers that were converted into schoolrooms after a twister leveled the school."

"When did your family settle in Kansas?"

"My father's folks came as squatters in the early 1850s. My mama's folks settled there after the Civil War."

"Historically, were your people Jayhawkers or bushwhackers?"

"I'm proud to say that they were Jayhawkers. They'd migrated from Massachusetts, and as Yankees were strongly antislavery. My great-great-grandfather was involved in launching raids into Missouri to attack proslavery factions. Unfortunately, he was a casualty during the Bleeding Kansas conflict."

Simone listened intently as Rafe revealed that because he'd grown up with farm animals, he knew where babies had come from by the time he was eight. His father bought a bull to mate with several cows, and the first time he saw a bull mount a cow he was transfixed by the act. When he told his father about what he'd witnessed, he was forced to endure a sermonlike lecture that wicked and licentious acts would damn his soul to hell.

"I was so screwed up in my head about sex that the first time I slept with a woman I couldn't bring myself to enjoy it. It took a while before I realized there was nothing wrong with me, but that my father's warped sense of morality made me feel dirty and guilty."

"Are you okay now?"

Rafe stopped, turned and cradled Simone's face in his

hands. Lowering his head, he brushed a kiss over her mouth. "Are you willing to help me out if I'm not okay?"

Sunlight slanting across her face turned her into a statue of bronze. "I agreed to date you. There's nothing in our agreement that we would sleep together."

A slight frown appeared between his eyes. "Are you telling me that there isn't a remote possibility that we can share a bed?"

"To me, sharing a bed is not the same as having sex. My sister and I shared a bed last night."

Rafe's frown deepened. "Must you always be so literal?" She nodded. He lowered his head again, pressing his mouth to her ear and whispered what he wanted to do to her. There was no mistaking her shock and embarrassment when a flush darkened her face. "Was that explicit enough for you?"

Simone closed her eyes, praying for the earth to open up and swallow her whole as Rafe's erotically ribald suggestion played over and over in her head. The flush that had suffused her face moved lower until she was unable to stop the tiny tremors that left her shaking uncontrollably.

Her knees buckled slightly, and she would've fallen if Rafe hadn't held on to her. The need, wanting and the desire she'd repressed for years surfaced with Rafe's sensually charged admission.

She opened her eyes, staring up at the man who made her feel things she didn't want to feel, a man who only days before had come into her home and into her life to make her aware that she was a normal woman who'd denied her femininity.

"It was very explicit." Her smoky voice was barely a whisper.

Tightening his hold around her waist, Rafe pulled her flush against his chest, permitting her to feel his rising desire. A hint of a smile tugged at the corners of his strong, masculine mouth. "As long as we understand each other, then I believe we're going to get along very well."

Simone didn't remember rising on tiptoe, or her arms finding their way around Rafe's neck, but what she did remember was his warm breath on her parted lips and the texture of his tongue when it met hers.

The heat from his body, his natural scent mingling with the clean metallic fragrance of his aftershave and the hardness between his thighs pressing against hers were magnified as Simone gave in to the passion heating her blood to a scalding temperature that threatened to incinerate her into millions of particles.

They sank down to the verdant lushness of the grass, becoming one with nature. Rafe wanted to devour Simone: her mouth and her body. His hands were in her hair, fingers undoing the loose plait. He didn't know how long he would have Simone Whitfield as his witness, but wanted to enjoy whatever time they were given.

His fingers feathered over her chest, then moved down to the hem of her T-shirt, gathering fabric and easing the cotton up and over her breasts. Pulling back, he stared down her breasts under a sheer bra that was an exact match for her tawny-brown skin.

"Don't," he whispered when Simone attempted to cover her chest with her hands. "I promise you that I won't do anything you don't want me to do. Just let me look at you." Her hand fell away and he visually feasted on what her clothes had artfully concealed. "You are so beautiful." There was no mistaking the awe in the four words. Moving down the length of her body, he feathered kisses over her flat belly. "So sweet, so good," he murmured over and over.

Rafe unsnapped her jeans, pressing a kiss to the hollow where her hipbones joined her pelvis. He worshipped her flesh, whispering a litany to her beauty. He was aware of the change in Simone's respiration, the soft moans coming from her throat and the barely perceptible movement of her hips.

He wanted her more than he'd ever wanted *any* woman, but knew he couldn't make love to her out in the open where someone could witness what he considered a very private act. He also couldn't make love to Simone because he wasn't able to protect her from an unplanned pregnancy.

Reluctantly, he raised his head and snapped her jeans, his eyes meeting Simone's. Passion had darkened them to a sooty-brown. "Thank you," he whispered.

Pushing to a sitting position, Simone combed her fingers through her hair and braided it again. "What are you thanking me for?"

Rafe stood up, offering his hand, and he wasn't disappointed when she placed hers trustingly in his; he eased her to her feet. "For allowing me to sample your goodies."

Simone presented him with her back as she adjusted her T-shirt. "Do I have grass stains on the back of my shirt?"

Here he was talking about making love to her and Simone was worried about grass stains. "No!"

She spun around, her eyes flashing fire. "There's no need to answer me in that tone."

It took all of Rafe's self-control not to actually raise

his voice to Simone. "Do you have blood or ice water in your veins?"

Her eyes widened. "What are you talking about?"

He took a step and pulled her close. "In case you weren't aware, I was ready to make love to you, but all you're concerned about is grass stains on your shirt. And what if there are grass stains? Would you sneak back into the house and change before someone figured out what we were doing?"

Rage made it difficult for Simone to draw a normal breath. "You're wrong, Rafe."

"No, I'm not wrong, Simone," he shot back angrily. "I wasn't wrong when I said you were a prude. What the hell did your ex do to you? Or were you a prude before you married him?"

Simone's eyes narrowed as she took a step. Rafe caught her around the waist, lifting her above his head. She screamed as tears filled her eyes. He knew she was afraid of heights.

"Let me down. Please," she pleaded.

Easing his hold on her body, he set her on her feet. They stood motionless, glaring at each other. "I like you better when I have you on your back," Rafe said in a quiet voice.

Simone rolled her eyes at him. "Bully." Lifting her chin in a haughty gesture, she headed back to the main house.

Smiling, Rafe stared at the curve of her hips in the fitted denim. "Sexy wench."

Stopping, Simone turned and faced him, her hands resting on her hips and a smile tugging at her mouth.

"Tormentor."

He took two steps, bringing them inches apart. "It takes

one to know one, because not only have you tormented me, but thinking about you has turned me an insomniac."

Simone blinked once, as she processed the lawman's erotic confession, hard-pressed not to laugh. "If that's the case, then you should think about taking an OTC sleep aid."

"I don't need a sleep aid."

"What do you need?"

"SIW."

Simone knew he was referring to her initials: Simone Ina Whitfield. She moved closer, her breasts flattening against his hard chest. "You will not get a piece of me until I decide whether I want to give up *my* goodies."

Rafe stared at her from lowered lids, the nostrils of his nose flaring with each labored breath. He'd forgotten to tell Simone that she unwittingly had become a tease—a very sexy tease. "That's all good," he drawled.

She went completely still. "It is?"

His expression was closed, almost somber. "Yes, Simone. I've never had to beg a woman for her goodies, and I don't intend to start now."

Her eyebrows flickered. "You're really a piece of work. Do you actually believe I'm going to beg you to make love to me?"

Time stood still when Rafe's steady gaze bore into Simone, as if he were attempting to commit everything about her to memory. And memories were all he'd be left with when this assignment ended.

"No," he said after an interminable silence. "What I'm hoping is that you'll want me as much as I want you right at this moment."

Simone was too startled by his confession to offer a

comeback. She did want Rafe, yet was too much of a coward to be as openly candid. Curving her arms under his shoulders she held on to him, feeding on the strength that made him so inherently *and* supremely confident. She smiled when his arms went around her waist. "It's going to come, Rafe." *I don't know when, but it is going to come,* she added silently.

Burying his face in her hair, he pressed a kiss to the fragrant curls. "I know, baby."

"We should head back or people will begin to talk."

"Let them talk, Simone. It's been a long time since I've cared about what other folks think or say about me."

"You may not care, but I do. These people are my family. I'll have to deal with them long after you're gone."

He didn't want to think of leaving her, yet he was realistic enough to accept the inevitable. He would leave her and she would continue her life as planned. Although he would walk out of Simone Whitfield's life, Rafe knew he would never forget her.

"You're right. Let's head back."

Chapter 10

Simone recognized Abram and William Sanborn's SUV and minivan parked near the garages as she and Rafe approached the house. "Micah's brothers are here." There was a slight tremor in her voice. She'd wanted to get to the house before they'd arrived.

"Are you sure you're all right?" Rafe asked when he reached for her trembling hand.

She gave him a bright smile. "Of course I'm all right. Let's go in."

They walked into the smaller of the two kitchens where the Sanborns had gathered. Simone's gaze shifted from her sister, sitting on a high stool at the countertop sipping coffee, to Micah, handing his mother a mug, and then to Bridget, who massaged her husband's back as he sat at a table, cradling his head in his hands.

"Oh, there you are, Simone," Rosalind announced when she saw her future daughter-in-law's sister.

Simone went completely still when she saw countless pairs of eyes staring at her and Rafe. She smiled at Micah's mother. A retired family court judge, the mother of four and doting grandmother of four, Rosalind Sanborn was blessed with a smooth, flawless peaches and cream complexion and brilliant topaz-blue eyes. The sixty-something matriarch was not only elegant, but unabashedly stylish.

"We went out for a walk." She chided herself for sounding like a child who was expected to explain her whereabouts.

Setting down her cup, Rosalind walked over to Simone. "I wanted to wait so you could introduce your young man to everyone. And I also want to thank you for the champagne. We'll be certain to open it for a special family occasion." Her husband had discovered the case of premium wine in the entryway with a tag reading: *From Simone and Rafe.*

Looping her arm through Rafe's, Simone met his amused stare. "This is my very good friend, Rafe Madison. Rafe, this is Micah's mother, Rosalind. The man wearing the Kiss The Cook apron is Edgar Sanborn, and his grandsons Jacob and Isaac are wearing Cook In Training aprons. The twins belong to William and Melinda." William nodded, while Melinda stared slack-jawed at Rafe.

Rafe nodded to Rosalind, then offered his hand to Edgar. "Thank you for offering your home."

Edgar Sanborn, who'd left the bench to teach law courses at Princeton, bore an uncanny resemblance to the late leading man Clark Gable. He patted Rafe's shoulder. "As Simone's friend, you're always welcome in our home."

Redheaded Melinda Sanborn stepped forward, her clear brown eyes sparkling like newly minted copper pennies, and extended her hand. "Hello, Rafe. Please call me Lindy."

All gazes were fixed on Melinda, whose flushed face was only a shade lighter than her dark red hair. William Sanborn cut his eyes at his wife. It didn't take a genius to discern that the mother of his children was gushing over Simone's boyfriend like a starstruck adolescent. He forced a polite smile. "How's it going, Rafe?"

"It's all good, William."

"I'm Isaac and this is my brother Jacob. We're going to be eleven tomorrow," William and Melinda's sons announced proudly.

"I'm older than he is," Jacob stated, pointing at his identical freckled-face, curly-red-haired twin.

Simone continued with the introductions as Rafe exchanged greetings with Abram and his very pregnant wife, Ruby.

"That's Bridget and her husband, Seth, sitting at the table."

Bridget Cohen glanced over her shoulder, smiling. Her hand stilled as she stared numbly at Rafe. Her green eyes widened appreciably in her freshly scrubbed face. "Nice meeting you. I apologize for my husband, who's not feeling well. He thought it was cute to indulge in tequila shots at a friend's bachelor party. What makes it so pathetic is that Seth is not a drinker." A scowl followed her acerbic explanation.

Rafe angled his head and a thick lock of honey-blond hair fell over his forehead. "I'm sorry to hear that," he said, deadpan.

Seth waved his hand, but didn't turn around. "Thanks, man."

"Forgive me for not getting up," Ruby apologized, "but I'm moving a little more slowly nowadays." She rested a hand over her distended belly. Her neatly braided hair showed off her very rounded dark brown face to its best advantage.

"Mama, Mama!" screamed a toddler, running into the kitchen. "Mari *afta* me!"

"Marisol, stop teasing that child!" Melinda scolded softly.

The toddler tried crawling up on her pregnant mother's lap, but was thwarted when Rosalind picked her up. "Was Marisol bothering Grandma's baby?" Rosalind crooned as she kissed Kimika's moist cheek.

Thirty-month-old Kimika pointed at her teenage cousin. "She *afta* me, Grandma."

"It's af-ter, Kimmie," Ruby said softly, correcting her daughter. Rosalind glowered at her daughter-in-law, but held her tongue. Her motto was: "Let the children breathe."

A wide smile split Marisol's face when she spied Simone. But it faded quickly when she saw the tall, blond stranger. "Please don't tell me that Brad Pitt is standing in my grandmother's kitchen."

Rafe bit back a smile, while shaking his head. "I'm sorry to disappoint you, but I'm definitely not Brad Pitt." Everyone laughed at the teenage girl's crestfallen expression.

Marisol gave him a suspicious look. At fifteen, the

teenage girl had begun attracting the attention of boys from her neighborhood and school, much to the chagrin of her overprotective father. Her olive coloring, long, black, curling hair and delicate features made her a standout among her peers.

She came over and hugged Simone. "He's hot," she whispered in Simone's ear.

"I think he's hot, too," Simone whispered back.

Edgar reached into a drawer under the countertop, took out an apron and extended to Rafe. "Do you cook?"

Rafe stared at the older man, wondering if he was being set up. "I do some cooking. Why?"

"Today the guys are cooking, so if you're going to be a part of the family, then you're expected to pitch in." He pointed to a door at the far end of the kitchen. "You can wash up over there."

Rafe took the bibbed apron, slipping it over his head and tying it at the waist. He wanted to tell the Sanborns that he wasn't going to become part of *the family* because once he was reassigned, he would never see them again. However, he didn't mind sharing in the cooking duties. After all, he'd sat sipping Jack and Coke and watching a ball game while Simone and Tessa helped Faith.

"What are *we* cooking?" he asked Edgar.

"First there's brunch, then later this afternoon we'll sit down to dinner. I took a vote and everyone agreed to eat outdoors. We'll fire up the grill, crack open a few beers and enjoy the afternoon, but I'll need a couple of volunteers to go into town and pick up a few tanks of propane."

"I'll go, Dad," Micah said.

"And I'll go with you," Rafe offered.

"Hey, Rafe," Abram called out across the kitchen,

"are you into playing some tag football? It looks as if we're going to be one man short. Unfortunately my brother-in-law is in his cups."

Rafe nodded. "Sure. I'll play."

"We can't drink beer, Grandpa," Jacob announced proudly, "because Daddy says we're not legal."

Edgar ruffled his red curls. "I know that, champ. The beer is for the adults. All, but Seth," he added quietly.

Bridget glared at her father. "Daddy!"

"Don't 'Daddy' me, princess," Edgar countered. "I wasn't the one downing shots last night."

Rosalind set Kimika on her feet. The toddler ran over to Simone, raising her arms to be picked up.

"I think Seth would feel better if he went back to bed," Edgar said.

Pushing back his chair, Seth shuffled out the kitchen, Bridget following closely behind him. His curly, dark hair looked as if he combed it with his fingers.

"That wasn't nice, Edgar," Rosalind said.

"What's not nice is him coming home to my daughter loaded. But I will give him credit for not driving himself home."

Rosalind frowned at her husband of more than forty years. "What you fail to realize is that your daughter is not a little girl. She's a married woman and no longer your responsibility."

Ruby pushed herself off the chair and, holding a hand to the small of her back, duckwalked to the refrigerator. "I'm sorry, but I need to eat something." She and Abram shared a surreptitious wink. Pleading hunger had successfully defused what could have become a heated debate about the elder Sanborns' only daughter.

Even before she'd married Abram, she'd heard that Rosalind accused Edgar of spoiling Bridget, while he accused her of being partial to Abram. The truth was Rosalind loved all of her adopted children equally.

Simone picked up Kimika and they greeted each other by rubbing noses. "Did anyone tell you this morning that you're beautiful, Kimmie?"

She'd fallen in love with the little girl on sight. Her velvety skin was the color of whipped mocha, and her soft fuzzy hair was always neatly braided into styles that complemented the tiny face with doll-like features.

Kimika smiled, showing off her tiny white teeth. "My dad-dee."

Simone rubbed noses with the toddler again. "Your daddy is a very smart man."

Rafe stared at Simone cradling the child in her arms as he headed for the half bath off the kitchen. She looked so natural holding Kimika that he wondered why she hadn't had children of her own. Then he remembered the reason why she'd divorced Anthony Kendrick. If the man hadn't been willing to support his wife, it stood to reason he wouldn't support his children.

Rafe washed and dried his hands in the charming bathroom and returned to the kitchen to find it filled with Sanborn men of various ages wearing aprons. He wasn't a Whitfield or a Sanborn, but strangely enough he felt a bond with the unconventional family he hadn't been able to experience with his own.

Two hours after the conclusion of brunch, everyone gathered on the lawn for the regularly scheduled Sunday football game. Rafe and Micah had returned with the propane, Seth had recovered enough to get out of bed, but had elected to sit out the game with Ruby and Faith, who, as promised, had come with Ethan. Once Faith made her condition known, Marisol was recruited to play with the adults for the first time. This left Kimika, Jacob and Isaac to sit on the sidelines as cheerleaders.

The teams were divided by gender: Edgar, William, Rafe, Micah, Abram and Ethan faced their female counterparts in Rosalind, Melinda, Simone, Tessa, Bridget and Marisol.

Rosalind gathered the women in a huddle, explaining the rules and the boundaries. "I'll guard Edgar. Lindy, you cover William, Simone, Rafe, Tessa, Micah, Bridget, Abram, and Marisol, you will guard Ethan." Her blue eyes sparkled like topaz when she smiled at the women on her team. "Does everyone understand what they're supposed to do?" Five heads nodded. She extended her hand, and one by one the hands covered the one above their own. "Well, let's do it!" they shouted seconds before breaking the huddle.

The men won the coin toss and when Edgar threw the ball to Rafe, Simone scooted in front him, intercepting the pass. She was fast, but he was faster. She hadn't taken more than three steps toward the end zone when he took her down. The first play set the stage for the lopsided score routing the women.

Animated rookie player Marisol scored the only point for her team and was honored when her father and uncles hoisted her on their shoulders for a victory lap for her gutsy play.

Simone made it into the house with the others to shower and relax before dinner. When she walked into the bedroom she'd shared with Tessa, she found Faith asleep on the bed and Ethan standing with his back to the window. He was still in his grass-stained sweats.

"Is she feeling all right?" Simone asked Ethan. She'd noticed that Faith had disappeared before the end of the game.

He nodded. "She tires very easily." He moved toward the bed. "I'll get her up."

"No—please don't," Simone insisted. "You stay with her. I just need to get my things."

"Where are you going?"

"I'll just hang out with Rafe."

The routine for Sundays at the Sanborns was the adults usually retreated to their bedrooms to rest up after the football game, while the younger children gathered in the theater room to watch movies before sitting down to dinner.

"Are you sure, Simone? I don't want to put you out."

"You're not putting me out. Besides, we both know that my cousin works much too hard."

An expression of concern came over Ethan's face. "Perhaps you should tell her that, because she refuses to listen to me."

She smiled at the former U.S. Air Force officer who now piloted elite clients around the world in his private jets. "I'll tell Tessa to talk to her. She'll listen to her before she'll take my advice."

Ethan smiled, flashing deep dimples. "Thanks, cousin."

"You're welcome, cousin." Simone gathered her clothes and personal grooming items, placed them into her overnight bag and left the room, closing the door softly behind her.

She made her way to the third floor, knocking on the

door to Rafe's bedroom. The door opened and before she could blink, he'd pulled her inside. His gaze caught fire when he saw her bag.

"Moving in?"

"I need to use your bathroom, because I gave up my room to Ethan and Faith. She's resting."

"Is she all right?"

Simone heard the concern in Rafe's query. "She tires easily now that she's pregnant. Do you mind if I shower first?" she asked, changing the topic.

Rafe combed his fingers through his damp hair. If Simone had come to the door one minute later, he would've been in the shower. "No, I don't mind. I'm going downstairs to see what the kids are watching."

"It's probably something rated G or PG. Edgar and Rosalind are very strict about the movies their grand-children watch."

"The three *Shrek* films and *The Polar Express* are my personal favorites," Rafe admitted.

Simone smiled. "I'm partial to *E.T.* The first time I saw it, I cried when I thought he was dying."

Rafe angled his head and smiled at the petite woman with the shimmering eyes that reminded him of emeralds and smoky quartz. She was scrappy, competitive and definitely unafraid to challenge anyone bigger or stronger than her. When he'd tackled her, he made certain to take her down gently to avoid injury, but Simone Whitfield didn't go down easily. She relented only when he exerted additional pressure, rendering her immobile.

He winked at her. "I'll see you."

Simone waited for Rafe to leave before undressing and then walked into the bathroom. She showered, shampooed her hair, singing loudly under the flow of warm water. Revived, she massaged a scented crème over her body, pulled a wide-tooth comb through her damp hair, leaving it out for faster drying, and slipped into a pair of shorts and sleeveless tee over her underwear. She lay on the bed where Rafe had tossed and turned restlessly the night before and closed her eyes. Unlike Rafe, sleep came easily as she gave in to the exhaustion from the strenuous activity.

Rafe stood in the doorway to the theater room, smiling at the reactions of the younger Sanborns to *The Transformers,* a live-action update of the popular 1980s cartoon with dazzling special effects. He stared at the images on the large screen for a quarter of an hour before retreating to the upper level to shower.

He walked into the bedroom to find Simone asleep in his bed. Moving closer, he stared at the cloud of reddish-brown curls covering the pillow where he'd rested his head hours before. Rafe had wanted Simone in his bed, not just to make love to her, but to feel the warmth and softness of her body against his.

Staring unbeknownst to her made him feel like a voyeur. Whenever he looked at Simone, he wanted her to be fully aware of his intent. Turning on his heels, he headed for the bathroom. The smell of her perfume and shampoo still lingered in the air. Stripping off his clothes and leaving them on the floor, Rafe opened the door to the shower stall and stepped in. The sight of the colorful bath sponge, bottles of shower gel and shampoo reminded him of another time when he'd shared a bathroom with a woman—a woman whom at that time he'd loved more than himself—a woman who professed to loving him, but had deigned to sleep with more than one man.

When the woman he'd lived with came to him with the news that she was pregnant, Rafe's first reaction was to propose marriage. However, his shock and joy was short-lived when Dorene admitted that the child she carried wasn't his. Although he and Dorene always used contraception, she hadn't with the man with whom she'd been working.

There were other women after Dorene, but none had tugged at his heart the way Simone did. What he liked most about his witness was her fire and spunk. She'd come at him knowing physically they were a mismatch, but that hadn't stopped her. There was something about Simone that reminded him of one of his mother's hens who wouldn't let anyone gather her eggs. In the end, the feisty little pullet had become the farm's best laying hen, turning out broods Gideon sold to other farmers in the area.

He forgot about Dorene when he turned on the water and soaped his body. Stepping out of the shower, Rafe wrapped a bath sheet around his body, toga-style, and walked into the bedroom. Simone hadn't stirred on the bed. Not even when he dropped the towel to pull on his underwear. She was still asleep when, fully dressed, he walked out, closing the door behind him.

An imperceptible restlessness wouldn't permit Rafe to sit and relax. Other than the children lounging on leather chairs in the theater room, the house appeared to be unoccupied. He walked through a narrow hallway outside the kitchen and entered an enclosed all-weather patio area. Pocket doors were open to let warm air in through the screens. A retractable awning covered a stainless-steel grill, tables and chairs.

Sliding back the screen, Rafe stepped into the warmth of a picture-perfect spring afternoon. Micah, who lay on a webbed recliner under one of half a dozen umbrellas beckoned to him. "I thought you would've been resting with Simone."

Rafe sat and swung his legs over a matching lounger, lay back and closed his eyes. "I'm not sleeping too well."

Micah peered over at the man responsible for protecting his fiancée's sister. "Does your problem have anything to do with a woman with curly hair and hazel eyes?"

Sitting up quickly, Rafe met Micah's knowing smile. "How did you know?"

Grinning, Micah also sat up, running his hand over close-cropped, gray-flecked hair. "It's as apparent as the nose on your face that you have a thing for my sister-in-law. Don't look so surprised. It was Ethan who first noticed it."

"Damn, I didn't think I'd be that obvious."

Micah sobered quickly, his expression impassive. His respect for the marshal had shot up appreciably. "I'm glad you didn't try to deny you have feelings for her."

With wide eyes, Rafe met the district attorney's steady stare. "How can I when supposedly my face is an open book?"

"You're a lot better than I was before I realized I wanted Tessa in my life. I liked her the moment I saw her, but what I couldn't accept was her telling me that she loved me."

"Why?" Rafe asked.

"I had issues—serious issues—about my biological mother abandoning me after she told me that she loved me."

"How old were you?"

"Four." A slight lifting of an eyebrow was Rafe's only reaction to Micah's disclosure. "What I didn't know at the time was that my birth mother was terminally ill and she couldn't take care of me, so she left me in the clinic of a hospital with a note pinned to the inside of my jacket explaining this.

"The Sanborns adopted me, giving me a childhood most kids fantasize about. And despite my achievements, I struggled with abandonment issues until I realized I was going to lose Tessa if I didn't face them."

"Why are you telling me this, Micah?"

"Your time with Simone will end when you're reassigned, and knowing her she'll move on a lot more quickly than you will. She has her business and extended family to keep her busy, while you'll be holed up in a hotel or safe house going stir-crazy with a talkative witness reeking of liniment." Attractive lines fanned around Rafe's eyes when he smiled. "Am I right, Brother Madison?"

"Sure you right, Brother Sanborn." Within seconds Rafe's mood changed, darkening. "She's not easy to get close to, Micah."

"Neither was her sister," Micah countered. "But would you like her if she was easy? Personally, easy women bore the hell out of me."

"I have to agree with that. I've always preferred a little *piquante* to bland."

"Hey, now," Micah drawled, touching fists with Rafe.

Rafe sobered again. He didn't want to think of Simone

and the feelings she evoked in him just by occupying the same space. "What's the word around the Brooklyn D.A.'s office about the attack on Judge Fischer?"

"Within minutes of the attack, the court went on high alert. Clerks were pressed into service to identify judges who presided over hate crimes. Faxes, e-mails and texts were streaking throughout cyberspace with requests from judges for the Marshals Service to install residential security systems in their homes. The number of senior inspectors and deputy marshals has also increased at the federal courthouses."

"I'm not going to let anything or anyone get to Simone," Rafe said after a prolonged pause.

Micah let out an exhalation of breath. He didn't want to imagine anything happening to Tessa's sister, who he now regarded as a member of his own family even before exchanging vows with Tessa.

"I know you won't." He nodded, and Rafe returned the nod. "I'm going into the house to get a bottle of water. Can I bring you one?"

"Please."

Rafe lay back on the lounger when Micah got up and went into the house. He hadn't known Simone Whitfield a week and he was mooning over her like a lovesick puppy. Perhaps if he hadn't had to be around her 24/7, then his emotions would be less intense.

Liar! a silent voice taunted.

He was no different than Micah Sanborn. The moment he saw Simone, he'd become enthralled with her. The difference was he didn't have abandonment issues. And despite Dorene's duplicity, he was still able to engage in a healthy relationship with a woman.

He hadn't lied to Simone when he'd revealed that he'd never begged a woman for her body. If it happened by mutual consent, then he enjoyed the intimacy, but if they didn't then he continued to see them, aware that some liaisons were better if sex wasn't an integral component of the relationship. He'd realized that when in college he'd unknowingly dated a rape victim. They dated for four months before she decided to end it, claiming she felt bad not sleeping with him. When he told her it didn't matter, she refused to relent. They parted as friends, and the following semester he got a letter from her informing him that she'd joined a group for abused women and was getting the help she needed.

He closed his eyes and thought about some of the women he knew and some he shouldn't have known. Then he thought about Simone. He didn't know if it was the woman, or if he was tired of being alone.

His assignments took him away from his home for weeks that sometime stretched into months, but that was a choice he'd made impulsively almost twelve years before. But living with Simone had changed him. He enjoyed waking up to seeing her, sharing meals and pretending she was his girlfriend. What she didn't know was that he didn't want the pretense. He wanted to play house for real.

Chapter 11

Rafe adjusted the wipers to a faster speed. Water sluiced down the windshield in rivulets, making it almost impossible for him to see the taillights of the car ahead of his.

"Did the meteorologist predict rain for today?" Simone asked as she squinted to see beyond the torrents lashing the landscape.

"I don't know. But at least it held off until later in the day, or we would've never gotten in the football game."

"You're feeling real cocky, aren't you, because you made five touchdowns?"

"Don't tell me you're jealous," Rafe teased, grinning.

"Of course I'm not. The next time you won't be so lucky."

"Oh? You attribute our spanking the ladies to luck?"

Simone wrinkled her nose at him. "You spanked us

because most of the guys on your team are jocks. I'm certain you work out, Ethan at the health club in his sub-division and Micah admits he still boxes with a few of the cops at his old precinct. And look at Abram. He's so broad he could easily masquerade as a Hummer."

"Micah said that sometimes they play mixed teams. If that's the case, then I want you on my team, because I like your aggressiveness."

"It's competitiveness, not aggression."

Rafe gave her a quick look. "My bad," he drawled in his best Midwest twang.

Simone glanced at the glowing number on the dashboard clock. It was minutes before seven. To say she'd enjoyed hanging out with the Sanborns was an understatement. Edgar and Abram had grilled marinated New York strip, bone-rib eye steaks and filet mignon to order for the adults and Angus burgers for the children. Potato salad, coleslaw, vegetable kebabs and grilled sweet corn on the cob were set out as side dishes, along with beverages that included cold beer, lemonade and bottled water.

Late in the afternoon, storm clouds and a rumble of thunder forced everyone indoors where copious amounts of food were devoured as if the assembled hadn't eaten all day. She and Rafe gathered their bags and raced to the Sequoia as the heavens opened, soaking them to the skin.

They were now stuck in slow-moving bumper-to-bumper traffic. Her skin felt cold and clammy, and the cool air coming from the vents had her nipples standing at attention through the damp material of her white tee.

Rafe smothered an expletive under his breath when the driver ahead of him hit his brakes, forcing him to do the same. Instinctually he stuck out his right arm to stop Simone from lurching forward, his fingers grazing her breasts.

He gave her a quick glance. "Sorry about that."

She closed her eyes when a tingling shot through her chest as her breasts grew heavy with a strange sensation that left her struggling to breathe. "That's all right."

Simone said it was all right when it was quite the opposite. Her body was on fire with a longing she hadn't thought possible. Raphael Madison had crossed her threshold five days before, his very presence evoking a longing and need she hadn't thought possible.

Simone wanted to be anywhere but sitting less than a foot away from a man who, despite not being her *type,* she craved like a drug addict. Inwardly she cursed the weather that slowed traffic to a crawl. The sound of the reverberating thunder and the powerful energy from the flash and crack of lightning ignited a burning passion that raced through her veins like a lit fuse. She closed her eyes, her heart thundering. The harsh, uneven sound of her breathing echoed loudly in her ears.

Rafe gave Simone another quick glance. Her labored breathing frightened him. "Simone. Baby, are you all right?"

Teeth clenched, she nodded. "I'm okay, Rafe." She'd lied twice in a matter of minutes. Pressing her knees together, she tried to still the pleasurable throbbing between her thighs. Miraculously it stopped before she embarrassed herself.

The storm moving in a westerly direction was in full effect when Rafe entered the city limits for White Plains. Lightning hit a tree, snapping thick branches as

if they were fragile matchsticks. Slowing, he came to a
stop when sparks from a downed wire skipped along the
wet roadway.

"What are you doing?" Simone asked when he
shifted into reverse.

"I have to take another route. There's an electrical
wire blocking the road."

"There will probably be some electrical outages
tonight."

"Do you have candles in the house?"

Simone nodded. "Yes. I also have an extra supply of
wood in the mudroom, so we can always start a fire for
light and heat." All the fireplace grates were filled with
wood. The only exception was her home office where
she'd replaced the wood with fresh herbs.

Rafe smiled. "Have you ever cooked over an open
fire?"

"No."

"I'll show you how one of these days."

"Now why would I cook over an open fire when I
have a range?"

"It's good to know in case of an emergency. One
winter, we lost power for three days after our county was
paralyzed by two feet of snow. We had to use oil lanterns
for light and the fireplace replaced our stove. We took
turns melting snow for bathing and cooking."

"It probably gave you a healthy respect for what your
ancestors endured to survive life on the prairie."

"It did."

"Do you think you'd ever go back to living on a
farm?" Simone asked Rafe.

"No," he replied much too quickly. "I left farm life

behind when I went to college. Of course I went home for holidays and during recesses, but I never wanted to be a farmer like my father, grandfather or great-grandfather."

"I'd asked you once where you went to college and you never told me."

Rafe remembered Simone asking, but he'd been reluctant to give her an answer at that time. But their relationship had changed, become more personal. "I went to Florida Memorial."

Shifting slightly on her seat, Simone gave him an incredulous stare. "Are you talking about Florida Memorial College in Miami?" He nodded. "But, that's a historically black college."

"I know that," he confirmed.

Her shock waning, she asked, "How did you feel—"

"The same if I'd attended a predominately white school," Rafe said, knowing what she was going to ask him.

"I'm sorry, Rafe. I didn't mean to insult you."

"There's no need to apologize, Simone."

The words were barely out of his mouth when the road went completely black. The streetlamps had gone out.

"Dammit," she swore softly. They were less than a mile from her home, and she prayed she still had power.

Lights blazed from the windows of the homes along the stretch of road leading to her house. Marshals in black sedans and SUVs with tinted windows were parked outside Judge Mitchell Fischer's house and property.

Seeing the vehicles was a reminder to Simone of her fate. She'd gone about her daily routine as if she hadn't become a government witness. The only exception was the man sharing her house. And even with Rafe as her bodyguard, she hadn't been made to feel like a prisoner.

They were complete opposites—physically and psychologically—yet complemented each other. He liked her and she liked him—a lot.

Rafe was already turning into the driveway when he heard Simone's soft sigh. The lamps flanking the front door were on. He touched the remote on the visor and the garage door opened. He pulled in and parked next to his Yukon. There was just enough space between the two vehicles for Simone to open the passenger-side door and squeeze out.

"I'll get your bag," Rafe offered, as he shut off the engine. He reached for the gun holstered to his ankle, tucking it into the waistband of his jeans and opened the door on his side.

Simone stood near the steps that led into an area outside her kitchen, waiting as Rafe deactivated the alarm and went inside. At first, she'd thought his command that she not enter the house until he came to get her overly dramatic because her house was wired. However, she did change her mind when she realized that even the most sophisticated security systems were compromised. She also realized he'd become her first line of defense if someone managed to bypass her security code; he would kill Rafe first before coming after her.

He returned and nodded. "You can come in."

Mounting the stairs, she handed him her tote and his bag. "Please leave them in the corner near the washing machine. I'm doing laundry tomorrow." She kicked off her running shoes. "I'm going upstairs to get out of these wet clothes. You should do the same. You're not going to be much use to me sick."

Rafe opened his bag and took out a toiletry case. "Will you take care of me if I do get sick?"

She flashed an attractive moue. "No. I'll just request another bodyguard."

Rafe smiled. "It's not going to happen, beautiful. You're stuck with me for the duration."

"Bummer."

"Isn't it?" he teased. "Go get out of those wet clothes before *you* get sick and I'll have to take care of you."

Simone blinked. "Would you?"

"Would I what?"

"Take care of me?"

"Isn't that what I'm doing now, Simone? Taking care of you?"

The seconds ticked off as they regarded each other like strangers. "Yes, Rafe," she said quietly, "you're taking very good care of me."

She turned and walked away before she blurted out something else. He was taking care of her, but she needed him to take care of something else: her body.

Simone walked slowly up the stairs to her bedroom, her thoughts a jumble of confusion. It was a sixth sense that made her so conscious of Rafe even with a room filled with people. She knew instinctively the exact moment when he was looking at her. Time after time, she'd turned to find his eyes fixed on her. She'd thought it was because he was her bodyguard that he hadn't wanted her out of his sight, but she realized it wasn't the case, because they didn't share a bedroom.

Making her way into her bathroom, she filled the claw-foot bathtub with water, adding a handful of lavender-scented bath crystals under the running water. She opened a drawer for a fire starter and lit candles lining shelves, ledges and the one on the table next to the upholstered chair in rose-pink toile.

She turned to put away the match when she saw the wood on the fireplace grate. Rafe mentioning cooking over an open fire reminded her that she hadn't taken a bath using only the light from a fire in the fireplace in weeks. It was usually after working nonstop to decorate a room or a tent with wedding flowers that she treated herself to a bubble bath.

Every winter she ordered cords of wood. Whenever she invited her family over for Thanksgiving, Christmas or New Year's, she used the fireplaces. The flame from the lighted match caught pieces of kindling, and within minutes a fire crackled behind a decorative screen.

Stripping off her clothes, Simone walked on bare feet over to a portable stereo unit on a shelf and pressed a button. The distinctive voice of Sarah Brightman singing a collection of Andrew Lloyd Webber compositions filled the space. Thankfully, she'd remembered to replace the batteries.

She turned off the lights, got into the warm water and closed her eyes. The scent of lavender, the sweet smell of burning wood and the clear voice of Sarah singing "Another Suitcase In Another Hall," from *Evita* lulled her into a state of total relaxation.

Rafe had just emerged from the shower closet when everything went black. He cursed under his breath. Their luck had run out. He managed to make his way back to his bedroom, and stubbed his toe not once but twice on furniture before he was able to locate the small flashlight that was a part of his official equipment.

He pulled on a pair of shorts, then left to check on Simone. She'd mentioned once that she wasn't afraid of the dark, but she didn't do well during the winter months because of seasonal depression. Usually she didn't leave the house unless she turned on lamps.

Training the beam of light on the floor, he walked into her bedroom, stopping abruptly when he heard music. His brow furrowed. How could she play the radio without electrical power? She wasn't in the bedroom, so he knew she had to be in the bathroom. Why, he wondered, hadn't she known the lights were out?

He entered the bathroom, stopping abruptly when he saw her sitting in the bathtub. The light from dozens of candles and the flickering fire behind a decorative screen made her look as if she'd been painted in layers of gold.

The hauntingly beautiful voice of Sarah Brightman drowned out his soft gasp when Simone sat up straighter, giving him a clear view of her full breasts. The flesh between his legs betrayed him and he gasped again, this time loud enough for Simone to know he was there.

Simone stared at the large figure filling out the doorway. "What do you want?" Her voice was low, breathless.

"The power just went out."

Her eyes widened like silver dollars. "Please wait inside the bedroom for me."

She hadn't realized the loss of electricity because of

the candles and the battery-powered CD player. Waiting until Rafe left, Simone got out of the bathtub and picked up a towel on a low stool beside the tub.

Simone tried to stop her hands from shaking as she blotted the moisture dotting her body. The look on Rafe's face when she realized he was watching her was imprinted on her brain. It'd been a combination of shock and awe. Tucking the ends of the towels between her breasts, she walked out of the bathroom and into the bedroom, encountering complete silence and darkness.

"Rafe? Where are you?"

"I'm right here," he said, his warm breath sweeping over the side of her face.

As if pulled by an invisible wire, Simone curved into the contours of his hard body, moaning softly when he cradled her face in his hands and brushed a kiss over her parted lips, the touch as feathery as the brush of a butterfly's wings.

She wanted him to quell the pulsing between her legs, to end her self-imposed eight-year celibacy, and she needed to lie with Raphael Madison to remind herself that she was a woman.

Rafe felt the tiny tremors shaking Simone's body. "Do I frighten you?"

"No."

His mouth moved to the area below her ear. "Are you sure?"

"Very sure," she whispered.

His hands went from her face to the towel and seconds later it pooled around Simone's feet. He wanted to see her—all of her, but nature had taken that option

from him. What he didn't want to do was turn on the
flashlight.

"Simone?"

"What is it, Rafe?"

"I want you—"

Her hand over his mouth cut off his request. Simone
didn't know if he was going to admit to wanting her, but
the truth was she wanted him—badly. "I want you to
make love to me."

"Do you know what you're asking?"

"I know exactly what I'm asking, Raphael Madison.
Wasn't it you who said you hope that I'll come to want
you as much you want me? Well, that time has come. I
want you—now."

"You know this is going to change everything between us, Simone."

Simone gritted her teeth. As long as she lived, she
didn't think she would ever understand what made a
man who he was. Rafe had talked about getting her into
bed, but now he was balking. "Nothing's going to
change. I'm still a government witness and you're a
U.S. marshal assigned to protect me."

Rafe wanted to tell Simone she was wrong. When he
made love to her, he wouldn't be a marshal but a man
who'd found himself in too deep. A man who'd found
himself bewitched by a slip of a woman with a sharp
tongue, quick temper and an inherent sexiness that she
either wasn't aware of or chose to ignore.

She may have been his witness, but she was also
something more—much more. If Micah Sanborn knew
Tessa Whitfield was that special woman the moment he
met her, then it was the same with Raphael Madison.

Living with Simone Whitfield for five days was akin to six months of Saturday night dates. They'd spent every waking hour together, and when he awoke it was her he thought of, sought out.

"We'll have to sleep in my bed, unless you happen to have condoms on hand that haven't expired."

Simone pressed a kiss over his heart. "It will have to be your bed."

Reaching into a pocket of his shorts, he handed Simone the flashlight. "Direct the beam on the floor."

That said, he swept her up in his arms and headed out of her bedroom, down the hallway and into his. Outside the house, the storm intensified as rain lashed the windows with increasing wind gusts. It was storming outside *and* inside.

Rafe placed Simone on the mattress, his body following hers down. This night was to be theirs, and he wanted their coming together etched in their memories—forever. "Don't run away, sweetheart. I'll be right back," he whispered near her ear.

"Where am I going to go butt-naked? And, don't forget, in the dark."

Rafe kissed her moist, parted lips. "I'll find you."

Easing the flashlight from her hand, he went over to a drawer in the dresser and took out a condom from a stash he carried in the case with his grooming supplies. He returned to the bed, moving over Simone. Flicking off the flashlight, he buried his face in her soft, scented hair, breathing a kiss on the fragrant curls. His mouth moved slowly to the side of her neck, pressing a kiss to the velvety flesh. He moved lower, down to her throat, tasting the sweetness of her skin. Even in the dark, she was a visual feast. He continued his oral exploration when his mouth closed over her breast, suckling until the areola pebbled like tiny seeds.

The sounds coming from Simone's throat was Rafe's undoing. Blood rushed to the area between his thighs, hardening his sex so quickly that it left him light-headed. He had to slow down or it would be over before it actually began. Taking deep breaths, he flicked his tongue over her nipples, worshipping the flesh covering her perfectly formed full breasts.

Rafe loved her smell, the way she tasted, and he knew that he was falling in love with Simone Whitfield—a woman he'd been ordered to protect with his life.

Simone felt as if she were drowning in erotic sensations that heated the blood coursing through her veins, taking her to a place where she'd never been. She had only one man with whom to compare Rafe's lovemaking, and there was no comparison. This was no frantic coupling, but a slow, measured seduction that had her craving his caress, his kiss.

She arched off the mattress when his hand moved up her thighs and covered the mound concealing her sex. Everywhere he touched her, he ignited a burning passion that grew hotter and hotter until she found herself gasping in the sweetest agony.

The barrier she'd erected after she'd ended her marriage was swept away with the onslaught of desire that weakened her defenses, and she opened her heart to welcome the pleasure that'd eluded her for years.

Rafe wanted to kiss and taste every inch of Simone's fragrant body, but wasn't certain whether she'd experienced a full range of lovemaking. She may have had sexual intercourse, but he wondered if she'd ever been made love to. And that's what he wanted to do—make love to her.

His touch and kisses became bolder as his tongue dipped into the indentation of her belly button. Attuned to the changes in her breathing, the slightest movement of her body, he took his time giving and receiving pleasure. Her hands went to his hair when he buried his face between her legs to inhale her distinctive feminine warmth and scent.

Her fingers tightened in his hair as her hips lifted. "Easy, baby," he crooned softly. "Let me make you feel good."

Simone tried to sit up, but the hand splayed over her belly stopped her. The intense pulsing that she'd experienced in the car had returned. This time it was stronger. "Rafe!" she screamed, not recognizing her own voice.

"Relax, darling. I'm not going to hurt you."

How was she going to relax when she felt as if she were coming out of her skin? And how was she going to relax with his head between her thighs? This was a lovemaking that was totally foreign to her.

Rafe applied the slightest pressure to keep Simone from closing her legs and pushed his face against the down as his tongue searched the opening he sought. A single sob escaped Simone before it dissolved in hoarse gasps that'd become music to his ears. He was relentless, his tongue flicking over the swollen bud of flesh until it swelled to twice its size. Her gasps were replaced by a low keening that had the hair standing up on the back of his neck.

He lessened his assault on her flesh, reaching for the foil packet and opening it. It took only seconds to slip the latex over his tumescence. Moving up Simone's moist, trembling body, Rafe positioned his erection at the entrance to her femininity.

"It's all right, darling." She'd stiffened when he pushed against her long-celibate flesh. "Breathe, baby. Just breathe," he crooned over and over, hoping to get Simone to relax enough for him to penetrate her.

Simone felt Rafe's hardness, the increasing pressure, as he eased his sex into her body, which flamed with fire one minute and trembled uncontrollably from cold the next. The hot and cold sensations continued until the heat won and love flowed through her like thick, warm, sweet honey. Her arms went around his back, holding him where they'd become heart to heart, flesh to flesh and soul to soul. Establishing a rhythm as if they'd choreographed their dance of desire, she discovered a pleasure that sent shivers of delight up and down her spine. Rafe had promised to make her feel good, and she did.

Rafe recognized the instant the dormant sexuality of Simone's body had been awakened, and as her passion spiraled, so did his. His love and desire to pleasure her took precedence over who he was and everything that had occurred in his life. The only thing that mattered was the woman who'd become one with him.

Everything in the world ceased to exist as he quickened his movements. Anchoring his palms under Simone's hips, he pulled her closer. "Oh baby, oh baby, oh baby," he chanted over and over until it became a litany.

Simone felt the contractions. They began slowly, increasing and growing stronger until she was mindless with an ecstasy that took her beyond everything she'd ever known. She screamed! Once, twice, then lost count as they kept coming. She dissolved into an abyss of satisfaction that swallowed her whole. She was too caught up in her own whirling sensations of fulfillment to register the low growl exploding from Rafe's constricted throat as he, too, climaxed. They lay together, savoring the feeling that made them one.

Simone moaned in protest when Rafe withdrew from her. Turning over on her side, she lay drowning in a maelstrom of lingering passion that lulled her into a sated, dreamless sleep. She never knew when Rafe left the bed to discard the condom, extinguish the candles in her bathroom and check on the embers in the fireplace. She was sleeping deeply when he returned to the bed, pulled her against his body and joined her in a slumber that was a long time coming.

Chapter 12

Simone opened her eyes, her breathing faltering. She wasn't in her bed, and the slight ache between her legs and the hard body pressed to her back silently communicated she wasn't the same woman who'd awoken the day before.

"Good morning, baby."

"How did you know I was awake?" she asked, because she hadn't moved.

Rafe pressed a kiss to her bare shoulder. "Your breathing changed."

She smiled. "How long have you been awake?"

Rising on an elbow, Rafe leaned over and pulled a wealth of curls off her cheek. "Awake long enough to eyeball my girlfriend's goodies."

Her face flamed. She sat up and clutched the sheet to her chest. "I can't believe I'm sleeping with a pervert."

The sunlight coming in through the windows slanted

over Rafe's face. Humor and tenderness softened his eyes. "Believe it, darling," he teased. Shifting slightly, he pulled her back down, one arm going around her waist. "You've turned me into a pervert."

"Why me, Rafe?"

"Why not you? You're smart and sexy—a most winning combination."

She smiled. "I thought men don't want smart."

"What do you think they want?"

"The sex is enough."

"Not for me," Rafe countered. He buried his face in her hair. "You can't talk to sexy once you finish making love. And what good is sexy once you leave the bed?"

"Maybe that's enough for most men."

"It's not enough for me, Simone. Sex may or may not play an integral part in a relationship, but it shouldn't be the glue that cements the relationship. There has to be respect and, above all, trust. Even if you have the most mind-blowing, explosive sex, it's nothing without the respect and trust."

"What about love, Rafe?"

"Anyone can say that they love someone, but do they really mean it? Some of the most amazing things are blurted out in the throes of passion."

"Do you include yourself in that mix?"

A soft chuckle rumbled in his chest. "Yes, I do."

Simone shifted into a more comfortable position. "Are you telling me now that I'm not your baby? Because that's what you were chanting in *your* throes of passion."

The seconds ticked off and the only audible sound in the room came from their measured breathing. "You're my baby in *and* out of bed, Simone."

Simone wanted to ask Rafe to define what it meant to be his *baby*. She was aware that it was a term of endearment similar to darling. "If I'm going to be your baby, then you have to be my darling."

Rafe pressed a kiss to her hair. "Baby had better get out of bed while she still can, because darling is having a problem with a certain part of his body."

Glancing at her lover over her shoulder, Simone stared at him under lowered lids. "What kind of problem?"

"Right now it has a mind of its own."

"What is darling saying, darling?"

"It says that he wants baby."

Turning over, Simone stared at the man who'd made the most exquisite love to her that she'd ever known. "I'm going to have to get up even though I'd love to linger in bed with you."

Rafe saw the barely perceptible expression of discomfort when Simone had turned to face him. "Did I hurt you?"

She shook her head. "No. I'm just a little sore from using muscles I didn't know I had."

He didn't know how, but Rafe knew Simone wasn't being completely truthful with him. Not only was she small, but also very tight. But it stood to reason because she hadn't had sex in eight years. "We don't have to make love again until you're ready."

A slight frown appeared between her eyes. "It's not about not being—"

He stopped her when he placed his thumb over her parted lips. "Please don't argue with me, Simone. You were very tight—"

"Is that a problem, Rafe?" It was Simone's turn to interrupt him.

He tightened his hold on her body. "No, it's not a problem, and don't try and make it an issue, Simone," Rafe countered, his voice rising slightly. "You have your reasons for wanting to sleep with me as I have mine for agreeing to sleep with you. What I want you to know and always remember is that I'm honored and humbled that you've chosen me and not some other man to share your bed after so many years."

Simone bit down on her lower lip to stop its trembling. "There's no need to get maudlin, darling. It's only sex," she lied smoothly.

"If it's only sex, then why have you waited eight years to sleep with a man? Why haven't you slept with some of the guys in your bowling league?"

Simone gathered more of the sheet, tucking it around her body as she slipped out of bed. She didn't have to explain to Rafe why she'd decided to share his bed. "Let's not make more of it than it is. We're both consenting adults, so let's leave it at that."

"The power's back on," he said as she walked out of the bedroom, the sheet wrapped mummylike around her lush body. The digital clock on the dresser was blinking twelve o'clock.

Resting his head on folded arms, Rafe stared up at the ceiling. He hadn't wanted to believe they'd had *sex*. That was something he could get from any woman. Simone had sex with him, while he'd made love to her.

What'd occurred between them hadn't changed the reality that he was a U.S. marshal and she a government witness. What had changed was that they were lovers.

* * *

Simone didn't want to think about what she'd shared with Rafe, because it only served to remind her of a longing that she didn't know she was capable of. Each time she recalled his slow, deliberate lovemaking, her body betrayed her.

She'd admitted to him that they'd had sex because she didn't want to fall victim to emotions that wouldn't allow her to let him go. And the time was going to come when she had to let him go. There was no way she was going to spend another eight years pining for what had been and would never come again. She'd made that mistake once and didn't intend to repeat it with a man who was just passing through.

She showered quickly, slipped into a pair of sweats and a tank top, then went down to the kitchen. Turning the radio to an all-news station, she listened to the announcer's update of the prior evening's violent thunderstorm. Two thousand Westchester County residents and businesses were still without electricity and utility crews were working around the clock to restore power as quickly as possible. One of her clients was in the business area affected by the power outage.

The soft chiming of the telephone caught her attention, she picking up the receiver after the second ring. "Hello."

"Good morning, Simone. Were you affected by the storm?"

"We lost power last night," she told her sister, "but it's back on now."

"I'm calling to remind you that we're meeting at my place tonight."

"I'll be there."

"I know you're coming with Rafe, so I made Micah promise to come home early. That way the guys can hang out together."

Simone smiled. Their bimonthly get-togethers always excluded men. "I'll let him know."

"Speaking of your bodyguard, how is he?"

"Sexy," Simone whispered into the mouthpiece, smiling.

"Oh, it's like that?" Tessa crooned.

"Yes. I'll tell you about it when I see you."

"Is that a promise?"

"Yes, Tessa, that's a promise." She saw movement out of the side of her eye. "I have to go."

Simone ended the call as Rafe walked into the kitchen, hoping he hadn't overheard her telling Tessa about him. Her dilemma was that he was sexy—very, very sexy. He wore his ubiquitous jeans, a pale blue pair with a matching long-sleeve shirt. He'd affected the solemn expression she remembered from their initial meeting. Had he, she mused, now regretted their passionate encounter?

"We need to talk about last night." The tone of his voice matched his impassive expression. Both were flat, lacking emotion.

Her eyelids fluttered wildly before she brought her fragile composure under control. She was right. He'd had second thoughts about sleeping with her. "Our sleeping together was a mistake." Her voice, colored in neutral tones, belied her disappointment. She'd experienced the most exquisite passion in her life, and the man responsible for giving it to her apparently had regrets.

Taking three long strides and closing the distance

between them, Rafe pulled Simone into the circle of his embrace, his expressive eyebrows nearly meeting in a frown. "Is that what you believe? That our making love was a mistake?"

Simone stared up at him, her heart pounding wildly. "Wasn't it?"

Rafe stared at Simone, complete surprise freezing his features. He couldn't believe she was so savvy when it came to her business, yet so naive, almost childlike, when it came to the interaction between a man and a woman. And it was her naiveté that was probably the reason she'd given her ex more chances than he deserved.

A hint of a smile started at the corners of his mouth before it became a full grin. "If it was a mistake, then it's one I'd like to repeat over and over and over."

Moving closer, Simone curled into the contours of his hard body. "I love making love with you," she murmured against his shoulder.

"Oh. I thought it was sex."

"*What-evah,* Rafe," she drawled sarcastically. Simone sobered. "There's one thing I want you to promise me."

There came a beat before Rafe said, "What's that?"

There was another pause as Simone composed her thoughts. When it came time for Rafe to leave, and it was certain he was going to leave her, she wanted it to go smoothly. No drama.

"When this *thing* we have with each other comes to an end—and it is going to end, Rafe—I don't want you to ever contact me again."

Rafe froze. Simone was talking about ending something that'd only begun. He didn't know how long they would be together; only the lead prosecutor in the case would determine that. Whether it was two, or maybe even three months, he didn't want to think about not being in Simone Whitfield's life. What he didn't understand was how after only five days their lives had become so inexorably entwined that he couldn't remember when he hadn't known her.

"Is that what you want, Simone?"

She nodded. "Yes. It's what I want."

He closed his eyes and exhaled inaudibly. Rafe didn't want to fight with her, because as it was he'd compromised his assignment as a deputy marshal by becoming involved with the witness he'd been instructed to protect.

He opened his eyes, and at the same time a wry smile twisted his mouth. Promising not to contact her was easier than telling himself not to fall in love with her. "I promise."

Simone flashed a brittle smile. She didn't know why, but she felt like weeping. She hadn't expected him to acquiesce so quickly. Although aware of her ambivalence as to her feelings about her bodyguard, she didn't want sex to be the defining factor for what would become their short-lived affair.

She'd asked herself, did she want more? And the answer was a resounding yes.

But should she expect more? And the answer was a resounding no.

Her decision to sleep with Rafe had been just that—*her* decision. For more years than she wanted to count, she'd denied her sexuality. Even when she continued to see Tony and he'd asked to make love to her, she'd refused, always aware that if she'd permitted him to crawl back into her bed he would also wend his way back into her life.

Her relationship with her bodyguard wasn't predicated on promises of love and happily ever after, but his keeping her alive so that she could testify against a man who'd tried to murder a federal judge.

"Thank you for not complicating my life," she said quietly.

Rafe didn't want to believe Simone could be so self-centered. She was only thinking of herself. He'd made it easy for her, but what about him? Did she believe it would be easy for him to walk away from her? Not fall in love with her?

"It's my job not to complicate your life."

Simone nodded. "I may have to adjust today's schedule because of last night's storm. The neighborhood where I'm scheduled to deliver flowers is still without power. I'll probably reschedule for tomorrow morning. I also have to go to Brooklyn. Even though it's a Whitfield women-only gathering, you can hang out with Micah."

"How long have you had these women-only get-togethers?"

Easing out his embrace, Simone smiled at Rafe. "It goes back more than sixty years. It started with my grandmother, continued with my mother and aunt and now me, Tessa and Faith. They meet once a month, while Tessa, Faith and I meet bimonthly. However, that will change once Faith has her baby. We'll also go to the once-a-month schedule."

Dipping his head, Rafe brushed a light kiss over Simone's mouth. "What else have you planned for today?"

"I'm going to put up several loads of laundry, then dust and vacuum downstairs. I also have to put together several bouquets for a noon pickup."

"What can I do to help you around the house?"

Simone successfully hid a grin. She'd thought Rafe much too macho to offer to do housework. "Strip both beds, gather the bath towels and empty the hampers."

"Anything else?" he teased.

"That's all for now, thank you."

Rafe angled his head as he studied the woman who unknowingly had him craving her night *and* day. "I'm surprised you don't have a cleaning service."

"I'd contracted with a service at one time, but after six months I decided not to renew because there was nothing for them to clean. Besides, the services didn't include windows or laundry. I'd reconsider if I had children or even a child."

"Do you want children, Simone?"

"Yes, I do," she said without hesitating.

She wanted children and so did he. At least that was something on which they could both agree.

"This isn't a legal parking space," Simone informed Rafe when he pulled into a space parallel to a No Parking Anytime/Tow Away Zone sign.

He'd elected to park on the street where Tessa had set up Signature Bridals in the tony Brooklyn Heights neighborhood rather than ride around looking for an empty space or park in a public garage. He cut his eyes at her, something she'd noticed he'd begun doing lately when he didn't agree with her.

Pulling down the visor, Rafe removed an official U.S. Government placard, leaving it in the windshield, while at the same time giving Simone a smug look. "Now you know why I wanted to take my vehicle."

She inclined her head in supplication. "I concede, O Wise One."

Rafe didn't know whether to laugh or kiss Simone. They'd spent the day playing house. She'd shown him how to operate the state-of-the-art digital washer and dryer, and while he did several loads of laundry, she'd made beds, cleaned both bathrooms, dusted and vacuumed.

He'd accompanied her to the greenhouse where she'd selected flowers for bouquets that were regularly scheduled Monday deliveries to Tessa and her aunt. She would've prepared one for her mother if Lucinda Whitfield hadn't been out of the country.

The courier, a part-time college student who was obviously infatuated with Simone, appeared disappointed that she hadn't come to the door to sign his receipt. It'd taken all of Rafe's self-control not to laugh at the young man's crestfallen expression.

"Micah's here," Simone said, pointing to the gray sports car parked in front of Signature Bridals. She waited until Rafe came around to assist her.

Simone led the way up the brownstone steps, Rafe following closely behind. She'd noticed that whenever they were in public, Rafe positioned himself slightly behind her, on her left, his gaze taking in everyone and everything around them.

Simone had seen footage with secret service agents guarding the president and other high-ranking government officials. Ever vigilant with listening devices, distinctive lapel pins and sunglass-covered gazes sweeping over crowds for anything out of the ordinary, they were ready to react within seconds of a perceived threat.

Tall and lanky with the natural grace of a big cat,

Raphael Madison seldom relaxed his guard. The only exception had been when they were in bed together. He'd taken her on a sensual journey of complete fulfillment with his uninhibited lovemaking.

Simone reached into her handbag for the key to Tessa's home out of habit before catching herself. She had to remember her sister no longer lived alone. She rang the bell instead. The intercom buzzed and she pushed open the oak door with stained-glass sidelights.

Tessa met them in the foyer. She looked very chic dressed in a white man-tailored shirt, black slacks and black patent leather loafers. A black velvet headband held her hair off her face.

"Welcome," Tessa crooned, flashing a bright smile. She kissed Simone, then Rafe. "Please come in."

Rafe closed and locked the door, his gaze sweeping over the tasteful furnishings in the foyer of the brownstone in the bucolic Brooklyn neighborhood. Pale oak floors reflected the warm glow from wall sconces and an Art Deco–inspired ceiling fixture. A winding staircase with a mahogany banister and newel posts led to the upper floors.

"Is Faith here?" Simone asked.

Tessa shook her head. "She's on her way."

"Why didn't she call me, Tessa? We could've picked her up." Faith, who owned and operated a tiny bake shop in Greenwich Village only blocks from where she rented a studio apartment, didn't own a car; she relied on taxis and car services to get around the city and the outlying suburbs.

"She's been with a client most of the day."

Simone remembered Ethan's concern that his wife

was working too hard, and made a mental note to ask Tessa talk to her. It was ironic that Faith's relationship with Tessa was better than Simone's relationship with her own sister. It hadn't always been that way before she married Tony.

Tessa smiled at Rafe. "Please follow me. Micah just got in, so he'll be down shortly."

Rafe winked at Simone as he followed her sister down a hallway. He stopped when the doorbell chimed.

"Please get the door, Simone," Tessa called out. "That must be Faith."

Turning on his heels, Rafe retraced his steps. "Don't move, Simone. I'll get the door."

Tessa went completely still; the imminent danger surrounding her sister hit her full force for the first time. The only one standing between Simone and someone seeking to prevent her from testifying was Rafe Madison. Her eyelids fluttered as she watched him push back his lightweight jacket to reveal the handgun at his waist at the same time Micah descended the stairs.

"Who's at the door?" he asked.

Tessa gave her fiancé a half smile. He'd changed from his business suit into a T-shirt, jeans and running shoes. "It's probably Faith. I just made a serious faux pas when I told Simone to open the door."

Micah looped an arm around her waist. "Simone may be your sister, but it's Rafe she must answer to, or she'll be taken to a safe house. She also faces the risk of being jailed if she refuses to cooperate."

Tessa nodded. "I know that now."

Micah affected a wide smile when Faith walked in.

Impending motherhood agreed with her. "Hey, cousin," he teased.

Faith dropped her large leather tote on the floor next to a table cradling the exquisite floral pink parfait bouquet of frilly lisianthus, fragrant carnations, velvety roses and double-petaled Angelique tulips. The assortment of flowers had become a personal favorite of Tessa's. The Wildflowers and Other Treasurers trademark arrangement had made her cousin a much sought-after floral designer.

"Hey, cousin," she said, greeting Micah, handing him a large box stamped with her shop's logo. "I brought dessert." Faith smiled at Rafe. "It's good seeing you again."

He nodded. "It's nice seeing you, too," Rafe said truthfully. He truly liked the Whitfields and the Sanborns. Both families were close-knit, supportive, friendly and unpretentious.

Micah handed the box to Tessa before resting a hand on Rafe's shoulder. "Are you ready to hang out in the man cave and get your eat and drink on?"

"What man cave?" Simone and Faith chorused.

Tessa rolled her eyes at the same time she shook her head. "Micah has claimed the parlor as his personal sanctuary."

"Are women allowed in the man cave?" Simone asked.

"Are men allowed at your bimonthly get-togethers?" Micah countered.

"Oh, no, you didn't go there, cousin," Faith whispered under her breath. "I don't know about you *ladies,* but Mama needs to eat."

Reaching for Faith's hand, Simone steered her in the direction of the kitchen. "Let's go, Mama, before you faint on us."

Chapter 13

This meeting of the Whitfield women differed from those in the past because they'd come together to discuss Tessa's upcoming wedding.

"How are the responses?" Simone asked her sister.

"Nearly seventy-five percent have confirmed." Tessa and Micah had decided to hold their wedding at Whitfield Caterers two months prior to it closing at the end of August. Both wanted a small, intimate gathering with family and close friends.

Faith took notes in a small notebook. "Please keep me updated so I know how many cake souvenirs I have to make."

Simone went down her checklist. "Have you purchased your guest book?"

Tessa nodded. "Yes. The programs are printed and we've applied for our marriage license."

Simone's gaze shifted from Tessa to Faith. "As soon as Mama gets back, we're going to have to set up an appointment for fittings."

Faith nodded. "I hope there's enough fabric in my gown to let it out in the waist and hips."

"How much weight have you gained?" Tessa asked her cousin.

"Three pounds." Simone and Tessa shared a look. "What was that all about?" Faith asked when she glared at the sisters.

"Faith Whitfield-McMillan I doubt if you're going to blow up in the next month," Tessa chastised in a patronizing tone.

"But I'm eating like a horse."

Simone placed her hand over Faith's. "That's because you're pregnant."

"How did Ethan react when you told him that he was going to be a father?" Tessa asked.

A scowl marred Faith McMillan's beautiful face. "He acted a fool, then told me that he's not going to make love to me until after my first trimester. He read somewhere that the first three months are when most miscarriages occur, so he's going to play it safe and abstain."

"You mean to tell me that he's not going to make love to you—"

"You heard what I said, Simi Whitfield," Faith countered angrily. "I truly want to hurt the man, because now that I'm pregnant I'm as horny as a mink in heat."

"Why don't you take cold showers?" Simone teased.

"I'm not you, Simi."

"What's that suppose to mean?" Simone snapped. She hadn't bothered to hide her annoyance.

"Aren't you the one who hasn't had sex in ten years?"

"It *was* eight years, thank you very much."

Tessa's gaze narrowed. "Was?"

Simone suddenly realized she'd used the wrong verb tense, but it was too late to retract it. A rush of heat suffused her face as she picked up her water goblet and took a long swallow.

"You did it, didn't you?" Tessa whispered. She doubted whether Micah or Rafe could hear her from the kitchen.

Faith blinked once. "She did what? What did you do, Simi?"

The seconds ticked off as Simone gathered her thoughts into some semblance of order. She didn't want to lie to her sister and cousin, but then again she didn't want to divulge too much because she didn't want a repeat of her doomed relationship with Tony.

"I'm going to tell you, but on one condition."

"What's that?" they asked in unison.

"I want you to promise that whatever happens between Rafe and me, it will not become a hot topic."

Faith looked confused. "Am I missing something here?"

Simone remembered she hadn't told Faith about her protective status. Leaning across the table, she told her everything about the day that'd changed her life. The pastry chef clapped a hand over her mouth as her eyes widened.

"Oh, damn!" she whispered between her fingers. She lowered her hand. "I thought he was someone you were dating."

Simone shook her head. "You know I'm not into blonds. He's more your speed," she added.

"It's not my fault that I attract men of all races,"

Faith said in defense of her dating men who weren't only African-American. "It didn't take long for me to realize that a frog is frog regardless of his skin color."

The three women shared a smile. Faith had dated so many losers that she'd begun referring to them as frogs. However, her string of bad dates ended when she met and married Ethan McMillan after a six-week courtship.

Propping an elbow on the table, Tessa peered at her sister over the rim of her glass of a cherry-cranberry concoction. She'd prepared a main dish of grilled tuna to accompany a white bean and charred onion salad and penne with pancetta, and spinach with a buttery crumb topping.

"Now, we want to hear everything about your sexy bodyguard."

Simone demurely lowered her gaze. Although she'd earned a reputation of being very vocal and at times vociferous, she was just as private about her sex life. It was only recently that she'd admitted that sex with Tony hadn't been that great.

"I'm embarrassed—"

"What are you embarrassed about, Simi?" Faith cut in. "You're an adult and so is Rafe, so what's there to be ashamed of?"

"I'm not ashamed, but we've been together less than a week."

"Since when is time a deciding factor when two people are attracted to each other?" Tessa stated.

Faith nodded. "I married Ethan six weeks after meeting him for the first time."

"And I slept with Micah after a week of meeting him for the first time," Tessa added. "You and Rafe are technically living together, so I'm certain that added to the sexual tension. Officially, he may be your bodyguard, but in reality it's goes a lot deeper than that."

Simone gave Tessa a questioning look. "What do you mean?"

"Open your eyes, Simone. The man's got it real bad. He can't take his eyes off you."

"Hel-lo, Tessa. It's his job to watch me."

"Not the kind of watching he's been doing," Faith mumbled behind a napkin. "You've closed yourself off from reality because you kept hoping and praying Tony would change, Simi. Raphael Madison is reality and then some."

Simone's gaze shifted from her cousin to her sister. "I'm not going to make the same mistake with Rafe that I made with Tony. First of all, I'm not in love with Rafe and secondly, I've learned how to let go. I don't know how long Rafe and I are going to be together, but I plan to enjoy it."

Looping an arm around Simone's shoulder, Faith kissed her cheek. "Good for you. Now you sound like a real Whitfield woman."

"On that note, I'm going to brew some coffee and serve dessert," Tessa announced as she pushed back her chair.

"I'll take herbal tea if you have it," Simone said, also coming to her feet. "Don't you dare move," she ordered Faith when she reached for plates to clear the table. "This past Saturday was the last time you're going to stand on your feet to cook for us. Whenever we meet at your place, we'll bring everything."

"Simone's right, Faith. You're working much too hard. You're on your feet for hours at the shop, then you work yourself into the ground baking for your private clients." Tessa held up a hand when Faith opened her mouth to defend herself. "I don't want to hear it, Faith," she continued angrily. "Get your priorities straight and think of that baby you're carrying."

Simone wanted to throw her arms around Tessa and kiss her, but managed to conceal her delight. Tessa was always able to get Faith to listen to her without the explosive confrontations she'd had with her first cousin.

A hint of a smile softened Faith's lips. "I hear you, Tessa, but you can save the rant because Ethan has been nagging me about the same thing," she said quietly.

"What are you going to do about it?"

"I've decided to sell Let Them Eat Cake."

"What!"

"I don't believe it!"

Simone and Tessa had spoken in unison.

"But...but when did you decide this?" Tessa sputtered.

"I've been thinking about it for a while. I didn't say anything, because I wanted it to be a surprise."

"Finding out that you're going to have twins is a surprise," Simone said.

Faith rolled her eyes. "Bite your tongue, Simi Whitfield."

She told the sisters about her husband having sold all but one of the Harlem properties he inherited from his physician aunt and uncle to finance the startup of his private car and jet service.

"He surprised me with a wedding gift of an East Harlem brownstone. Ethan had the contractor put in an industrial kitchen on the first floor for Signature Cakes.

We've decided to use the second and third floors as our living quarters."

Simone gave Faith a dazzling smile. "Ethan is truly a prince."

"He's the best," Faith confirmed. "Now, Miss Divas, do I have your permission to cook when it's my turn for our get-togethers?"

Tessa looked sheepish. "I guess so, now that you won't have the responsibility of running the shop."

Rising, Faith bowed gracefully. "Thank you, Divas."

"Have you told Ethan about selling the shop?" Tessa asked.

Faith shook her head. "I'll let him know tonight."

"I'm sorry to interrupt," said a deep voice at the entrance to the kitchen, "but may I come in and put up a pot of coffee?"

Simone wrinkled her nose when she saw Rafe standing behind Micah. He'd removed his jacket and the hem to his shirt hung outside his waistband. Honey-blond fell over one eyebrow, making him appear devilishly rakish.

"What's the matter, dudes? No coffee in the *man cave?*" she teased.

Micah exchanged a look with Rafe. "Brother, your woman has some mouth."

"I know, but there's not much I can do about it," Rafe remarked, deadpan.

"Micah!" Tessa whispered. "Leave it be." She didn't want her fiancé and sister to get into a verbal exchange because Simone would give the assistant district attorney a run for his money. Simone had honed her debating skills in high school when she led her school to the state's semifinals. "I'll bring the coffee."

Simone cleared the table and stacked dishes and pots in the dishwasher while Tessa brewed coffee and tea. Faith was left to sit and watch the activity going on around her. She didn't know why everyone was treating her as if she were an invalid, but decided to enjoy the inactivity because when the baby came she would appreciate doing absolutely nothing.

Rafe and Micah joined the women in the kitchen as they drank coffee and devoured every morsel of the tiramisu Faith had baked earlier that morning.

Ethan arrived as Rafe and Simone were leaving. She whispered in his ear that Tessa had read his wife the riot act, to which he gave her a thumbs-up sign. She knew he would be overjoyed once Faith revealed her intent to sell her business.

Rafe said his goodbyes, then waited at the door for Simone as she hugged and kissed her family. He escorted her to his truck, then maneuvered away from the curb in one smooth motion.

Simone pressed the back of her head to the headrest and closed her eyes. She'd eaten more in the past three days than she'd eaten in a very long time. Not only was she full, but also sleepy. The motion of the vehicle lulled her into a state of complete relaxation as she fell into a deep, dreamless sleep.

Rafe stole a quick glance at the woman sitting beside him. Micah was right about her mouth. She was outspoken and brutally honest, traits he admired in a woman because of his mother's passivity. He'd never heard his schoolteacher mother challenge her husband, not even when she knew he was wrong. Esther Madison had taken a vow to obey her husband, and she had.

The reason he'd found himself intrigued with Simone was because she was so vocal. However, he'd gotten her to understand why he insisted she not go against his orders because he'd been instructed to protect her, with his life if necessary.

He drove back to Westchester County with the sound of Mozart's "Requiem" filling in white noise. It wasn't rap or hip-hop, but a religious-inspired classical opera. As much as he tried, it was almost impossible for Rafe to escape his staid upbringing.

He pulled into the driveway leading to Simone's house and parked. Not wanting to wake her, he did something he'd never done before. He carried her into the house without checking it first. She stirred in his arms, but didn't wake up as he climbed the stairs to her bedroom.

Placing her on the bed, he undressed her, his penetrating gaze taking in every detail of her body that he hadn't seen the night before. He hardened quickly when he stared at the fullness of her breasts. She'd accused him of being a pervert, but the reality was he never tired of staring at her—with or without her clothes. He covered her nakedness with a sheet and lightweight blanket, turned off the bedside lamp and then, turning on his heels, walked out of her bedroom when he wanted nothing more than to lie with her.

Rafe retreated to the bathroom where he washed his face and brushed his teeth. Walking into his bedroom, he slipped the handgun off his waistband and placed it on the night table, then folded his body down to the rocker and stared out the windows.

Midnight was two hours away, the beginning of

another day, and with it came Ian Benton's scheduled arraignment; it was about to begin and it brought him one day closer to when he would have to leave Simone Whitfield. Leaving her was something he couldn't afford to think about. Staring out the window at the star-filled sky, he lost track of time as he willed his mind blank. He didn't remember when he closed his eyes or fell asleep, but something startled him and he came to his feet. Within seconds he was reaching for the gun.

"Rafe?"

The husky sound of Simone's voice stopped him as his fingertips grazed the grooved handle. "What's the matter, baby?" He didn't realize how fast his heart was beating until he turned on the lamp. His hand was shaking.

Simone stood in the doorway dressed in a delicate white nightgown that made her look fragile and virginal. Her hair flowed around her face in sensual disarray. She was staring at him as if he were a stranger.

"I don't know whether I imagined it, but I heard a noise."

His fingers tightened around the butt of the gun as he pushed it into his waistband. "What kind of noise?"

She shook her head, a cloud of curls moving with the motion. "It sounded like breaking glass."

Taking two steps, Rafe caught her upper arm and pulled her forcibly out of the bedroom and into the bathroom across the hall. "Stay in here until I come for you," he ordered after he closed the door to the closet concealing the shower stall.

The questions whirled in his head as he made his way down the darkened hallway. Had someone leaked the name of the government's witness to Benton's people? Had they sent another assassin to make certain she'd never appear in court to testify against their hired killer?

He counted the number of the steps it took to reach the top of the staircase. The only illumination came from the soft green night-lights Simone had placed in the many outlets. Grateful that he'd chosen to wear a dark shirt and slacks, Rafe blended into the shadows. He reached for the gun and pressed it against his thigh. Moving silently, he checked each and every window on the first floor, finding them all intact. He checked the alarm. The red light indicated it was armed.

Then, he heard it. It hadn't been Simone's imagination. Someone outside the house was breaking glass. Rafe weighed his options: call the White Plains Police Department and report a trespasser or contact the team of marshals guarding Judge Fischer's house to inform them that someone was attempting to get to his witness. The latter was preferable because he didn't want to involve the local police in a matter out of their jurisdiction.

There came a pounding on the front door, then a man's voice calling Simone. "Open the door, Simone. It's Tony! I need to see you."

He smothered a savage curse. Simone's ex-husband was screaming her name as if he were auditioning as Stanley Kowalski in Tennessee Williams's *A Streetcar Named Desire*. Simone told him that it'd been six months since she last heard from Anthony Kendrick, but like bad luck he was back.

Punching in the code on the keypad, Rafe disarmed the alarm and opened the door. Kendrick didn't have time to react when he found his throat in a chokehold.

Rafe nearly lifted him off his feet. "What the hell are you doing here?"

Anthony Kendrick clawed at the fingers around his throat. "Let me go," he gasped.

Rafe eased his grip. "Not until you tell me what you're doing here."

"I came to see my wife."

Shaking him much like a mastiff would a toy poodle, Rafe curbed the urge to hit the man who'd inflicted untold emotional pain on the woman whom he knew he was falling in love.

"She's no longer your wife."

Anthony, buoyed because the hold on his throat had eased, felt a rush of bravado. He squinted at Rafe through a beer-induced haze. "Who the hell are you, and what are you doing in my wife's house?"

"I ask the questions, buddy," Rafe drawled.

Anthony swayed slightly then righted himself. "I don't have to say anything to you."

"Yes, you do. Either you talk to me, or talk to my friend." Rafe raised his left hand for the first time. Light from the porch lamps glinted off the lethal weapon. He gestured with the gun. "Inside."

Flicking on lights, Rafe directed Anthony into the kitchen. "Sit down," he ordered once they were in the kitchen. Anthony obeyed like a child, sitting down at the smaller of the two tables.

Concealing the gun under his shirt, Rafe picked up the wall phone and dialed 911. He gave the operator his name, the address to Simone's house and the reason for the call.

Three minutes later, he left two White Plains police

officers in Simone Whitfield's kitchen with her intoxi-
cated ex-husband and went to get her.

Knocking lightly on the door, he called her name.
"It's all clear."

The door opened and Simone emerged with wide
eyes. "What was it?"

"Put something on over your nightgown and come
downstairs."

"What aren't you telling me, Rafe?"

He ran the back of his hand down her cheek. "Please,
baby, just do as I ask." She nodded.

Rafe waited until Simone covered up her revealing
nightgown with an oversize nightshirt and then escorted
her downstairs.

"Oh, sweet…." The words died on her tongue when
she recognized the man sitting in her kitchen with two
White Plains police officers. Shock gave way to rage.
"What the hell are you doing in my house?"

Simone almost didn't recognize Anthony Kendrick.
He'd lost a lot of weight, his eyes were sunken and from
the fumes wafting in the air, she knew he'd been drinking.

She glared at the dissipated man, unable to believe
she'd loved him despite his shortcomings. At first she'd
been caught up with his Billy Dee Williams' good looks;
then it was his intelligence. But unfortunately his lack
of ambition proved a detriment to their sharing a future.

Anthony pointed a finger at Rafe. "He pulled a gun
on me."

"I'm licensed to carry a gun," Rafe said quickly when
the officers turned in his direction.

"Do you have some ID?" asked Sergeant Timmons.
Reaching into a pocket of his slacks, Rafe handed him

the small leather case with his photo and shield. The police officer exchanged a look with his partner. "He's good. What's your connection to Miss Whitfield?"

"She's my fiancée." It was the first thing that'd come to Rafe's mind.

"Miss Whitfield?"

Simone knew he was asking her to confirm or deny Rafe's assertion. "We are engaged," she lied smoothly.

The other officer ran a hand over his face. "I hate these damn domestic disputes," he said through clenched teeth.

"This is not a domestic dispute," Simone said, correcting him. "This man is trespassing." She pointed at her ex. "We've been divorced for eight years, and he's never lived here."

Sergeant Timmons stared at Simone. "You can always get a restraining order, Miss Whitfield."

Moving closer to the man seated on the chair, Rafe glared at Anthony Kendrick. "She's not going to need a restraining order. It's obvious Mr. Kendrick has been drinking, so I suggest that when he sobers up you'll impress upon him that if he comes within ten feet of my fiancée again I'm going to shoot him."

Anchoring a hand under Anthony's shoulder, the sergeant eased him to his feet, eyebrows lifting when he was assailed by the smell of stale beer. "Let's go, buddy. We're going to take you somewhere so you can sleep it off."

Anthony struggled to escape the strong grip. "Take your hand off me."

The other officer moved over to assist his partner. "You're quickly running out of options, Kendrick.

Either you can come peaceably, or we'll take you out in cuffs. But then we can always walk out and leave you here to catch a bullet."

Anthony sobered at the mention of bullet. He glared with rummy eyes over his shoulder at Simone. "Do you want to know why I cheated on you?"

"Get him out of here!" she screamed.

"I slept with other women because you're a frigid bitch!"

What happened next was a blur. Rafe hit Anthony, the savage blow knocking him to his knees. He drew back his arm to hit again, but one of the officers had Anthony's arms behind his back, fastening a pair of handcuffs around his wrists.

Simone stood stunned as the police officers forcibly hauled her ex-husband out of the kitchen, Rafe following. She was still in the same spot when he returned.

"I'm sorry you had to see me clock his ass," he said quietly.

She blinked once. "Better you hit him than me frying pan him." She gestured to the large cast iron pan hanging from an overhead rack.

The seconds ticked as they regarded each other. "You now have your answer about whether he'd cheated on you." Rafe's voice was soft, comforting.

Simone closed her eyes. "I don't care. I stopped caring a long time ago."

Bending slightly, he swung her up into his arms. "Let's go to bed."

Simone buried her face between his neck and shoulder, feeling the raw, unleashed power in his upper body.

"Please don't leave me tonight," she whispered as he climbed the staircase.

She was pleading with Rafe to stay with her because she was tired, tired of pretending to be strong, tired of putting up a brave front for others because that was what others expected from her and tired of being "poor little Simone."

Rafe wanted to tell Simone that he wanted to spend this night and every night for the rest of his life with her. He carried her past her bedroom and into his. Light from the table lamp cast long and short shadows throughout the space.

His gaze met and fused with hers as he lowered Simone to the bed. He took his time undressing. Turning his back, he stepped out of his boxer-briefs.

Rafe hadn't needed Simone to touch him to get him aroused. Just looking at her, inhaling her distinctive scent was enough for him to achieve full erection. He sat on the bed, turned off the lamp, swung his legs over the mattress and lay with his back to Simone, not wanting her to see his arousal. He'd promised not to touch her for several days, but keeping that promise tested the limits of his control.

"Good night, baby."

Simone snuggled against his back. "Good night to you and to *darling*."

His deep, rich laugh filled the room. "You know?"

"I saw it," she teased.

Placing her arm over Rafe's waist, she pressed a kiss to his back. She didn't want to think of Anthony's allegation that she was a "frigid bitch." There were times when she'd doubted herself, but it was never sexually.

Oh, yes, there were times when she refused to let him make love to her, but only when she'd suspected that he was sleeping with other women.

Anthony Kendrick could say anything he wanted about her, but there was one thing of which Simone was certain—she wasn't frigid.

Chapter 14

Rafe sat in Malcolm and Lucinda Whitfield's parlor, waiting for Simone, who'd come to tell her parents why a strange man was living with her.

Not only were he and Simone living together, but they were also sleeping together. He'd made love to her a second time, again awed by the passion she had elicited from him. It was as if he couldn't get enough of Simone Whitfield. He stood up in one smooth, fluid motion when her father entered the room.

Tall and slender with close-cropped curly graying hair, hazel eyes and a trimmed mustache and goatee, Malcolm Whitfield exuded breeding and sophistication. Simone had informed him that her parents had returned from celebrating their thirty-eighth wedding anniversary in Bermuda, the same place where they'd gone for their honeymoon.

Malcolm offered his hand to the man responsible for safeguarding his daughter. "I'd like to thank you for taking care of my daughter."

Rafe shook his hand. "There's no need to thank me, Mr. Whitfield. It's my job." What he didn't add was that it wasn't his job to sleep with his witness, but doubted whether Malcolm would be pleased with that piece of news.

"Job or not, I still want to thank you."

"The government is very grateful that Simone is cooperating with them. With her eyewitness testimony, they'll be able to lock up a very dangerous criminal for the rest of his life."

Malcolm studied the tall, casually dressed federal officer, whose gaze never faltered. He judged people, men in particular, by their ability to look him directly in the eye, and Deputy Marshal Madison had passed his test.

"Lucinda and I would love to have you stay for dinner."

"We can't, Daddy," Simone said, walking into the room. "I have bowling."

Turning around, Malcolm smiled at his eldest daughter. Despite all that was going on in her life he'd never seen her look better. Even when she'd retold the horror she'd witnessed, she didn't appear at all frightened that she would have to sit in a courtroom and identify the man who'd stabbed her neighbor.

Of his two daughters, Simone had always been the gutsy one. She preferred playing sports to ballet lessons, roughhousing with boys to playing with dolls. She'd also married young *and* chosen badly.

Malcolm had lost track of the number of times his

baby girl had come to him crying about her good-for-nothing husband. But there was little he could do about her dilemma. He couldn't make Anthony Kendrick get a job any more than he could force Simone to leave him. He and Lucinda had assumed a mind-one's-business attitude where it concerned their children's romantic entanglements, because they knew survival and common sense would eventually prevail. When Simone had had enough of Anthony Kendrick, she left him.

Placing an arm around her shoulders, Malcolm dropped a kiss on her hair. "When can you make time for your old man?"

Tilting her chin, Simone smiled up at her father. "You're not an old man, Daddy. We're coming over Saturday morning for a fitting."

"Okay. I'll see you Saturday."

On tiptoes, Simone kissed her father's cheek. "Bye, Daddy."

He tugged at her hair the way he'd done when she was a little girl. "Stay out of trouble." It was something he'd said to her over and over whenever she went out to play with the kids in their neighborhood.

Simone nodded to Rafe. "I'm ready."

Malcolm walked his daughter and her bodyguard to the door and stood on the porch watching as they got into a large black sport utility vehicle. He was still standing in the same spot when Rafe Madison backed out of the driveway.

"Is she going to be all right?"

He turned to stare at his wife. Her eyes were puffy, which told him that she'd been crying. Taking a step, he folded her to his chest. "Of course she's going to be all right, Lucy. That young man is going to take very good care of our daughter."

Lucinda Whitfield wanted to believe her husband. She'd also wanted to believe her daughter when she reassured her that having a live-in bodyguard allowed her the freedom she wouldn't have had if she were at a safe house or sequestered in a hotel or motel room. She wanted to believe them, but her doubts came when she was introduced to Raphael Madison. He looked nothing like she would've envisioned a federal marshal to look.

"That young man you speak of looks like a rock star."

"That's not such a bad thing, Lucy, because looks can be deceiving."

"I hope you're right, Mal."

"Have I ever been wrong, Lucinda Whitfield?"

His wife patted his chest. "I can remember the time you stood me up to go out with Christina Wright."

He smiled. "But I made up for that gross error in judgment when I married you."

Lucinda raised her head and smiled up at the man whom she'd loved for most of her life. "Yes, you did."

Rafe found it hard to believe that it was only a few weeks ago that he'd come to White Plains to protect Simone Whitfield. His life had become a roller coaster—speeding up, slowing down and then speeding up again. And he hadn't wanted to get off as long as Simone was along for the ride.

He'd met her parents, reassuring them that he would keep their daughter safe. What he hadn't told them was who would protect Simone Whitfield from Raphael

Madison. He was in love with her, and refused to think of the time when he'd leave her.

Ian Benton had been arraigned at the White Plains Federal Courthouse, pleading not guilty to charges of conspiracy, attempted murder, aggravated assault and assault with a deadly weapon. His attorney had gone through the formality of requesting bail, but it was denied. He'd spoken to the press at the conclusion of the arraignment, stating he was going to seek a change of jurisdiction because he doubted whether his client would get a fair trial because of the judge's popularity.

Rafe had viewed the news footage with disdain. Bail or no bail, guilty or not-guilty plea, Ian Benton was going to spend the rest of his natural life behind bars.

The noise in the bowling alley had reached ear-splitting decibels. It was the last game of the season and the stakes were high as to which team would come in second. Simone's team was the undisputed first-place winner, but the fight for second had grabbed everyone's attention with three teams vying for the position.

The league had been set up to raise money for the children and widows of police officers who'd lost their lives during 9/11. Winning wasn't about trophies, but bragging rights.

Rafe glanced at his watch for the fifth time within the hour. Never one to sit on the sideline, he had always been a participant when it came to sports. Whether it was basketball, football or baseball, he'd been a competitive *and* an aggressive player. His high school and college coaches liked him not only because he played hard, but because he played to win. He'd recognized Simone's competitive spirit within an hour of their initial meeting and knew he'd found his female counterpart.

Cheers and applause thundered throughout the alley. The Long Blue Line bowling season had ended.

Simone made her way over to Rafe, the thrill of victory showing in her smile and eyes. Rising on tiptoe, she wrapped her arms around his neck, pulling his head down. She kissed him, not a quick brushing of the lips. Her lips parted seconds before her tongue slipped into his mouth, simulating his making love to her.

"Let's go home."

Rafe lifted his eyebrows. "Aren't you going out with the others to celebrate?" The bowlers had planned to celebrate the end of season at a City Island seafood restaurant.

Simone shook her head. "No. The last time I hung out with these folks I wound up with a hangover."

"How many drinks did you have?"

"Only one," she admitted.

"Maybe I should've said what did you drink?"

"I had a Long Island iced tea."

Rafe affected a grimace. "It's no wonder you were sick. Do you know what makes up a Long Island iced tea?"

"I know now. As soon as I change my shoes we can leave."

"Hey, Simone, are you hanging out with us tonight?"

She smiled one of the female officers. "I can't. I have to get up early tomorrow."

"So, do I," quipped a twenty-year veteran who'd just submitted the necessary documents for retirement, "but I'm still going."

There came a chorus of "come on," and "you gotta go,"

until Rafe grasped Simone's hand and escorted her out of the bowling alley. She knew if he hadn't been there she probably wouldn't have been able to make as smooth an exit. There was something about Rafe when he went into deputy marshal mode that was intimidating.

Rafe drove back to White Plains, relieved that Simone hadn't elected to stay and celebrate with the others. The less she interacted with crowds, the easier it was for him to protect her. The risks to her survival increased exponentially whenever they weren't in a controlled environment.

"I'm glad you decided not to go out celebrating tonight," he confessed to Simone, as he carried her up the stairs to the second story.

"Why's that?"

Lowering his head, his gaze lingered on her lush mouth. The soft gold light from a wall sconce highlighted the gold in her hair, eyes and skin. "I want you all to myself."

Simone stared up at him through her lashes. "I didn't realize you were so selfish."

"I'm..." He stopped himself before admitting that he was jealous, jealous of every man who looked at or spoke to Simone. He suspected they wanted her as much as he wanted her and would always want her.

At first Rafe believed he'd been lusting after Simone. But that all changed once they shared a bed. Sleeping with her made him aware of who he was and what he wanted for himself and his future.

He'd realized a boyhood dream to become a Major League ballplayer, but his dream was short-lived when he was forced to walk away from baseball to resolve a family crisis.

He'd believed his two-year liaison with Dorene Eustace would eventually lead to marriage and children, but he'd had to walk away again when she confessed to carrying another man's child.

And now it was Simone Whitfield. She'd claimed their sleeping together was "only sex," but to him it'd become more—so much more.

"I'm tired." He'd told her a half truth.

Rafe was tired, tired of hiding his feelings, tired of pretending that protecting Simone was his official duty as a U.S. deputy marshal.

"It's no wonder you're not falling on your face, Rafe Madison," she chided softly. "You were insatiable last night."

If he'd been insatiable, it was because Simone had also been insatiable. As promised, he'd waited a few days before making love to her again. Just when he was ready to sleep in late, Simone informed him that she wanted to go jogging. He'd tried talking her out of it, but she claimed she was ready to return to the place where she'd witnessed the assault on her neighbor and faced down a would-be attacker.

"I'm tired because I had to get up at the crack of dawn to run around a track with my fiancée."

"How did I go from being your witness to your girl-friend and now your fiancée in a week?"

He flashed a Cheshire cat grin. "I don't believe in wasting time."

"I suppose we'll be husband and wife by the end of the month, and the parents of twins before the end of summer."

"Now that sounds like a plan."

"Rafe!" Simone's husky voice had gone up several octaves.

"Simone!" he said in falsetto.

"I'm serious."

"And I'm not?" Rafe asked her.

Her shock yielded to a slowly rising annoyance. "You've lost your mind if you think I'd marry you."

Rafe came to a complete stop at the top of the staircase. "On a scale of one to ten, ten being the highest, I believe I'd score higher than your *ex-husband*. I'd never permit my wife to support me or *our* children. And whatever goes on in our bedroom stays in our bedroom."

"Despite what you might believe, I do recognize your good qualities, Mr. Madison."

"You don't have to patronize me, Simone."

"I'm not trying to patronize you. I'd like to get married again, and when I do I'd like to have children. But that's not going to happen now, because it's only been six months since I decided to let go of Anthony Kendrick. Six months is insignificant when compared to sixteen years."

Rafe shifted the slight weight in his arms and continued down the hallway to his bedroom. "We're not engaged, which means we're not getting married. So there's no need for further dialogue," he stated matter-of-factly.

Simone pushed against his chest. "I wasn't the one who referred to you as my fiancé."

Walking into the bedroom, he deposited Simone on the bed, his body following and covering hers. "Enough," he whispered harshly against her parted lips.

Placing her hands on his shoulders, she attempted to

push him off her. "Don't you dare tell…" His mouth covered hers, stopping her tirade.

What had begun as a battle of wills, a struggle for dominance faded, replaced by a rush of desire that set Simone on fire. His hands were everywhere: her face, hair, searching under fabric to touch skin.

Her hands were just as busy when she pushed his hair off his face and forehead before moving down to the front of his shirt. Rafe gently pushed her hands away when he removed his firearm and placed it on the nightstand on his side of the bed. Clothes and undergarments were strewn on the bed and floor in their rush to become one.

"Let me love you," Simone whispered against Rafe's throat. "Last night was yours. Let this night be mine."

Rafe nuzzled the side of her neck. "Do you know what you're asking?"

Reaching over, she switched on the bedside lamp. The smoldering flame in her lover's eyes sent a shiver of anticipation throughout her body. "I know exactly what I'm asking—darling."

He smiled. "What do you want me to do—baby?"

Going to her knees and leaning forward, Simone pressed a kiss over his heart. "Sit down. Please sit down," she repeated when he looked at her as if she'd spoken a language he didn't understand.

Rafe complied and pressed his back to the headboard. He felt like the pervert that Simone had once accused him of being when his gaze feasted on her full breasts rising and falling above her narrow ribcage. He'd always proclaimed himself a leg man, but had changed his mind when he saw her naked for the first time the night of the storm. The image of her oil-slick

breasts with succulent, dusky brown nipples were forever imprinted on his brain.

He couldn't stop the groan that slipped out when he
felt his sex harden. "Do you want to put on the condom?"

Suddenly Simone felt awkward. It was her intent to
seduce Rafe, to do all the things to him that he'd done
to her that wrought the most exquisite pleasure imagin-
able. She shook her head. "No, you can put it on. But
not until I tell you," she added after he'd taken the small
packet out of the drawer to the nightstand.

She sat back on her heels and stared at the stranger
sharing her home—a stranger who made her feel and do
things that were totally inconceivable to the old Simone
Whitfield-Kendrick. Everything she'd wanted to share
with Tony she'd offer Rafe.

Her marriage, fraught with disappointment, frustration, repressed rage and discontent had made her less
than a willing bed partner. It was only when Tony turned
on what'd been his two-hundred-watt charm that she
submitted to his subtle seduction.

Tall, muscled, golden and unabashedly virile Raphael
Madison made her ache with desire. He'd pretended
they were engaged, that they'd planned to marry, but
he'd lied. They were a man and a woman, and in the
week their lives had become entwined and they'd
become lovers.

Moving closer, she straddled his thighs. They shared
a smile. The throbbing of his blood-engorged sex
against her belly kept time with their laboring breathing. "Don't touch me," Simone ordered in a quiet voice
when his hands came up.

Bracing her hands on either side of Rafe's head, she

breathed a kiss over his mouth. The feel of her mouth on his was barely perceptible; she pulled back as he sought to deepen the kiss. She beckoned, he came and then without warning she withdrew, leaving him frustrated and wanting more.

Simone became bolder when she embarked on an oral journey that began at the hollow of Rafe's throat. Her rapacious tongue flicked over his shoulders, breastbone and over nipples darkening like ripe cherries as she suckled him as a baby its mother.

Rafe felt as if he were being held underwater. If he didn't breathe, then his lungs would explode. He wanted to put Simone on her back, bury his swollen sex inside her moist heat, but banished the notion when he remembered her warning not to touch her.

Everything, everyone he'd known or met faded into obscurity when he felt another kind of moist heat—her mouth. Rising off the mattress, Rafe bellowed like a wounded bull.

"Please, baby! No!"

What was wrong with him? He was pleading with a woman to stop the most exquisite pleasure he'd ever experienced. Then, without warning, he felt a familiar tingling sensation at the base of his spine.

Reaching over, he forcibly pulled Simone's head from between his thighs, flipped her over on her back and entered her in one strong, swift motion. It took only seconds to realize she felt different. He'd forgotten to put on the condom.

Simone emitted a small moan of protest when Rafe pulled out, yet sanity returned seconds later, her body opening and receiving his latex-covered sex. Bending her knees, she looped her legs around his waist, holding him fast as he rotated his hips, each thrust deeper, harder.

She felt the pulsing that began like gentle waves washing up on the beach. They grew stronger, more turbulent, as gusts of fiery desire shook her from head to toe. She trembled like a fragile leaf in a storm.

The hot tide of passion took over completely, and Rafe and Simone surrendered simultaneously to the uncontrollable joy that made them one with the other.

As she lay savoring the aftermath of the lingering passion, a wave of sadness swept over Simone. She'd lied to Rafe and to herself. Sleeping with him wasn't just sex. It was about making love, and she'd made love with Rafe.

A silent prayer escaped her parted lips as she prayed for strength. She had to remain emotionally detached, or she would find herself making the same mistake of not being able to let go.

I will be able to let him go. The silent vow reverberated over and over in her head. By the time sleep came calling, Simone believed that she could and would.

Chapter 15

Simone sat on a stool at the workstation in the mud-room, gathering the supplies she needed for a wedding bouquet made of stephanotis. Because she didn't grow the exotic star-shaped white flower called Madagascar jasmine, she had special ordered them from a local florist.

Reaching for a plastic box filled with wires to support the stems of flowers to prevent the heads from breaking off, she went completely still when an arm went around her waist.

"Don't, Rafe."

"Don't what?" he whispered near her ear. "Don't touch you? Don't want you? Or maybe don't even like you? Which one is it?"

Resting the back of her head against his chest, Simone closed her eyes. "None of the above," she admitted.

Rafe tightened his hold around her body. "When are you going to stop and take a break? You've been in here for more than five hours."

After he'd accompanied Simone to a local florist where she'd picked up a special order, she'd returned to the house and retreated to an area in the mudroom that to Rafe resembled a shoemaker's workshop. She informed him that as soon as Ian Benton was sentenced, a contractor would begin laying the foundation for the outbuildings for a state-of-the art greenhouse, a large area to store her supplies and spacious counters to assemble her floral designs and a laboratory. Her pronouncement of "I'm going to be tied up for a while" translated into her working nonstop for more than five hours.

"It will probably be another five before I'm finished." Simone opened her eyes to see Rafe scowling at her. "What's that look all about?"

"When are you going to eat?"

"I'll eat when I'm finished with the bridal bouquet." She'd spent the morning and afternoon making boutonnieres for the father of the bride, the groom, four groomsmen and four attendant bouquets for a Friday-evening wedding. The trend of Friday-night weddings had become increasingly popular over the years. And as with most wedding flowers, most were assembled the day before the wedding.

Easing her back against his chest, Rafe lowered his head and kissed her eyelids. "Can I at least bring you something to drink?"

A soft smile parted Simone's lips. "I'd like some raspberry iced tea, please."

Shifting slightly, his mouth found hers. "Raspberry iced tea it is."

Waiting until Rafe left, Simone resumed the arduous task of poking a wire through the center of each star-shaped stephanotis flower, pushing out its green center, and replacing it with a rhinestone. The bouquet was not difficult to make, but very time consuming. She'd glued seventy-five rhinestones to stephanotis wire stems. Once completed, she'd make three rhinestone-studded wire flowers into a triangle-shaped cluster, twist an eight-inch piece of wire around the wire stems and tape them. In all, she would have to make twenty-four clusters. Even after completing the bouquet, she still had to cover the handle of the bouquet with inch-wide white ribbon and glue the remaining rhinestone trim up the handle in a spiral design. Yards of three-inch wired sheer decorative ribbon, which she would make into four two-loop bows, wouldn't be attached to the bouquet until shortly before the ceremony.

When Simone met with the prospective bride earlier in the year, she'd been stunned with the stark simplicity of the gown the bride had chosen, suggesting a bouquet with the rhinestones. It was only after seeing a photograph of the completed bouquet that the young woman agreed to go with the flowers with a subtle perfume and an ability to stay fresh through the wedding day and night.

Rafe returned with a tall glass of the chilled liquid. Simone removed her gloves, picked up the glass and took a long swallow. "Oh, that's good. I hadn't realized I was so thirsty."

Sitting on a stool next to her, Rafe massaged the back of her neck. "What can I do to help you out?"

She gave him an incredulous stare. "You really want to help me?"

"No, Simone," he drawled. "I just want to sit here and count the number of freckles on your face."

"I don't have freckles."

"Yeah, you do." He touched her cheek. "You have one right here, and another one over here. Oops, I missed one."

Smiling, she squatted at his finger. "Stop, darling."

He caught her hand, holding it firmly in his larger one, then studied it as if he'd never seen it before. The color contrast between hers and his wasn't as startling as he thought it would've been. Perhaps it was because Simone spent so much time indoors, or when working in the greenhouse she always used gloves to protect her hands from the chemicals she used to grow her flowers. Even when assembling her bouquets, she wore latex gloves to avoid bruising the petals or transferring the oil from her body to the delicate blooms.

"What's the matter, Rafe?"

He met her questioning gaze. Today Simone appeared so much younger than any time before. It could be because she'd parted her hair in the center and braided it into two thick plaits. Or maybe it was the enchanting wisps around her face. Or perhaps it was because she hadn't bothered to put anything on her face. Even if she didn't apply makeup, she rarely went without lip gloss.

"Why did I just suddenly feel like I've been sleeping with a girl?" A slight frown appeared between the wide eyes that had the power to seduce him with a single glance.

"Who are you talking about, Rafe?"

"I'm talking about you, Simone Whitfield."

Her frown deepened. "What about me?"

He blinked slowly and a sweep of hoary lashes touched the tops of his cheekbones, and now it was Simone's turn to look at the man she'd been sleeping with—really look at him. There was something about his perpetually tanned face that made him look exotic. Perhaps it was his coloring or the slight slant of his eyes or even the shape of his mouth, but whatever it was it made him shockingly attractively. Marisol Sanborn had likened Rafe to Brad Pitt, but the "world's sexiest man" couldn't compete with Raphael Madison. Her bodyguard claimed a raw, sensual masculinity that was almost palpable. She'd watched other women's reactions when seeing or meeting him enough to know what she felt was not imagined, but very real.

And everything she shared with Rafe was real—at times too real. Like that morning. Their lovemaking had been particularly tender, passionate, and moments before she climaxed, Simone knew that she'd fallen in love with her bodyguard. It'd taken all of her resolve not to blurt out what lay in her heart. The tears fell, and when Rafe asked her if he'd hurt her, her comeback was it was that time of the month. Her menses came *every* twenty-eight days like clockwork, and she expected to see it before the end of the day.

But the shift in her hormone levels had nothing to do with the ache in her heart. For the second time in her life she'd fallen in love with a man, but this time she knew she would have to let him go. She wouldn't leave him. He would leave her.

"Right now you look no older than sixteen. But if you push it, then maybe eighteen."

"In some states a lot of girls are married at sixteen, or even younger."

"The average age for marriage in New York is somewhat higher than sixteen," Rafe argued in a quiet voice.

"I can assure you that I'm not sixteen, and I have no wish to ever be sixteen again."

"Not even knowing what you know now?" Rafe teased.

Simone shook her head. "No. Not even knowing what I know now."

A comfortable silence ensued as they stared at each other. It was something that was occurring more often now. They'd sit across the table or relax on the back porch reading, then without warning look up and find the other staring. A shared wink and smile, and then they'd return to whatever it was they were doing at the time.

Rafe smiled, a tender light illuminating his eyes. "Show me what you want me to do."

She handed him a spool of twenty-one-gauge wire and a pair of wire cutters. "I need you to cut twenty-four, eight-inch pieces of wire. You can use the yardstick on the other counter."

He moved over to an adjoining countertop where Simone had glued a yardstick to the edge. Unrolling the wire, he quickly cut the required length and quantity. "Done," he announced proudly. "What's next?"

"Hey, you're fast."

Rafe opened and closed the cutters. "Do you have anything else I can cut?"

Simone reached for large roll of three-inch-wide wired sheer ribbon stamped with decorative medallions and edges made of wire so finely woven it resembled silver thread. "I need you to cut this into twenty-four-inch lengths."

"How much is on the spool?"

"Four yards."

Rafe appeared deep in thought, then his expression brightened. "You'll need six lengths."

Simone's smile was dazzling. "Not only are you quick, but you're dangerous with that wire cutter. Why is it that you write and do everything with your left hand, but cut with the right?"

He hoisted the cutters. "What can I say about being a lefty in a right-handed world? If you had a left-handed cutter, I'd still use my right hand."

The fact that he was left-handed and a pitcher had made him a much sought-after candidate for the major leagues. His obsession with all that was baseball began when his maternal grandfather took him to St. Louis to see the Cardinals play the Chicago Cubs. The roar of the crowd, the smell of hot dogs and peanuts all paled as he'd sat wide-eyed and transfixed, watching what had become a duel when opposing pitchers threw a ball over home plate with a speed and accuracy that made his heart pump wildly in his chest, while at the same time rendering him mute. Whenever his grandfather asked him a question, all he could do was either nod or shake his head.

Spending his birthday weekend in St. Louis with his grandfather had become the highlight of his six-year-old existence. He returned home and began using pieces of corn cobs as his ball and a hand-drawn target affixed to the side of an outbuilding where his father kept farm equipment as home plate. It took years and intense concentration to perfect hitting the target dead-center, but by the time he'd entered high school and joined the baseball team, he had total control of all of his pitches: curves, splitters, sinkers and his celebrated fastball.

Gideon was opposed to him becoming a ballplayer because he wanted him to go to college and make something of himself. Well, he did make it to college on academic and athletic scholarships, earned a degree in criminal justice, and was drafted to play in the major league. But his lifelong dream was cut short with a single telephone call from his sister, who told him that their father had threatened to kill their mother because he'd heard voices telling him that she was evil and that he'd been given the responsibility of ridding the world of iniquity.

Two days before the end of the season, he flew back to Kansas to take care of family business while his team headed into the postseason playoffs with a chance of playing in the World Series. They lost every game, and the press had a field day when he was accused of bailing on his team. Rafe wouldn't give his agent permission to talk to the media about his personal life, and when contract negotiations came up post–World Series, he stunned everyone when he not only opted *not* to re-sign with his team, but quit baseball altogether.

He walked away from his dream with the proceeds from his initial multimillion dollar contract and a degree in criminal justice. Everyone said he was crazy when it was his father who was certifiably crazy. He applied for a position with the U.S. Marshals Service and hired a fraternity brother as his investment consultant.

There were occasions when he regretted giving up

his baseball career, but it was short-lived when he remembered why he'd been forced to leave. And as the years passed, he became less repentant, and now that he had fallen in love with Simone Whitfield, it'd all been worth it.

He'd found her changed, softer and less angry. Pretense or not, they'd become a couple—in and out of bed.

What would've taken Simone more than three hours to complete by herself she was able to do in two with his assistance. She misted the bouquet, put it into a large plastic bag and placed it on the shelf in the refrigerator with the other wedding flowers.

Looping her arms under Rafe's shoulders, she pressed her breasts to his back. "Thank you. I may have to hire you as my assistant."

"Will I have to interview for the position?"

Standing on tiptoe, she breathed into his ear. "I don't know yet."

"Do I detect some reluctance?"

Simone inhaled the scent of his cologne mingling with the detergent she used doing laundry. "I don't know how long I'll be able to work with you before I decide to seduce my employee. And I'm certain you're quite familiar with laws about sexual harassment in the workplace."

Grasping her hands, Rafe turned and faced Simone. This was a Simone he'd never seen before: sexy and teasing. "How would you seduce me?"

Pulling her hands from his loose grip, she rested her palms over his pectorals and undid the buttons on the front of his shirt, exposing his chest. Slowly, methodically, she placed feathery kisses to his breastbone before venturing lower to his flat belly.

Rafe sucked in his breath when she unsnapped his jeans and her fingers searched under the waistband of his underwear to find him hard from the desire she evoked just by them occupying the same space.

Simone closed her eyes, enjoying the feel of the heavy flesh throbbing in her hand. "If you want my goodies, then you better take them now because after today you're going to be on lockdown for the next eight days."

It took Rafe a full sixty seconds before he decoded her cryptic statement. He met her amused gaze with astonishment. "What happened to three or five days?"

"Not *moi*."

His eyebrows lifted. "Are you sure? After this morning, I'd think you'd want to take a few days off."

Releasing his sex, Simone began to button his shirt. "Well, if you have a headache, then I'll understand." If Faith admitted that she was horny as a mink, then Simone knew how she felt, because since she'd begun sleeping with Rafe her dormant sex drive had kicked into high gear. It was as if she couldn't get enough, that she had to make up for eight years and that she was ready to overdose on Raphael Madison.

Gently pushing her hands away, Rafe relieved Simone of her tank top and bra, hard-pressed not to smile. "You really have some mouth on you, Simone Whitfield."

"What's the matter, darling? You don't like it?"

His hands went to the waistband of her drawstring pants, untying and pushing them off her hips. "I like the mouth. It's what comes out of it that I find a bit shocking at times."

Simone opened her mouth and stuck out her tongue. "You told me that you like my tongue when I—"

Rafe lowered his head and caught the tip of her tongue between his teeth, pulling gently until she moaned softly. He released it, glaring at her under lowered lids. "That's enough, baby."

This was one time when he wanted to make love to Simone where they stood, but he didn't want to risk getting her pregnant although that was exactly what he wanted to do—if only it would permit him to hold on to her.

Rafe had observed her with Kimika Sanborn, awed by the tenderness in her touch, the softness in her eyes when interacting with the toddler. It was obvious Simone was quite fond of the adorable little girl and vice versa. She'd admitted to wanting children, and so had he.

He'd asked himself from the very first time he'd slept with Simone if she was the one who'd make him question what exactly he wanted for himself and his future. He'd gotten his answer earlier that morning. Their love-making was different—tender, unhurried and uninhibited. Her response had stripped him bare where he'd almost blurted out to Simone that he loved her.

He'd believed himself in love with Dorene, yet never told her. They'd lived together, shared a bed, and because he never told the woman that he loved her, she'd slept with another man who wasn't afraid to verbalize his feelings. He'd loved and lost once, but swore it would not happen again.

His heated gaze moved from Simone's face to her bare breasts and came to rest on the candy-striped panties exposing more than they concealed. Going to his knees, his teeth closed over the silk ties at her hips, pulling them free. Triangles of red-and-white silk settled atop the pants around her ankles.

Rafe stood up, and at the same time he lifted Simone off her feet, she cradling his face between her palms. "Where are you taking me?" she asked when he headed out of the mudroom.

"Upstairs."

"Ah, sookie, sookie," she crooned. "I got something to take care of my darling's head."

"Now, which head are you talking about, baby?" Simone averted her gaze. "What's the matter, darling? Cat got your tongue?" Rafe teased.

Nothing was said when he finished undressing her, then himself. Their gazes were locked in a battle of wills when he paused to slip on protection until Simone held out her arms, welcoming him into her embrace and inside her body; their silent communication ended amid moans, groans and shared sighs of fulfillment.

Chapter 16

Rafe leaned against the door frame leading into the dining room, watching Simone adjust a crystal water goblet and matching wineglass on the damask-covered table. She'd decided to break with decades of tradition to cancel her Monday-night Whitfield women get-together to host a Friday-night dinner party. Tessa, Micah, Faith and Ethan confirmed their attendance, with her sister and future brother-in-law electing to spend the weekend in Westchester County because Tessa was scheduled to oversee a wedding reception in Croton-on-Hudson.

The week before, Lucinda Whitfield called Simone to tell that her only son, daughter-in-law and grandsons would arrive in New York in time for the annual Whitfield Memorial Day cookout.

Simone was forthcoming when she disclosed to Rafe

that Vernon and Yolanda Whitfield, who'd resigned their teaching positions, were expected to return to New York in time to join the rest of the family for what was regarded as an unofficial family reunion.

When Malcolm Whitfield told his son that a developer offered to purchase the land where Whitfield Caterers had conducted business for a quarter of a century, he and his brother decided to accept the offer because business had been steadily declining as a number of hotels went up along the interstate. After conferring with his wife, Vernon and Yolanda decided to return to New York to help the Whitfield brothers with their new business venture: a bi-level bowling alley with a game room for children and a jazz club for adults.

Although Simone expressed that she had mixed feelings about the demise of Whitfield Caterers, she knew her father and uncle were grateful for more than two decades of success that had afforded them the opportunity to purchase homes, educate their children and live quite comfortably into old age. However, she looked forward to interacting with her brother and his family more than summer vacations and every other Christmas.

"It looks perfect."

Simone's head came up at the sound of the familiar voice with its distinctive Midwest twang. There were times when she thought Rafe sounded like a Southerner. She gave him a tender smile. "Thank you. I still haven't decided what flowers I want to use as a centerpiece."

"What about tulips?"

Her eyebrows lifted. "What color tulips?"

Walking into the dining room, Rafe approached Simone, his penetrating gaze leisurely taking in the sun-browned face glowing with good health. They'd spent the past two days outdoors, taking their meals in the gazebo and relaxing on loungers on the patio. She'd wanted to fill the hot tub, but he'd nixed the idea. Sitting in the warm water, wearing next to nothing was too risky in case he had to react quickly.

"I like the yellow ones with the crinkly orange edges."

Simone nodded. "Parrot tulips." She ran her fingertips down his stubbly cheek. "Good choice. I have some orange- and lemon-scented candles that will complement the tulips." She'd gotten up earlier than usual to set the table for the evening's dinner before going to jog. "I'm ready."

They left the dining room, stopping in the entryway to slip on sunglasses. Simone felt a rush of excitement she hadn't had in a long time. She'd made an appointment at a local salon to have her hair cut and styled, eyebrows waxed and a manicure and pedicure. Cutting her hair symbolized a new beginning.

When she told Rafe that she wanted to host a dinner party in lieu of the Monday-night gathering, he'd offered to help with the cooking. It'd taken hours before they finally decided on a menu with dinner for six: asparagus with *beurre blanc,* salmon scallops with sorrel sauce, julienne carrots and string beans, risotto, crème caramel and Kir Royales. Rafe reassured her that although the dishes bore fancy names they were easy to prepare.

Shortening his stride, Rafe fell into step with Simone. "What time do you expect to be finished with your hair?" He'd tried talking her into changing her appointment because they had to cook later that afternoon, but she told him that she'd made the appointment weeks before and didn't know when her favorite stylist would be able to fit her in again.

"I should be finished by noon. Remember, I've already called in my food order, so we just have to pick it up." She'd ordered the salmon from a fish market, the vegetables from a gourmet grocer and all that remained was to pick up several bottles of champagne and a bottle of crème de cassis—a black currant liqueur. "Why don't you get your hair cut while you're waiting for me?"

"Is there something wrong with my hair?"

"Yes. It's too long. Either you get it cut now or four weeks from now. There's no way you're coming to my sister's wedding looking like a throwback to the Seventies."

"For your edification, Miss Whitfield, men had beards *and* long hair in the Seventies."

"Whatever," she drawled. "Knowing Tessa as I do, she'll have a BF if you show up with your hair hanging around your face."

"What's a BF?"

"Bitch fit!"

Rafe winced. "If that's the case, then I'll cut my hair."

"Oh? You'll cut it for Tessa, but not for me?"

"If you'd asked me to cut it for you, I would've."

"But I did," she said, protesting.

"No, you didn't, baby. Just think about what you said."

Simone's steps faltered, as they usually did each time she came to the spot where the man had sprung from the trees to plunge a knife into her neighbor's chest. She thought going back to the crime scene would help her face her fears, but it wasn't working. Rafe had assured her that she would always feel uncomfortable, but at least she hadn't let her fear paralyze her so that she wouldn't be able live a normal life.

Judge Fischer was still in the hospital, with marshals guarding his room around the clock. He was making progress, albeit slowly, and doctors predicted he would be able to return to his home at the end of the first week of June.

Simone found it hard to fathom that she'd known Rafe only three weeks when it seemed as if it'd been so much longer. They slept together every night. There were nights when they got little or no sleep because the passion between them never seemed to wane, but then there were nights when they lay together without exchanging a word. These were the times she treasured most. It was uncanny that they were now able to communicate without speaking.

Without warning, she found her wrist caught in a viselike grip when Rafe jerked her back against his body. Within seconds the gun in the holster around his ankle was in his hand.

"Coyote," he whispered hoarsely.

At first glance, Simone thought it was a dog. "It's so small," she whispered.

"It's a pup, which means his mother is somewhere around."

"Don't shoot it, Rafe," she pleaded.

"I'm not going to shoot it, Simone, unless it comes at us. A lot of wild animals are carrying rabies, so their behavior can be somewhat unpredictable."

"I want to go back home now."

Rafe hadn't taken his gaze off the coyote pup who appeared dazed. "We will as soon as it moves."

"Make it move, Rafe."

He nodded when he heard the panic rising in Simone's voice. Just as he made a motion toward the animal, it ran off into the woods. Bending slightly, he returned the automatic to his ankle. "Okay, let's go back."

"You must really think I'm a coward—"

"Don't say it, Simone. There's not a cowardly bone in your body. I wouldn't mind having you watch my back."

"The only weapon I'd have is a frying pan."

"You did all right with your Mace."

"It was pepper spray. It's illegal for me to carry Mace."

As they walked back to the house following their pre-empted jog, Rafe suggested eating breakfast at a diner. Simone was quick to agree. She liked going out with Rafe because it made her feel more like a girlfriend and less like a witness.

The doorbell chimed and Simone and Rafe shared a glance. Their first guests had arrived.

Rafe wiped his hands on a towel. "I'll get the door."

Simone shot him a knowing look. She'd stopped going to the door whenever the bell rang and rarely answered the telephone without Rafe standing close enough to overhear her conversations. The only time she was afforded a modicum of privacy was in the bathroom.

Rafe went to the door and peered through the security eye. He opened the door, successfully concealing a smile when Tessa's jaw dropped. *Simone made me cut it,* he mused. He knew Tessa was staring at his close-cropped hair he'd permitted to grow much too long. If he'd been assigned to courthouse security or transporting prisoners he would've gotten a memorandum about his appearance.

But on the other hand, he planned to get a haircut once he was notified of a date for the trial. What he didn't want to do was think of the time when he'd have to escort Simone into the courtroom for the first time. Not only would it signal the beginning of the end of Ian Benton's reign of terror against the justice system, but it would also signal the beginning of the end of his relationship with a woman he'd come to love beyond description.

"Come in," he said smiling. Bending his head, he kissed Tessa's cheek and then pumped Micah's hand.

Micah handed Rafe a shopping bag. "There's wine in there for Simone and a bottle of Jack for you." The two men shared a knowing smile.

Tessa glanced around the entryway. Colorful flowers in shades of yellow and orange complemented and repeated the colors in lighted scented candles under chimneys. Her sister's gift for the aesthetics was extraordinary. Whether it was choosing flowers for a bouquet, setting a table for formal dining or shopping for antiques, Simone was without peer.

"Everything looks so pretty."

"Your sister is incredible," Rafe remarked as he led the way through the living room, down a hallway and into the kitchen.

Incredible in which way? Tessa mused, reaching for her fiancé's hand. Rafe was good for her older sister. He'd changed her into the young woman she'd remembered before Simone had married Anthony Kendrick. And after she married him, it was as if she'd forgotten how to laugh or even smile. There were times when Simone was so moody Tessa couldn't bear to be around her. Most times she ignored Simone, but Simone and Faith went at each other like a cat and dog. Whenever Simone got into a funk, the Whitfields kept their distance until her dark mood passed.

Tessa entered the kitchen, stopping abruptly. Her eyes widened when she saw Simone's hair. "You did it! You finally cut your hair."

Simone glanced up from stirring a saucepan with finely minced shallots in white wine vinegar. With the addition of unsalted butter it would become the *beurre blanc* that she planned to serve with steamed asparagus.

"It is about time, don't you think?"

Tessa walked over to her sister, wrapping her arms around her neck. "You look fabulous!" And she did. The shiny corkscrew curls framing her face showed off her delicate features to their best advantage. The shorter hair made her appear older and more sophisticated. Now, Simone Whitfield looked like the woman she was.

She smiled at Rafe. "I like your haircut, too." The shortened strands, ranging in color from flaxen, palomino-gold to jonquil lay against his scalp in perfect precision. Rafe's gaze went to Simone. "Did my sister make you cut your hair?"

"No," Rafe lied much too quickly. "I decided it was time I began looking human. With the next full moon, I'd probably turn into the Wolf Man."

Micah sniffed the air. "Something smells wonderful." Leaning over, he kissed Simone's forehead. "Nice hair."

The doorbell chimed again, and Rafe went to answer it. He and Simone were cooking and hosting a dinner party together, something that he'd never done before. It reminded him of the time when his sister invited him to the tea parties she gave for her dolls.

Six years Rachel's senior, he'd humored her, pretending to sip tea from the tiny cups and eat cake off the small plastic plates filled with gumdrops or cookie crumbs. Rachel promised that when she grew up she would invite him and his wife to her home for a party, not behind the barn, but in a real garden. Whenever he went to San Diego he sat in his sister's garden, eating and drinking tea, but not with a wife.

Dinner had become a festive, relaxed affair for the three couples, eating and drinking while sharing stories about childhood antics, quirky people they'd encountered, national and world politics. When the topic segued to sports, Simone, Tessa and Faith rose from the table and retreated to the enclosed back porch.

Faith dropped to a cushioned chair, resting her bare feet on a footstool. "Now that Simi has a live-in chef, I think we should meet here every other Monday."

"That's not going to happen," Simone said as she sat on the love seat next to her sister. "Remember, Rafe's only going to be here until the sentencing phase."

Faith closed her eyes. "Is there anything you can do to convince him to hang around after the trial?"

Simone shook her head. "No, Faith. I made him promise that when he leaves he'll never come back."

Faith opened her eyes. "Why would you have him promise that?"

"I don't want a repeat of what I had with Tony."

"Simi Whitfield, Rafe Madison is no Anthony Kendrick. You give a bum half your life and now when you find a real man, a very good man, you send him packing. You make me so mad that I—"

"Calm down, Faith," Simone warned. "Remember you're carrying a baby."

"Mama and Daddy like Rafe," Tessa said as Faith and Simone embarked on what would become a stare-down. The cousins got along just fine until Tony's name came up.

"That's because he's very charming." Simone didn't know why she felt she had to validate her lover's easy-going personality.

Faith's expression brightened. "Ethan says he's fun to hang out with."

Tessa chuckled. "Micah claims if you turn one of your rooms into a man cave, then he, Rafe and Ethan would hang out here every weekend to watch the games while sitting in the hot tub."

"Oh, heck, no!" Simone sputtered. "I'm not about to turn my home into a sports bar. Let them go to a real sports bar to drink beer and make as much noise as they want."

"Sorry, Simi, but Ethan doesn't particularly like beer."

"Then Jack and Coke," Simone countered.

Tessa wagged a finger at her sister. "That's your man's drink of choice."

"What do you expect? He does admit to being a little country."

"A little?" Faith and Tessa chorused.

"He's real country," Faith crooned. "Country *and* fine as hell."

The sisters nodded in agreement. The three women talked quietly until Rafe walked into the room to inform them that coffee and dessert was ready to be served.

Chapter 17

When Rafe turned down the street where the Whitfields lived, the aroma of grilled food hung in the humid air. It'd rained Sunday night, but let up and then stopped altogether for those off from work and school to celebrate the holiday, cooking and dining outdoors.

Simone jumped out of the Yukon as soon as Rafe came to a complete stop. Her brother and his family had arrived the night before, and she couldn't wait to see her nephews. Each time they returned to New York for a visit, they appeared to have grown several inches. She noticed a number of New Jersey license plates on cars parked along the street. Lucinda and Malcolm had invited the Sanborns to come across the river to celebrate the holiday with them.

Not bothering to go into the house, Simone went around to the backyard where she saw Vernon with

Faith's father. Henry Whitfield, Malcolm's identical twin, was older by minutes and was quick to apprise everyone of that statistic.

The Sanborn twins, Isaac and Jacob, were hanging upside down from the jungle gym Lucinda and Malcolm had erected for their grandchildren, while Kimika, sitting between Marisol's legs, giggled uncontrollably as they came down the slide.

"Vern!"

Vernon Whitfield turned at the sound of his sister's voice. Smiling, arms outstretched, he closed the distance between them. Picking her up, he swung her around as he'd done when they were children. Vernon had inherited his mother's coloring, dark eyes and hair color, but his father's height.

Setting her on her feet, he kissed her cheeks. "You look wonderful. I like the short hair."

Simone, still grinning, ran her hand through the curls grazing the nape of her neck. "Thank you. Where are Yolanda and the boys?"

"I dropped them off at her parents' last night. Yolie just called to let me know she's on her way over. What…" Vernon's voice trailed off when he saw the tall, blond man carrying a large wicker hamper. "It can't be! White chocolate!"

Simone turned to see who her brother was talking about. All she saw was Rafe with the hamper filled with fresh melons, an assortment of cheese and seasonal fruit. A slight frown furrowed her forehead. "Who are you talking about?"

A wide grin split Rafe's face. "VW?"

"White chocolate," Vernon repeated.

Simone's gaze shifted from her lover, to her brother and then back again. "You two know each other?"

Setting down the hamper, Rafe pulled Vernon Whitfield into a rough embrace. When he'd been assigned to protect Simone Whitfield he never would've connected her to Vernon Whitfield. He'd thought the name familiar, but the Vernon he knew had always been called VW.

"Brother Madison."

"What's up, Brother Whitfield?"

It was the *brother* that raised the red flag for Simone. "You two are fraternity brothers?"

"O noble Kappa Alpha Psi, the pride of all our hearts. True manliness, fidelity, thou ever dost impart!" Rafe and Vernon sang at the top of their lungs, their arms over the other's shoulder.

What, she thought, were the odds that her brother and bodyguard had pledged the same fraternity? Rafe admitted to attending FMU and Vernon was a Tuskegee alumnus, both historically black colleges.

An expression of enlightenment brightened Simone's face. He'd accused her of being biased and into stereotypes. She narrowed her gaze at him. "Are you really a *brother?*"

A mysterious smiled tilted the corners of his mouth at the same time he nodded. "I'll tell you about it later."

Vernon clapped a hand on Rafe's shoulder. "What are the odds that one of my frat brothers would hook up with one of my sisters?"

Rafe gave him a sheepish grin. "Try a hundred thousand to one."

Henry Whitfield took his niece's hand, pulling her gently away from Vernon and Rafe. Ducking his head, he kissed her cheek. "It's been a long time since I've seen you look so happy."

"That's because I am, Uncle Henry."

"Does your young man have anything to do with it?"

Your young man. She and Rafe had perfected their act to the point where everyone believed they were actually a couple. She'd come to Mount Vernon to share breakfast with her parents before she, Faith and Tessa were measured for their gowns. They were scheduled for a final fitting two weeks before the wedding. During brunch, Lucinda had fussed over Rafe as if he were a rare hothouse orchid. This amused Simone, while her bodyguard took it all in stride.

Raphael Madison was a man who'd sworn an oath to protect his witness, but he was also her brother's fraternity brother, her lover and, above all, a man she'd fallen in love with, a man who would walk away from her and never look back. That was their agreement.

However, the revelation that he and her brother were Greeks—members of the same fraternity—changed everything. Would Vernon, who'd relocated his family from North Carolina to New York, maintain contact with Rafe?

Simone knew she'd changed, had matured enough not to repeat the mistakes she'd made with Tony with Rafe. It'd taken sixteen years for her to learn to let go of someone who hadn't changed because he hadn't wanted to change.

A single incident had shattered her cloistered existence and the result was she was forced to step outside her imagined existence and into the real world. For years she'd affected a "should I" or "shouldn't I" posture with her ex-husband while denying her femininity with self-imposed celibacy.

Then, Kansas-born U.S. Marshal Raphael Madison swept into her life with the power of a Great Plains twister, protecting her, but also helping her to see who she could actually be—for that she would be eternally grateful. He was able to defuse her quick temper with a warning look and the single word—"enough."

She enjoyed being Rafe's temporary girlfriend and lover. She'd come to look forward to preparing meals with him and having him assist her whenever she designed her floral arrangements. What had really surprised her was that her macho lawman actually liked playing house.

"Auntie Simone!"

The sound of her nephew calling her name pulled Simone from her reverie. Before she could turn around she found herself wrestled to the grass as eight- and ten-year-olds tag-teamed her.

"Give up?" the older of the two shouted.

Squirming and flailing, Simone shook her head. "Never!"

The eight-year-old wrapped his arm around her head, applying what he considered a headlock. "Give up, Auntie Simone?"

"I give up!" she screamed as they both applied modified headlocks.

"Nicholas and Quincy Whitfield!"

The two boys, their eyes as big as silver dollars, scrambled off their aunt and the grass when they heard their mother's voice. Yolanda Whitfield's attempt to glare at her sister-in-law failed when Simone lay on her back, arms and legs outstretched.

"Welcome home, Yolie," Simone said, grinning. Her

sister-in-law had changed her hairstyle—yet again. Her chin-length hair was a mass of tiny twists that flattered her perfectly rounded face.

Yolanda's dark brown eyes shimmered with warmth and humor. "When are you going to stop rolling around on the ground?"

"Hopefully never." A shadow fell over Simone as Rafe extended his hand.

"Need help getting up?" She placed her hand in his, and he pulled her up in one continuous motion. "You have grass stains on your shirt," he whispered close to her ear.

Simone blushed. She remembered another time when she'd asked him if she had grass stains on her shirt—a time when he stated that he liked her better on her back. He'd gotten his wish because she'd lost count of the number of times she'd lain on her back whenever they made love.

She knew she would miss Rafe whenever he left her, but he wasn't all she would miss. She would miss their passionate lovemaking, because whenever they came together they gave the other all of themselves, holding nothing back.

Her arm went around Rafe's waist. "Rafe, this is Yolanda, Vernon's wife and the mother of my two would-be professional-wrestler nephews, Nicholas and Quincy." The boys had run away to join the Sanborn children in the playground area of the expansive backyard. "Yolanda, this is my very good friend and Vernon's frat brother, Rafe Madison."

Rafe smiled and extended his hand. "I'm honored to meet you."

Yolanda took the proffered hand, her eyebrows lifting

slightly. "It's always a pleasure to meet one of Vern's frat brothers."

Vernon walked over and brushed a kiss over his wife's lips. "I see you've met white chocolate."

Yolanda gasped audibly. "Vernon!" Her shocked expression spoke volumes.

"Yolie, please. Don't let the blond hair and blue eyes fool you. Brother Madison is a *brother* and pitched in the majors."

It was Simone's turn to gasp, as she wondered how many more surprises she would experience before the day ended. The man she'd been sleeping was mixed race and at one time had been a Major League ballplayer. What was next—a wife and children in Kansas?

Faith walked over to the small group, looking every inch a model in a pair of lemon-yellow slacks she'd paired with a crocheted top with an Empire waist. Her eyes were shielded from the sun by a pair of oversized shades.

"Hello, everybody!" She handed out hugs and kisses to Yolanda, Vernon, Rafe and Simone like a celebrity. She rested a hand on Vernon's arm. "Cuz, can you and Rafe help Ethan bring in a few things from the car?"

"Sure."

"No problem."

Rafe and Vernon had spoken in unison.

Yolanda stared at Simone from under her lashes. "Where did you find *him?*"

Simone smiled. "*Him* found me," she teased.

Yolanda rolled her eyes upward. "White chocolate or dark chocolate, he's fine as hell."

Faith frowned. "Yolanda Evans-Whitfield, what are you babbling about?"

"Simone's man. He's Vernon's frat brother."

Faith lifted her glasses. "You mean he's a *brother?*" Yolanda and Simone nodded at the same time. "No wonder Ethan and Micah call him brother."

"Do you think they knew?" Simone asked.

Faith settled her sunglasses on her nose while sucking her teeth. "Heaven knows what they talk about whenever they get together. They're a perfect example of the old boys' network."

"Mommy, mommy!"

The three women turned to see Quincy running toward them, Isaac, Jacob and Kimika Sanborn following closely behind. "Grandpa is cooking a pig in the ground!"

"The pig has eyes!" Jacob said.

"Big eyes," Isaac confirmed.

"Pick me up," Kimika demanded of Simone.

"What's the magic word?" Simone asked the toddler.

"Please."

Simone swept her up in her arms and rubbed noses. "Let's go and see this pig everyone's talking about."

She headed for the area in the back of the house where Malcolm Whitfield had a contractor put in an outdoor pit and fireplace. This would be the first year Malcolm would cook and serve his celebrated roast pig. It was a favorite of those who held their affairs at Whitfield Caterers. It saddened Simone that her father and uncle were closing the establishment at the end of August, but the decades-old, family-owned business had allowed the brothers to purchase homes, educate their children and maintain a very comfortable lifestyle.

An era would end when they sold the land to a developer, along with the two-story Revival Regency-style mansion with stone-colored brick, a bowed entry and portico constructed on sloping lawn that overlooked an English garden and a pond filled with water lilies and a family of magnificent, graceful swans. Malcolm and Henry would leave the catering business to begin another, this time with another generation of Whitfield man: Vernon.

It was close to midnight when Simone returned to White Plains with Rafe. They would've left Mount Vernon earlier, but the women had gathered in Lucinda's kitchen, talking nonstop, while waiting for their men to finish watching a baseball game that had gone into extra innings. The game still hadn't ended when William and Abram loaded their sleepy children into their vehicles to head back to New Jersey.

Dropping her handbag on a chair in the entryway, Simone stared at Rafe's back when he locked the front door and set the alarm. "I'm going upstairs to take a bath."

Rafe nodded, but didn't turn around. "I'm going to hang out down here for a while."

She waited for him to turn around to face her, but when he didn't she headed for the staircase. There was so much more she wanted to know about Raphael Madison, yet was reluctant to ask. He wasn't authorized to reveal anything more than his name and/or official identification, so her wanting to know more wasn't an option.

Rafe paced the length of the enclosed back porch like a restless cat. Spending the day with Simone's family and the Sanborns was one he'd remember for years. Reconnecting with a fraternity brother had been a surprise, just as much of a surprise as the fact that he'd fallen in love with the man's sister.

He hadn't planned to become emotionally involved with his witness, make love to his witness or fall in love with her. He and Simone Whitfield were complete opposites, and despite their differences she'd become an integral part of whom he'd become.

She was fresh, exciting and sensual. Everything about her appealed to his masculinity, and he didn't want to think of the time when he'd have to leave her. Simone made him promise that he was never to contact her once he was reassigned, a promise he was tempted to break.

How could he walk away from her and pretend what they'd shared never happened?

Even when Simone was in one part of the house and he in another, her essence lingered. When he least expected it, he'd catch a whiff of the lavender that made up her body wash and shampoo. And of all of the flowers she grew and cultivated in her greenhouses, she'd become the rarest, most exotic of them all.

Knowing he couldn't put off the inevitable, Rafe double-checked all of the doors and windows, then climbed the staircase to the second story.

His footfalls were muffled in the carpeting running the length of the hallway as he made his way toward his bedroom. Then, without warning, Rafe stopped and retraced his steps and walked into Simone's bedroom. Instead of waiting for her to come to him, he would take the initiative.

A knowing smile deepened the laugh lines around his

eyes when he encountered darkness. He felt as if it were a repeat of the night of the storm, when he'd made love to Simone for the first time. He heard the music coming from the radio and detected the flicker of candlelight through the half-opened bathroom door.

As he'd done that night, he stood in the doorway, watching Simone as she lay in the bathtub, eyes closed and her head resting on a bath sponge. And despite the warm temperatures inside and outside the house, a fire crackled in the fireplace. Moisture dotted her face, turning her into a statue of molten gold.

Taking a backward step, he undressed in the darkened bedroom, leaving his firearm on the table next to the king-size iron bed. Whistling softly and hoping not to startle her, he smiled at Simone when she opened her eyes.

"Would you like company?"

Sitting up straighter, Simone held out her hand. "I would love company." Moving toward the other end of the tub, she giggled as Rafe stepped in and sat behind her. "If I'd known I was going to have company I would've used another fragrance."

Wrapping his arms around her waist, Rafe eased Simone back against his chest. "We wind up smelling like each other whenever we make love," he whispered, pressing a kiss to her damp hair.

Tilting her chin, she smiled up at him. "You don't mind smelling girly?"

He returned her smile. "That's all good as long as I don't turn into a girl."

"What's wrong with being a girl?"

"Nothing. As long as I stay a guy."

"You like being a guy?"

Rafe angled his head and kissed her forehead. "I suppose I've taken being a man for granted until I met you." He wanted to tell Simone that he wanted to make love to her every night for the rest of his natural life.

Simone shifted until she settled into a more comfortable position, her cheek pressed to his heart. The bathtub was definitely not large enough for two people—especially one as tall as Rafe. "If I had to wait eight years to sleep with a man, then I'm glad it was you." A pause ensued, with only the sound of Anita Baker singing "You Bring Me Joy," breaking the comfortable silence.

Rafe splayed his fingers over her flat belly. "I guess you want to know about me?"

"At first I wanted to know who you really are, but to know more would only complicate what we have."

"How's that?" he asked.

"We're already in too deep, Rafe. I'm certain you don't make it habit to sleep with—"

"I've never slept with a witness," he said, interrupting Simone. "You're the first *and* I promise that you will be the last."

"Who you sleep with once you leave—"

"Please don't say it, Simone. Let's not talk about the future."

"What do you want to talk about?"

"We need to talk about us—now."

"No, we don't, Rafe. What we need to do is enjoy the time we have left."

Rafe wanted to shake Simone until she was too breathless to say anything. "We are going to do that. But—"

"But nothing," Simone interrupted, yet again.

"Micah's right when he told me that my woman has some mouth."

Don't, a silent voice warned her. *Think before you say anything.* She counted slowly to ten as she swallowed back her acerbic retort. Simone knew she'd changed, because in the past she would've come back at Rafe like a lit fuse seconds from detonation. She wasn't certain what had brought about her change in attitude, but she liked the new Simone Whitfield.

"Do you like my mouth?" she asked instead.

"You have the sexiest mouth of any woman I've ever had the pleasure of kissing."

"And how many women have you kissed, Raphael Madison?"

"I plead the Fifth."

She smiled. "Did you have groupies when you were a baller?"

Rafe's jaw tightened. "I was never what you would refer to as a baller," he said between clenched teeth. "There were no women waiting for me at hotels or stadium exits when the team traveled from city to city."

"Did you have a special girlfriend?"

"Yes," he said truthfully. "I was in a relationship."

"Was it serious?"

A wry smile twisted his mouth. "It was more serious for me than it was for her."

"She cheated on you." Simone's query was a statement.

"I don't want to talk about it, Simone."

"What do you want to talk about?"

"I've wanted to talk about us for the past five minutes, but you keep interrupting me, baby."

"Talk, Rafe," she drawled.

"I didn't tell you..." His words trailed off when a loud pop from burning wood, followed by a shower of embers came from behind the decorative wrought-iron fireplace screen. "I didn't tell you that I'd pledged a black Greek fraternity because you probably wouldn't have believed me. Even when I told you that I'd attended FMU you looked at me as if I'd grown an extra eye. There's no need for me to go around with a sign pasted on my back that I'm African-American because I know who and what I am."

A loud snapping sound reverberated throughout the bathroom, stopping all conversation. Simone and Rafe stared at the showers of embers lighting up the bathroom like flashes of lightning. They sat, watching the fire shower in an awed silence.

Chapter 18

"Which one of your parents is black?" Simone asked Rafe when the impromptu fire show ended.

"My mother. She's a direct descendant of former slaves fleeing Louisiana after Reconstruction. Her family settled in Nicodemus, Kansas, which is now a national historic site under the U.S. Park Service. It also holds the distinction of being the only remaining all black town west of the Mississippi that was settled in the 1800s."

Simone heard the pride in her lover's voice. "How did she meet your father?"

"My father, who lived in Waterville, was driving to Topeka when he was involved in a multiple-car pileup on the highway during an ice storm."

The bubbles disappeared, the water cooled, the fire blazed less brightly and the candles grew smaller as

Simone listened to Rafe talk about his family. Esther offering to let Gideon Madison sit in her warm truck because his had sustained severe front-end damage was the beginning of what would become a courtship when Gideon drove more than two hundred miles from Waterville to Nicodemus to see Esther every weekend. They'd decided he would save time, money and lots of gas if they married.

Esther, a college-educated teacher, gave up her career to become a farmer's wife and stay-at-home mom. Her thirst for teaching never waned when she taught her son and daughter to read before they celebrated their fourth birthdays.

Simone was unable to control the shiver that raced throughout her body when Rafe spoke of Gideon admitting to hearing voices. His increasing paranoia, violent outbursts and eventual break with reality came when he'd imagined everyone was trying to kill him.

"I'd signed a three-year, multimillion-dollar contract to pitch for the San Diego Padres, traveling to a different city every four or five days and going back to Waterville every chance I got. I knew something was wrong, but I couldn't put my finger on it. Everything came to a head when my sister called to tell me that my father was threatening to kill my mother because the voices told him she was evil.

"I asked the team's general manager for emergency family leave to return to Kansas. He was reluctant to approve it because the team had earned a spot in the postseason playoffs. He wanted me to promise that I'd be back in time for the playoffs, but I couldn't."

Simone closed her eyes. "Did you make it back in time?"

Rafe shook his head. "No. We lost and I was accused of selling out my team. Then came the threatening phone calls and hate mail, and when it came time to renegotiate my contract, I opted not to sign and quit baseball."

"What happened after that?" Simone's voice was barely a whisper.

"I moved my mother and sister into the house I'd bought in San Diego, then returned to Waterville to take steps to have my father committed so that he could get the help he needed. Meanwhile, I'd applied to the U.S. Marshals Service. While I waited for them to complete a background check, I used that time to get a graduate degree in criminal justice with a concentration in pre-law."

"You want to become a lawyer?"

"I don't want to practice law. I'd like to teach it."

Now Simone understood why Rafe had spent so much time talking to Micah and Edgar Sanborn. Edgar taught at Princeton and Micah was a district attorney. "When do you plan to go to law school?"

If someone had asked Rafe that question before he met Simone Whitfield, he would've said in ten years. Now, he wasn't so certain. He didn't want to leave Simone. He'd grown tired of sleeping in strange beds in hotels, motels or safe houses in different cities when called upon to protect a witness. At thirty-five, he wanted and needed stability.

"I'd planned to give the Marshals Service another ten years, but now I'm not that certain."

"What made you change your mind?"

"There are a number of reasons, and the first one is age."

"What about your age?" Simone asked.

"I'll be forty-five by the time I start law school. I don't want my classmates to mistake me for their instructor instead of a student."

"Can't you transfer to a department within the Marshals Service where you don't have to do a lot of traveling, or one where you have set hours? Then you can attend law school part-time. That's what Micah did."

"I could apply for court security."

"There you go," Simone said proudly. "See, you just solved your own problem."

"No, baby. You just helped me solve my problem."

Simone managed to turn and lay atop Rafe without splashing water onto the floor, her oil-slick breasts flattening against his hard chest. "I think it's time we get out of this tub before I shrivel up like a prune."

Gasping and breathing heavily, Rafe closed his eyes when he felt his sex swell. "Don't do that, Simone."

"Do what, darling?"

"Hump me."

With wide eyes, she gave him a look of pure innocence. "I'm not humping you."

Placing his hands over her bottom, he pressed her hips to his groin. "Feel that?"

Simone smiled. "What, pray tell, in the world is that?"

"You don't know?" Rafe loved Simone even more when she was soft, teasing.

"No, darling, I don't know."

"I suppose I'll have to show you." Bracing an arm on the edge of the tub, he pushed to his feet, bringing Simone up with him.

They stood in the bathtub, sharing a smile reserved for lovers. Anchoring an arm around Simone's waist,

Rafe stepped out onto the shaggy rug, bringing her with him. He took his time drying her body with a thirsty towel from the stack on the nearby stool. It was her turn to dry him; she lingered over hard planes of his body and between his legs until his desire for her superseded their tactile seduction.

Bending slightly, Rafe swept Simone up off the rug and carried her through her bedroom and down the hallway to his bedroom. It'd been ten days since he last made love with Simone—ten long, agonizing days where she slept beside him and he couldn't touch her.

He paused to protect her from an unplanned pregnancy, even though it was the last thing he wanted to do. And when he found himself inside Simone, he knew then that he wanted her as his wife and the mother of their children.

"I don't want my daughter's wedding to look as if we're under siege." Malcolm Whitfield's voice was low, angry.

Rafe didn't drop his gaze. "I can assure you, Mr. Whitfield, that my men are trained to be unobtrusive enough to blend in with your wedding guests. I will post two at the door as security. They'll be responsible for matching names with your daughter's guest list. Two will be in the parking area and the last two will circulate among your guests."

He'd called the lead U.S. attorney on Benton's case and put in a request for six marshals to provide backup at Simone Whitfield's sister's wedding. It took less than thirty-six hours for his request to be approved and earlier that morning half a dozen marshals in business suits arrived at Whitfield Caterers.

"And I can assure you that nothing's going to jump off here with half the guests representing the NYPD."

"Simone is not a witness for the New York Police Department, so it's the Feds' responsibility to provide protection for her."

Malcolm ran a hand over his face, knowing he was fighting a losing battle with the taciturn lawman "playing house" with his daughter. That was what Simone told him when she explained why a man had moved into her home. Whenever he observed the marshal with Simone, he'd detected a vaguely sexual magnetism between them. He'd never been one to get involved in his children's lives, but he wanted to tell Raphael Madison that his taking added precautions to provide witness protection for Simone went above and beyond the call of duty.

Nodding, Malcolm blew out a breath. "Okay. I'll allow them, but the minute I see a gun or pair of handcuffs, they're out of here."

It was Rafe's turn to nod. He didn't want to warn Simone's father that he would be the one in cuffs if he sought to interfere with the government's attempt to bring Ian Benton to justice.

Rising to his feet, Rafe offered his hand. "Thank you, Mr. Whitfield."

Malcolm stood up and took the offered hand. "You can dispense with the Mr. Whitfield and call me Malcolm. After all, you are *living* with my daughter."

Rafe's expression didn't change with the older man's veiled innuendo. He inclined his head. "Malcolm it is."

Malcolm glanced at his timepiece under the French cuff to his dress shirt. "You have twenty minutes to get your men into position." Reaching for the jacket to his tuxedo, he slipped his arms into the sleeves. "Now, if you'll excuse me I have a daughter to give away in marriage."

Rafe walked out after Malcolm, signaling to the heavily armed men standing in the hallway. He quickly gave them their orders, then went to look for Simone before the ceremony began. She told him that she was doing triple duty as wedding planner, floral designer and bridal attendant.

He'd found it hard to believe it'd been seven weeks since he'd come face-to-face with Simone Whitfield for the first time. And what was more amazing was the deep, abiding love for her that had nothing to do with them sleeping together. He wanted her awake or asleep, in and out of bed. They'd established a ritual of retreating to the back porch after dinner to sit and watch the sunset. Most times they sat silently, each lost in their private musings.

It was a time when Rafe mentally rehearsed for the day and time he would have to leave Simone. He'd told himself to be strong, stay strong, over and over until he believed he was. But would the mental calisthenics sustain him when he returned to his Poughkeepsie condo to kick back and relax before the next assignment?

Coming to a stop in front of the door to the room where he'd left Simone with the other members of Tessa's wedding party, Rafe rapped lightly on the door. He identified himself when a feminine voice asked who was it. When the door opened, he went completely still as Simone stood before him in a strapless silk chiffon gown in a robin's-egg-blue that shimmered against her skin, the color of burnished gold. Delicate feathers dyed the same blue color covered the crown of her head and curved under her jaw to her chin. A pair of large Tahitian pearl earrings suspended from a drop of bezel-set diamonds was her only jewelry.

"You look so incredibly beautiful." Simone's eyes appeared abnormally large and bright, and he attributed it to anticipation and excitement.

"Thank you. Why are you here?" she asked, lowering her voice to a whisper.

He took a step, lowered his head and brushed his mouth over her ear. "I came to tell you something."

Simone closed her eyes and inhaled deeply. She knew whatever he had to tell her was related to the Benton case. "What is it?"

"Open your eyes, Simone."

Her eyelids fluttered wildly until she focused her gaze. "Why?"

"I want you to look at me when I tell you that I love you."

Her lips parted. "No," she whispered.

Anchoring a hand on the wall over her head, Rafe leaned in closer. "Yes! I love you, Simone Whitfield." Pushing off the wall, he turned and made his way into the sanctuary where Tessa Whitfield was expected to exchange vows with Micah Sanborn.

All eyes were trained on the bride and groom as Tessa raised the hem of her gown with one hand and grasped Micah's with the other. They jumped over a ceremonial broom tied together with a bow in the same robin's-egg-blue silk of Simone's gown. The velvet-stemmed Tweedia flower added "something blue" to the white-on-white bridal bouquet of sparkling white roses and orchids tied together with satin-silk ribbon and corsage pins. Rafe's gaze was fixed on Simone.

It was uncanny how quickly he'd learned the different names of flowers, recognizing them by sight. Simone had worked tirelessly for three days to design flowers for the reception: the entryway, bar decorations, centerpieces, the bride and groom's chairs, the buffet table, the cake table and the powder rooms.

Tessa had confided to him at the rehearsal dinner that she'd wanted a church wedding, but the minister hadn't been able to accommodate her because there were two other weddings scheduled for the same day. The only alterative was to hold the wedding and reception dinner at Whitfield Caterers.

His gaze caressed Simone's delicate profile and the velvety smoothness of her bare arms and shoulders. He'd told her that he loved her, confessed what lay in his heart and she could only say no. Had she said no because she didn't want to hear it, or was it a "No, don't love me," or "I don't love you"?

Rafe directed his focus on the wedding party. Tessa exemplified the beauty and elegance of a Signature bride in a white silk-satin strapless Asian-inspired wedding gown with a kimono-style platinum-hued sash that accentuated her slim waist. Faith, as Tessa's matron of honor, wore a backless gown in a gunmetal gray with a large satin bow attached on the left side of the waist. Marisol Sanborn's black curly hair was blown straight and ended at the waist of her pale blue A-line satin gown with narrow straps tucked into a bow at the small of her back.

Micah had selected his father as his best man and his brothers William and Abram as his groomsmen. The family of the groom had elected to wear varying shades of gray while the bride's family had selected varying shades of blue.

After the exchange of vows and rings, the officiating judge, a Sanborn family friend, declared Micah and Tessa Sanborn husband and wife.

"Look this way, Simone, and lift your chin just a tad. Yes, that's it."

Simone fixed a smile and stared directly at the photographer as he shot several frames before suggesting another pose. Her distraction was a direct result of Rafe's unexpected declaration of love. It'd taken all of her concentration to walk down the white carpet without glancing over at Rafe. At first, she thought she'd imagined him telling her that he loved her because that was what she'd wished, hoped and prayed for.

Why, she mused, hadn't he told her the night before, when they'd sat in her mother's parlor talking after everyone had gone to bed? They'd talked about any and everything but themselves.

And in keeping his promise, wherever she went, he was there: when she'd decorated the rooms where the Whitfield-Sanborn party was to be held, gone to the rehearsal dinner at Franklin Lakes with the Sanborns and returned to Mount Vernon to spend the night with her parents. She'd slept in her old bedroom, while Lucinda had offered Rafe one of the guest bedrooms.

She met his gaze briefly as he stood in a corner, watching the picture-taking session. Simone wanted to tell Rafe that there was no need to watch her because she was among family and friends.

The photographer held up a hand. "That's it for now, folks."

There came a collective sigh from everyone in the wedding party as they filed out of the room. Simone had instructed someone on the waitstaff to bring Faith a small plate of fruit and vegetables to sustain her during the hour-long photo session, while the wedding guests were enjoying the cocktail hour before the wedding party arrived for a buffet dinner.

After they entered the ballroom to rousing applause, it took less than half an hour for Simone to develop a healthy respect for her sister's profession as a wedding planner. She had to make certain the servers refilled trays and platters of food favorites: shrimp, lobster, sushi and tempura. Tessa had hired a band and a DJ. Recorded music would play during the cocktail hour and dinner, and the band would perform for dancing.

Simone noticed several men in business suits lingering, while not eating or drinking. Walking over to her father, she tapped his arm to get his attention. "Daddy, who are the men standing around doing nothing?"

Malcolm gave his daughter a slight smile. "Ask your boyfriend."

"I will." Turning on the heels of her silk-covered stilettos, she searched the crowd for Rafe, finding him sitting at one of two tables for single guests. A very attractive young woman with short black hair clung possessively to his arm. His bored expression spoke volumes.

Simone, having removed her hairpiece, lifted the

hem of her flowing gown with one hand. She caught Rafe's gaze, and he rose to his feet.

"May I please have a word with you?"

Rafe nodded to the woman who'd latched on to him as soon as he sat down. "Excuse me, please." He escorted Simone a short distance away.

"Who are the guys in the black suits?"

"They're my men," Rafe admitted. "I wanted a little extra manpower because of the number of people here."

A slight frown furrowed her smooth forehead. "It's a bit much, Rafe. The NYPD's police commissioner and several high-ranking department officials are scheduled to arrive at any moment, so I don't believe anyone would attempt anything with all the police personnel."

"Assassins have shot presidents despite all the precautions taken by the Secret Service." His expression hardened. "The men will stay until the end."

She knew arguing with him would yield nothing. "Okay, but you should let them get something to eat. The head chef outdid himself tonight."

A hint of a smile softened Rafe's mouth. "When are you going to eat? Right now you should be sitting at the bridal table eating."

"I have to make certain everything's running smoothly."

"Wrong, Simone. Your father and uncle have owned and operated a very successful catering establishment for the past twenty-seven years, making certain everything runs smoothly. Now, go sit down, eat and enjoy your sister's special day. Everything is perfect."

"You think?" she teased.

He smiled. "I know." Without warning, he sobered. "I'd like you to save me one dance."

Her eyebrows lifted. "You dance?"

"Yes, Simone Whitfield, I dance. You think I'd only do the Cotton-Eyed Joe or the Texas Two-Step?"

A slight blush touched her cheeks. "Are you ever going to let me live that down, farm boy?"

"Never, city girl. Just remember to save a dance."

"Just one?"

He nodded. "We can share another one when we get back to White Plains."

"What we have to do is talk, not dance."

"We'll talk *and* dance."

Simone nodded. "Now, please tell your men that they can eat and drink."

Rafe resisted the urge to salute Simone. "I will."

She returned to the dais and found Micah standing off to the side with a very dark and drop-dead gorgeous man wearing an exquisitely tailored suit that had to have been made to measure expressly for his tall body.

Micah beckoned to her. "Simone, I'd like you to meet my law school mentor, Kyle Chatham. Kyle, this is my sister-in-law, Simone Whitfield."

Simone extended her hand. "It's nice meeting you, Kyle."

She remembered from the seating arrangement chart that Kyle was seated at one of the singles' tables. She couldn't tear her gaze away from his angular face with chiseled cheekbones, deep-set, slanting, catlike, warm brown eyes and close-cropped black hair with a sprinkling of gray that looked like diamond dust.

Kyle's eyes took in everything about Micah's sister-in-law in one, sweeping glance. Cradling her hand in his much larger, well-groomed one, he raised it to his lips and kissed her knuckles. "The pleasure is mine, Simone. May I call you Simone, Miss Whitfield?"

A rush of color darkened her expertly made-up face. There was no doubt Kyle Chatham was flirting with her *and* she liked it. "Yes, you may, Kyle."

Kyle let go of her hand. "Will you save me a dance? A very slow dance," he added, smiling and exhibiting a set of perfect white teeth.

He was the second man within minutes that had asked her to save him a dance. "I'll save you one, but I don't know how slow it'll be."

He winked at her. "I'll take my chances."

Simone gave the gorgeous man a polite smile. "Please excuse me. I have to get something to eat." Two waiters were assigned to see to the needs of those at the bridal table. Tessa preferred buffet to sit-down because it made for a more relaxed dining atmosphere. Guests were permitted a wider array of choices, and they could refill their plates as often as they wanted. Rolling bars were positioned strategically for beverage orders.

"I'll bring you what you want," Kyle volunteered smoothly.

Simone met his gaze. She knew he was interested in her, and there was no doubt she would've been into him if she hadn't been so in love with Raphael Madison— a man who'd confessed to loving her.

As a thirty-three-year-old woman, she was beyond playing games. She and Rafe had reached the point where their relationship had to be resolved.

Rafe watched with narrowed eyes as the impeccably dressed man leaned in a little too close to Simone to be polite. There was no doubt the man was interested in or flirting with her, but it was all for naught. Simone Whitfield was still a single woman, but he prayed she wouldn't be much longer. He planned to propose marriage and put a ring on her finger—but only if she agreed to marry him. If she claimed she didn't love him, then he would give her all the time she needed to come to love him as much as he loved her.

Have your fun now, because it's me she's going home with tonight. Rafe took one more lingering glance at Simone and the man cheesing at her, then made his way to his fellow marshals to give them permission to eat.

Voices lowered appreciably when the band members took their places. As soon as the octet launched into a soulful rendition of Marvin Gaye's "Got To Give It Up," couples crowded the dance floor.

Rafe watched Simone dance with her father, brother and Micah's brothers, waiting his turn. When the male lead singer took the microphone to sing Marc Anthony's "I Need You," he crossed the dance floor with long strides and tapped the shoulder of the man who'd hovered a little too closely to his woman.

"Excuse me, but my date did promise me this dance."

A stunned expression froze Kyle Chatham's even, masculine features. "Your date?" he asked Simone.

Smiling, she nodded. "Yes. We're living together."

Taking a step back, Kyle bowed elegantly to Rafe. "You're a lucky man."

Rafe inclined his head. "I know. And thank you." Taking Simone's hand, he led her out to the area set aside for dancing.

Folding her close to his body, he pressed a kiss to her hair. "I'm glad you told him that we're living together."

"It's not as if I lied," she said quietly. "He's very nice, but I didn't want to lead him on to make him believe that I'd be available to date him, given my current situation."

"What is your current situation, baby?"

Leaning back, she stared up at Rafe. "I'm living and sleeping with a man who picked the wrong time and place to tell me that he was in love with me."

"Why was it wrong?"

A mysterious smile parted her lush lips. "Because he didn't give me time to tell him that I'm also in love with him."

Rafe missed a step, but caught himself as he spun her around and around, the flowing skirt of her dress sweeping around his trousers. He hummed, then sang along with the vocalist, "Girl I really need you, need you. Babe, oh baby. Won't you marry me. Won't you marry, marry me. I love you. Oh, I need you."

Simone pressed her face to his shoulder, fighting not to break down and cry. "Don't do this to me, Rafe. Not here."

"Then where, baby?"

"Let's go somewhere and talk."

Rafe caught the eye of one of the marshals as Simone led him out of the reception hall and into her father's office, the officer following and standing outside the closed door.

A table lamp provided the only illumination in the small space filled with photographs of the many clients who'd used Whitfield Caterers for their special celebrations. Rafe sat on the edge of the desk and pulled Simone to stand between his legs.

"What do you want to talk about?"

"Us, Marshal Madison."

Rafe tried not to smile. "What about us, Miss Whitfield?"

"What's happening with us, Rafe? We've done everything we weren't supposed to do. In other words, we've broken all of the rules."

A dazzling smile brightened his face. "But it worked, didn't it?"

"You tell me, darling."

He angled his head. "I love you and you *claim*—"

"Claim! I told you that I love you."

"Okay. I stand corrected. I love you and you love me, and because we're living together *and* fornicating, I believe it's only right that we get married."

She patted his chest. "Oh, no, you didn't say fornicating."

"Yeah, I did," he said, laughing softly. "When do you want to get married?"

Her jaw dropped. "How are you asking about a date when you haven't asked me whether I'd like to marry you?"

He went to knees while holding her hands. "Will you, Simone Whitfield, marry me?"

Simone felt as if she were drowning in twin pools of sapphire as she saw something in Rafe's gaze that hadn't been there before: love. She'd recognized passion, but not love.

Her eyelids fluttered as she struggled not to cry. Tough girl Simone Whitfield was not prone to tears, but she was close, very, very close, to breaking down completely.

"Yes, Raphael Madison, I will marry you."

Coming to his feet, he pulled her close and kissed her with all the emotion he could summon at that moment. With Simone, he would right all the wrongs, realize his dreams and look forward to a future he never would've imagined.

"You know I'm going to have to talk to your father to get his permission."

"But...but you've already asked me. Isn't that enough?"

Rafe shook his head. "Don't forget that I'm a simple farm boy who was raised the old-fashioned way."

"Don't forget country."

"Hey! Ain't nothin' wrong with country."

"Sure, you right," she teased.

"Now who's country?"

Stepping back, Simone swirled around gracefully. "Not me. You're getting a city girl, darling, and don't you forget it."

"I'll talk to your father later on tonight, then tomorrow we'll hit a couple of jewelry stores to buy you a ring."

Putting her arms around his waist, Simone kissed his warm, tanned throat. "I'd like to have a winter wedding."

"What about a Christmas Eve wedding?" Rafe suggested.

"I'd love a Christmas wedding. Wherever we have it, I want my wedding flowers to be white poinsettias. What about children, Rafe? Do you want to wait a year or two or begin trying as soon as we're married? And what about your job? Are you—"

"Enough, baby," Rafe crooned, then covered her

mouth with his in an explosive kiss that sucked the air from her lungs.

Eyes bright, lips slightly swollen from his rapacious kiss, Simone nodded numbly. "Okay." It was the only word she could think of as Rafe escorted her out of the room, nodding to the man standing off in the shadows.

They returned to the reception as Tessa and Micah were cutting the cake Faith had designed. It was an exquisite Asian-themed four-layer rectangular creation featuring Chinese symbols for love, luck, happiness and prosperity—all of the things Simone would have as Mrs. Raphael Madison.

Chapter 19

Three days after Simone Whitfield officially announced her engagement to Raphael Madison, they'd returned from their early morning walk to find a man sitting on her front porch.

"It's all right," Rafe said when Simone moved behind him. "He's my supervisor."

She was grateful she and Rafe hadn't been holding hands. But then she couldn't remember a time when he'd been less than professional whenever they were out in public.

The tall, spare man rose to his feet with their approach. He wore a dark blue windbreaker over a white shirt and dark slacks.

He nodded to her. "Miss Whitfield. I'm here to see Deputy Marshal Madison."

Simone walked to the far end of the porch, staring

out past the sloping lawn to the landscape across the river. Something told her that the strange man's presence did not signal good news. As much as she tried, she wanted to shake off a feeling of foreboding.

Not now, she thought. Not when her life was as perfect as she could've imagined it to be. Rafe had had a lengthy talk with not only Malcolm, but also Lucinda, reassuring her parents that he would love, comfort and provide for their daughter and the children he prayed they would have together. He'd also discussed the risks that came with being a marshal, but when he told them of his plan to attend law school they appeared visibly relieved.

Later that afternoon, they'd gone shopping for rings, and Simone had selected an exquisite square-cut emerald surrounded by near-flawless diamonds instead of the ubiquitous diamond solitaire.

When she'd called Faith to give her the news, her cousin had offered her East Harlem brownstone for the wedding and reception, claiming the third-floor ballroom was projected for completion by summer's end. She would have to wait to tell Tessa her good news because her sister and new husband were honeymooning in the Greek Isles.

Simone didn't have to wait long to uncover why the man had been waiting for Rafe when he came around the porch to get her. "Yes, Rafe."

Cradling her face in his hands, he gave her a sad smile. "It's over. Benton decided to take a plea."

"What does that mean?"

"The federal prosecutor offered him a deal of twenty-five to life in lieu of a trial."

Her eyes grew wild. "Are you telling me the government bargained with a murderer? That he'll spend twenty-five years in prison, then get out to murder again? How old is he, Rafe?"

"Forty-two."

"He'll get out when he's sixty-seven. And that's certainly not too old for him pick up where he left off. You used me! The government used me! All the talk about putting him away for life meant nothing." She pounded Rafe's chest with her fist. "Nothing!" she shouted.

Holding her wrists firmly, Rafe pulled her up close. "Even if he gets out in ten years, he won't be able to hurt you."

"And why not!" she spat out.

"Because he's losing his sight. He's been diagnosed with retinitis pigmentosa. It's a progressive degenerative eye disease marked in the early stages by night blindness. That's why Benton's attacks were always committed during the day. By the time of his release, if he makes it, he'll be blind. He's being transported to a supermaximum security federal facility as we speak."

Simone closed her eyes, trying to slow down her runaway pulse. "Where?"

"Illinois."

She nodded. Illinois was far enough from New York where she wouldn't have to keep looking over her shoulder. "What happens now, Rafe?"

"I have to go, but I'll be back."

"When?"

"Give me a couple of weeks."

"You promise?"

"Yes, baby, I promise. I'm going inside to pack my things. Now, I want you to go inside the kitchen and stay there until I leave."

She blinked once. "Why?"

The seconds ticked off slowly as they stood staring at each other. Holding out his hand, he gave her the keys to the house. "I want you to walk away from me, because right now I can't bear to walk away from you."

Curbing the urge to kiss the man to whom she'd pledged her future, Simone rounded the porch and unlocked the front door. She didn't see the man standing on the top step waiting for Rafe. She couldn't see more than a foot in front of her face because of the tears distorting her vision.

She lost track of time as she sat at the table in the dining nook, waiting and listening. She couldn't hear Rafe's footfalls on the staircase or the soft click of the door closing behind him. What she did hear was the sound of his SUV when he started up the engine. Then there was nothing—no sound and no movement.

The house appeared abnormally empty. It was the way it'd been before Raphael Madison had walked arrogantly through her front door. Light coming through the trio of windows reflected off the precious stones on her left hand. Seeing the ring was a reminder of the promise he'd made when he'd slipped it onto her finger. A promise she knew in her heart he would honor forever.

The rain began at two that afternoon, coming down in torrents before subsiding, only to start up again. With the onset of the intense summer heat Simone had begun relaxing on the front porch. The smell of the rain-soaked earth was an aphrodisiac that heightened the fragrance of the flowers she'd planted around the front of the house.

She slept in Rafe's bed the first night he left, the second, third…and now it'd been more than two weeks and she hadn't returned to her own bed. She closed her eyes, listening to the gentle patter of rain on the roof. Simone didn't know how long she'd slept when something woke her. She opened her eyes to stare at a broad back under a black T-shirt. A man sat on the top step of the porch, legs outstretched, staring out at the rain. Her heart was beating so fast she feared moving or it would stop beating entirely.

"Rafe." His name came out in a breathless whisper.

Raphael Madison stared over his shoulder at the woman in the rocker. He'd been waiting weeks to see her. "How's my baby?"

Simone sprang from the chair at the same time he stood and caught her up in his arms. "She's good now!" Holding on to his neck, she placed tiny kisses all over his face. "When did you get here?"

"I've been here for about twenty minutes."

She kissed him hard on the mouth. "Why didn't I hear you?"

He shrugged a shoulder. "I don't know. I thought you would've heard me when I drove up."

She peered over his shoulder and saw the racy black sports car parked behind her SUV. "What's going on, Rafe?"

"There's nothing going on."

"Are you working now?"

Rafe set her on her feet, then pulled her over to the love seat. He sat, pulling her down to his lap. "I'm on vacation for the next month. I don't know what's on your schedule, but if you can take a few days off I'd like you to come to San Diego with me so you can meet my family. I also want to stop in Kansas to introduce you to my father. He may or may not be lucid, because most times he's heavily sedated."

"When do you want to leave?"

"It's up to you, baby."

Simone nodded. She had to admit that Rafe looked wonderful. His face was a little thinner, hair longer, but overall he looked incredibly fit. "I'll check my schedule."

"I put in for a transfer," Rafe volunteered. "I asked to be assigned to the White Plains Federal Courthouse."

Simone bit down on her lower lip to still its trembling. "Do you think you'll get approval?"

A hint of a smile deepened the lines around his eyes. "There's a good chance I will. I spoke to Judge Fischer and told him that I'd planned to marry the woman who saved his life, and he said he would put in a good word for me."

"That smacks of favoritism," she said accusingly.

"The expression is not how you do it, but did you do it. I did what I had to do because I don't want to be away from you again."

"Nor I you. I have a confession to make."

"What?" Rafe asked, combing his fingers through her curls.

"I've been sleeping in your bed since you left."

"At least you've been sleeping. I'm back to being an insomniac."

"Why don't you take a sleeping aid?"

"Why should I when I have Simone Whitfield? She's all the drug I'll ever need."

Rising, holding her tightly, Rafe made his way across

the porch to the front door. Simone opened and closed the screen door, latching it.

She buried her face between her fiancé's neck and shoulder as he climbed the staircase. Instead of walking the hallway to the room where he'd made love to her countless times, he walked into her bedroom.

There was only the sound of measured breathing and the whisper of fabric as they undressed and lay together on cool, floral sheets. They took their time rediscovering each other's body and when Simone opened her arms and legs to welcome Rafe home, she knew this coming together would be different from their other encounters. He would make love to her in what would become their marriage bed. Even without exchanging vows, they'd become one.

Simone sighed audibly, enjoying the aftermath of an ebbing passion that left her unable to move. "I can't believe I've missed you so much."

It was a full minute before he was able to reply. "I don't ever want to leave you alone this long again."

"Even if you have to go away, there's going to come a time when I won't be alone."

Lifting his head, Rafe stared down at the woman under him. "What are you talking about?"

"Babies, Rafe."

His face lit up like a two-hundred-watt bulb. "Are you pregnant?"

"No. But I will be if I don't go on the Pill." They'd made love without protection.

Reversing their positions, she gave Rafe a long penetrating look. "Do you want to start a family now?"

He nodded. "We can get married in Vegas before we

go to San Diego. Then we can always have a little something for the family around Christmas."

"That's what Faith and Ethan did."

"What's good for one Whitfield woman should be good for another."

Simone warmed to the idea. "If my mother has a fit, then you're going to have to deal with her."

"I doubt if she would complain about having another grandbaby."

"You're right about that."

Rafe dropped a kiss on her nose. "I love you."

Simone closed her eyes. "I love you, too."

And she did. She'd fallen in love with her bodyguard the night of the storm when they'd made love for the first time. Neither knew that it was the beginning of a love that promised to last forever.

Rafe withdrew from Simone, but he didn't release her. He held her close to his heart until they both fell asleep. He'd come back to plan his future with a woman whose arms would cradle their children and in whose arms he wanted to breathe his last breath. Simone Whitfield had become his love, his passion, his life and his reason for every decision he'd make.

She unknowingly had become his everything.

NATIONAL BESTSELLING AUTHOR

ROCHELLE ALERS

invites you to meet the Whitfields of New York....

Tessa, Faith and Simone Whitfield know all about coordinating
other people's weddings, and not so much about arranging
their own love lives. But in the space of one unforgettable year,
all three will meet intriguing men who just might bring them their
very own happily ever after....

Long Time Coming

June 2008

The Sweetest Temptation

July 2008

Taken by Storm

August 2008

ARABESQUE®

www.kimanipress.com

KPALERSTRIL08

Meet the Whitfield sisters—

experts at coordinating other people's weddings,
but not so great at arranging their own love lives.

NATIONAL BESTSELLING AUTHOR

ROCHELLE ALERS

Long Time Coming

Book #1 of The Whitfield Brides trilogy

When assistant D.A. Micah Sanborn and Tessa Whitfield wind up
stranded together all night in a citywide blackout, they discover a
passion most people only fantasize about. But their romance hits a
snag when Micah is unable to say those three little words.

**Coming the first week of June
wherever books are sold.**

ARABESQUE®

www.kimanipress.com   KPRA0520608

Dark, rich and delicious...how could she resist?

NATIONAL BESTSELLING AUTHOR

ROCHELLE ALERS

The Sweetest Temptation

Book #2 of The Whitfield Brides trilogy

Faith Whitfield's been too busy satisfying the sweet tooth of others
to lament her own love life. But when Ethan McMillan comes
to her rescue, he finds himself falling for the luscious pastry
chef...and soon their passions heat to the boiling point!

Meet the Whitfields of New York—experts at
coordinating other people's weddings, but not so great
at arranging their own love lives.

Available the first week of July wherever books are sold.

ARABESQUE®

www.kimanipress.com

KPRA1020708

DON'T MISS
THIS SEXY NEW SERIES
FROM KIMANI ROMANCE!

THE BRADDOCKS

SECRET SON

*Power, passion and politics
are all in the family.*

HER LOVER'S LEGACY by **Adrianne Byrd**
August 2008

SEX AND THE SINGLE BRADDOCK
by **Robyn Amos**
September 2008

SECOND CHANCE, BABY by **A.C. Arthur**
October 2008

THE OBJECT OF HIS PROTECTION
by **Brenda Jackson**
November 2008

www.kimanipress.com

KPBSS0808

The first title in a passionate new miniseries…

THE BRADDOCKS

SECRET SON

*Power, passion and politics
are all in the family.*

Her Lover's Legacy

ADRIANNE BYRD

Gloria Kingsley's affair with her late boss's son Malcolm
Braddock has Houston society's tongues wagging. Can
Malcolm step into his powerful father's shoes amidst hints
of scandal? And can Gloria entice Malcolm to overcome his
commitment resistance?

Available the first week of August wherever books are sold.

KIMANI
ROMANCE